RIGHT IN SIGHT

Elaine Braman

Margarete Johl

WP

Whimsical Publications, LLC

Florida

To purchase the authorized electronic edition of *Right In Sight*, visit
www.whimsicalpublications.com

Cover art by Traci Markou
Editing by Brieanna Robertson

Published in the United States by
Whimsical Publications, LLC
Florida

ISBN-13: 978-1-936167-70-8

Printed in the United States of America

"She's not married." Her stern gaze peered at me over her glasses. "At least in the legal sense, if you know what I mean, and according to her application, of course."

"How old is she?"

"Um, I'd say mid-twenties. Got that baby face still."

I raised my brows and Sadie chuckled. "That's from memory, not the application."

"Of course." I laughed with her.

"She works the swing shift at Bob's. Always pays her rent on the first. In cash too."

"Huh. Well, I'll go on over and knock on her door."

"You go on and do that," Sadie said. She waved her arms, shooing me out. "Mind you stop back in here when you're done. Fill me in on whether I was helpful for your next CSN article."

"CSN?"

"Yeah, *City Scope News*." She giggled.

I thanked her and headed over to the next building.

Stairways at each end zigzagged up three flights and the downstairs small patios jutted out beyond the landing overhead.

Rosa Lynn Kohl's unit was the second apartment on the second floor. I knocked. My stomach somersaulted. I wiped my sweaty palm on my slacks and waited. Masking tape with the occupant's name and a little stenciled heart stuck to the door beneath the unit letter *B*.

Footsteps, then the door popped open the length of the security chain and cigarette smoke rolled around the doorjamb. I peered through the gap and spied a bulbous nose, and one dark brown eye smudged with chocolate mascara.

"Yeah?" she said.

"I'm Kate Lambrose, from *City Scope*—"

"I don't want the paper." She slammed the door.

I knocked again. "Look. I'm not selling subscriptions." No answer. I knocked again. "You're Rosa Kohl, right?"

The chain yanked and the door flew open. "What about it?"

My eyes met a well-endowed bust restrained by the thinnest tank top material. I tilted my head back and peered up the flaring nostrils of the largest woman I had ever encountered. "You wouldn't happen to uh..." I swallowed hard. Insanity equaled asking an angry giant if she used an alias. "Use the name Rosalyn Kohler?" She took a step towards me. Her bare, flat feet slapped the concrete deck, and I stepped back to avoid a nipple in the eye.

"Does it say Rosalyn Kohler?" She smacked the door where the tape held fast.

I flinched. "Do you know anyone by the name of Abby?" No time to explain my crusade, I valued my life.

"What are you, a cop?"

I shook my head and back stepped as she took another step toward me. My butt bumped against the balcony rail.

"FBI? CIA? ICE?" She fired initials at me.

"CSN reporter." I managed to get my mouth working again.

Obviously, she had buried lies, but not out at sea and she was not my Rosalyn Kohler, thank God. The Amazon woman scared me gray, especially after she threatened to drop kick me over the railing. *Baby face? Maybe if her daddy went by the name Jolly Green. Paranoid? Absolutely, and definitely in need of anger management classes.* I beat feet down the steps. Next stop, Abbot's pharmacy for Summer Brunette hair dye to wash away my gray.

My knees were still shaking when I stopped at the rental office and thanked Sadie Arnold. She was sorry her lead hadn't panned out, but thought she might have info on the Alien Baby headline.

On the drive back from Hudson, I compartmentalized all my facts, which wasn't much. After my run in with Rosa Lynn Kohl, my imagination ran wild and tangled with the words from my phone threat. "Leave it go before you're gone." Giant woman's paranoia infected me, and I spun conspiracy plots in my head. Maybe Sadie Arnold's tip had merit. Maybe Rosa Lynn Kohl really was Rosalyn Kohler and somehow tied to my phone threat in ways I hadn't suspected. I checked my rearview mirror repeatedly during the ride back to Yardman, as if I could spot a tail. Just to be certain, I skipped the first exit off the highway and opted for the second. A slight detour and it put me on the south end of Yardman. I vowed to watch fewer murder mysteries.

ACKNOWLEDGEMENTS

We shout thanks to our publisher Janet Durbin, at Whimsical Publications, for recognizing our potential. And a special thanks to Brieanna Robertson for her professional editorial skills and keeping us honest with our commas, periods and italics. Much thanks and appreciation to Jamie Morris at Woodstream Writing Workshop for her expert guidance. *'I knew it was perfect when I heard it'* is her comment about our first person point of view voice.

Love and admiration to Darrel for his undying positive *rah rah* support and the hours spent with a highlighter. Thank you my dear sister Donna, for being here when writing came first.

With love and gratitude to David who was left to wrangle the dogs from underfoot and keep the house reasonably quiet, to Heather who listened patiently to one sided ramblings, and my brother, Detlef, who gave me the means to continue my dreams.

We are thankful to all our family and friends (you know who you are) for egging us on and we dedicate this debut in memory of our mothers, Pauline Braman, and Paula Johl.

CHAPTER 1

The overhead fluorescents flicked a quick two-step and the elevator doors outside the city desk office resounded. I looked up from my desk and waited for the frosted glass doors to fly open. A shadow darkened the glass, making the etched banner visible. *City Scope News* read backwards from my point of view, in many ways. Habitually, I referred to the newspaper office as the newsroom rather than the city desk, also etched in the glass door. After all, Yardman, Massachusetts was incorporated as a town and not a city, but Town Scope News would further diminish the size of the local newspaper.

The shadow elongated and the drone rolled closer, like a cartoon fly buzzing—didn't anyone else notice? My jaw locked and my pencil seesawed between my fingers. The lead tapped SOS dots on my desk blotter.

"Brosy...Brosy." Mack crashed his cart through the doors and my pencil split in half. "Joyce, Franklin, Suenoski, and Beck." He barked mail call.

And I, aka Brosy Brosy, once again sprang to my feet and stabbed my pencil into my four-foot cubicle wall. "It's Kate...Kate Lambrose," I hollered, and snapped the jagged edges off my pencil; splinters littered my keyboard. Calling me Brosy irked me as much as his damn squeaky mail cart.

Mack—the Mackerel, I secretly named him, bordered on seventy-six years old and chewed a stale, unlit cigar like a goldfish sucked food.

"Yeah, what ya say," he said.

Dan Suenoski snickered from behind me. "He's not going to get it, Kate," Dan said. "Besides, he enjoys rattling you. He wins."

"Yeah, rattle like a snake, if you ask me."

"I know what rattles a snake, Kate," Ondrea Franklin

said. "Those mongoose teeth of yours and saucer ears."

Joyce Hendrix leaned over into Ondrea's cubicle. "Oh, that was just downright nasty."

"Hey, the only reason he hollers Joyce instead of Hendrix is because he's hoping for a first-rate plug when you write his obit. Besides, Kate knows I'm only joking, right, Kate?"

"Sure, there's a jester in every kingdom. Glad you found your place."

Dan laughed and shot me a high-five. Simon Rutter slapped his hand on his desk and grinned at me. In the on-going battle to knock Ondrea off her perch, I scored the first goal of the day. I bared my mongoose teeth in a glorious smile and bowed, accepting congratulations.

I plopped back on my chair, which instantly adjusted its height a few inches lower. A guilty reminder I had five pounds to shave off my one hundred-thirty pound frame, or clean out the ten-pound tote looped over my chair.

Mack pushed his dated cart through the eight-cubicle maze centered in our office. The century old hewed ceiling logs did little to absorb the echo that bounced off the brick walls. He delivered rubber-banded clumps of mail to each desk. Except mine, he dribbled piece by piece over my cubicle on my head and snickered as he shoved along. Three weeks ago, after Phil, our past mail runner, moved out of state, the upstairs team hired Mack to replace him. I missed Phil. He had a quiet calmness about him where Mack had ragged edges.

I rolled my chair back, creaking over the pine boards, and tracked his left gimp to Beck's office. Helen Beck secluded herself behind a glass wall and held the coveted office as our Managing Editor. Behind her desk, six marble-framed arched windows stretched to the ceiling. The daylight blackened her to a silhouette. She anonymously scrutinized her team of columnists and reporters over rimless eyeglasses perched on the tip of her nose.

I had only worked at *City Scope News* for thirteen months, not enough time to understand the relationships in this home-grown newspaper. And I didn't expect enlightenment to happen today either when I witnessed the oddity of Beck laughing or Mack stroking her cheek. My attention zeroed in on them like a roadside car wreck. I looked over my shoulder into the copydesk office. Eugene Kennan, our Copy Editor, also watched the scene through his glass-walled office. He turned back and caught my stare. We nodded and shrugged.

I tugged on Dan's jet-black rattail that I jokingly threatened to cut off. My own personal tug toy when I needed to grab his attention, in a quiet sort of way. Besides, Dan would never part with his last leftover from his Harley boy days. He favored the mean look, simply to hide his big, burly, teddy bear self.

"Hey, what's with those two?" I asked.

"What? Who?" He spun around and followed my pointing finger in Beck's direction. Dan was the town dirt bag, meaning he harbored many secrets no one in town wanted disclosed. He did it with the same dedication and sincerity that made him Yardman's All-star Athlete in 1985.

"They're related somehow," he said.

"Huh, so much for complaining to the boss about Mack dropping mail on my head."

Dan spun back around. "Make conversation with him, uncover his cozy side. It might help."

Nothing riled Dan. His simple philosophy taped to his cube wall read, *What you reflect, reflects back to you.*

Okay, so perhaps I did reflect a bad attitude toward Mack, maybe men in general. Men tumbled across my path, skewing my life. I nabbed my coffee mug off my desk and shot off my chair to bump paths with Mack as he exited Beck's office.

"Mack, I hear you were a security guard at some government building in Washington." I wanted to say—*in your younger days*, but opted to flash my toothy smile.

"Yes, ma'am."

At forty-two years old, I didn't view myself as a ma'am yet, but I'd accept the respect.

"What agency?" I expected him to puff out his chest.

He stopped and pivoted deliberately to face me, forcing me to step back out of his space. Stale stogy fumed the air around him. He snapped his hand up toward his face and I flinched. He intended to slug me. My God, did he? A wily grin bent the deep parenthesis around his mouth and he rubbed his chin with his smoke-stained finger.

"Not your concern, missy."

"Whoa." I held up my hands. "Just making friendly conversation," I said, and sidestepped into the cafeteria.

The wheels on his cart squeaked once again until the elevator doors groaned shut and swallowed the sound. I peered out the door, all clear, and sprinted to safety, my cubbyhole.

Cozy side be damned. My attempts at good karma with Mack the Mackerel abandoned me today. If my father were still alive, he'd be the same age as Mack, which was probably why I continued to befriend Mack to no avail. I guess I wanted to slip between the cracks in Mack's defensive wall, to find a father figure. I could imagine the similarities. If I combined Phil's calm mirth with Mack's age and his cigar smoking, I'd almost have a clone of my father, although my dad only smoked a cigar on special occasions. It hurt almost as much as missing my father that Mack targeted me for no reason. Perhaps, I reminded him of someone he despised or vice versa. Whatever, I cast Mack from my mind and gathered up the downpour of mail.

CHAPTER 2

It tickled my ego that my column, *In Sight*, had survived for close to a year and my devoted readers kept me busy despite technology and the Internet. With a little self-initiative, our readers could investigate and resolve their own missing links without me. But, my compassionate humor kept them returning for weekly entertainment. Plus, the letter from the editor invited readers to send in their lost and found requests, promising success.

I gave birth to *In Sight* completely by accident. Armed with my new tote bag and a fresh film roll, I landed an assignment covering the Yardman's school committee lynchings. When Joe Deeter, the committee chairperson, was a no-show, the secretary suggested the "reporter"—air quotes and all—walk around the school to hunt down the MIA member.

Huh, why me? My brows knit into one joker style unibrow, but I went in search of Joe Deeter's lemon Subaru anyway. I found old Joe passed out, face down, blowing bubbles in a rain puddle. After I wrote a tongue-in-cheek feature about Deeter's misguided use of cold medication, I developed a fan base. Readers requested more lost and found humor. The *City Scope* received hundreds of letters and emails weekly from readers who asked for my assistance in locating their lost items.

At first, I thought my readers invented their lost item stories just to test my humor and my resourcefulness. On occasion, I still thought that.

Today, I received at least a dozen letters, and I fanned them like playing cards. One too square and the size of a thank you note fought against me. The letters sent to me via snail mail came from the non-computer aged generation who generally sought ancestral possessions long ago lost.

I removed each letter, stapled the envelope to the back-

side of each letter, and made a neat pile in my inbox, savor-
ing the card for last. Beck would grab the collection, hang
over my cube reviewing which requests interested her, offer
her anecdote, and provide me with the word count needed
for the column. I wanted her job. I could do her job, but I
wasn't the daughter-in-law to the owner.

I fanned my hot-flashed face with the card before slicing
it open. Curious to find the sender's name, I flipped the envelope front to back, and a delicate whiff of gardenias filled
my nostrils. I loved gardenias. I sniffed the card with a long
inhale. Odd, the sender neglected to include a return address, but the postmark read Boston.

An ocean scene decked the front of the paper-thin card,
the type received in bulk mail begging for a worthy donation.
The scene highlighted a cliff side lighthouse overlooking a
heaving ocean dotted with white caps, and a distant ship
cruised along the horizon.

Inside the card, hurky jerky cursive mixed with upper-
case printed letters stretched across the card in a downhill
slant—four lines of text and a signature line.

Seeking my conscience to be set free.
Find Rosalyn Kohler out at sea.
Before death severs all ties.
Surface the buried lies.
Hurry, Abby.

Speed-reading through the note, my brain twisted
threads to connect the card to a personal sentiment. The odd
prose and staggered wavy letters triggered a vertigo attack.
The words confused me, and I squeezed my eyes into slits,
expecting to ooze a clear understanding from my brain. I
read it again, one line at a time. The second line rhymed with
the first. The fourth line rhymed with the third. A shiver rattled up my spine. My shoulders shuddered.

A bona fide puzzle and I just smeared my fingerprints all
over the card. I tossed it on my desk. My eyes narrowed at
the poem slanting across the card. Clubbing it with my pencil
eraser, I dragged it closer to mull the stanza again. I hated
poetry, always had. Poems disguised words with ambiguity
and left the interpretation open to the reader. Abby's poem
was no different. Except, the first line admitted she wanted

rescue from her guilt. Second, Rosalyn Kohler who was out at sea anchored Abby's guilt. Clearly, this was the most eccentric request I had received and my first real attempt to locate a person. A quest I could grind my teeth on, more worthy than searching for *The Scarlet Letter*, accidentally sold at the library's yard sale. Far more adventurous than hunting for lost cell phones, old recipes, a diamond ring, or vintage Jack Benny records to play at the nursing home. Abby's poem even won over the lost and found request for a brown teddy bear hamster with a diamond-shaped white patch on his forehead.

I was so engrossed in deciphering Abby's poem that the murmur of phone conversations in the newsroom went unnoticed. At least until Joyce cried out, "Oh my God," and a thud vibrated my desk. I jumped.

"Sorry, I'm sorry, sorry," Joyce said.

"Jeez, Joyce, you scared the crap out of me," Dan said.

"Me too."

"Well you might as well tell us what has your panties in a bunch," Ondrea said. "Seeing as how you've interrupted our pace."

"I have to go to Dodd's right away," Joyce said.

Dodd's was the favorite funeral home in town, which Joyce frequented. She met with the families at Dodd's and wrote flowery obituaries. When she wasn't consoling families, she did fact finding and research for us.

"And?" I asked.

"Mr. Batley died," she said.

Until this point, our cubicle walls muffled our voices, but now we all stood, even Simon. Most days we ignored Simon for self-preservation more than anything else. He managed display-advertising layouts and the classified section for *City Scope* superbly. He spent his day on the phone, and his spiel never changed. Even I could recite it word for word. He wore black polyester pants with a white pin-striped shirt daily. I trusted he owned more than one set. Dan referred to him as the copy boy. Simon copied what he said, he copied what he wore, and he could fix the copier. If Eugene was within earshot, Simon copied what Eugene said. Appropriately, I referred to him as Simon Says.

"Selectman Batley?" Ondrea asked.

"Yes."

"Oh, that's not good," Dan said. "How'd he die?"

"Apparently, he was at Rubys yesterday eating lunch and just keeled over."

"I told you so. That food will kill you," Ondrea said. "Damn. He liked me too. He always let me interview him."

Ondrea's beat covered the town government, including the school department. She inherited that beat from me.

"It's not about you, On," Dan said. "He was the one selectman that wasn't intimidated by the little Sicily boys."

"What are you implying?" I asked Dan.

"Nothing, just that, is all."

Dan sat down and Simon quickly followed, then Ondrea and Joyce disappeared from view.

"Well, I just received a unique request for my column," I said, wanting to share my excitement since the work bubble had burst and I was not to blame.

Ondrea snickered. "Hold the press, Kate has another lost sock in the dryer caper."

"Yeah, what?" Dan asked.

I read Abby's poem aloud and just as I asked for opinions, the damn fire alarm squealed overhead. Joyce screamed and everyone jumped to his or her feet again. Ondrea bolted out the door without even a backward glance. I slapped my hands over my ears. Simon flipped on his baseball cap, and Dan stuffed ear buds in his ears.

Helen Beck jogged from her office and yelled, "Everyone exit the building, now."

"What's this, the third time this week?" Dan asked.

"I know. Wish they'd fix it." Although, I was clueless who *they* were that could fix it, but enough with the false alarms.

Within fifteen minutes, we were back in the building, except Joyce who hurried off to Dodd's, and I dove back into un-riddling Abby's poem.

In my opinion, Abby wrote her poem backwards. It made better sense to read it; Surface the buried lies, before death severs all ties. Find Rosalyn Kohler out at sea to set my conscience free. I supposed Abby harbored a secret that nagged her conscience about Rosalyn Kohler, and she desired forgiveness before one of them died. That sounded right, made sense with the signature line, *Hurry*. Unless Abby was a survivor and Rosalyn Kohler was a ship like the *Edmund Fitzgerald* or the *Titanic*. I loved that movie. Drama, romance, and a woman that survived and went on to live a life she chose despite circumstance. Perhaps RK, Rosalyn Kohler, lived aboard a ship, or was she buried at sea?

Ooo, the hair on my neck puckered my skin and I swiped away the heebeegeebees. I leaned forward in my seat and rubbed my hands together. *Maybe I'm on the right track*. I plowed on, enthralled in Abby's mysterious poem.

I turned toward Dan to ask for his opinion, but his headset clamped both his ears and he scribbled, nodded, and scribbled. Simon and Ondrea diligently pounded their keyboards and didn't bother to raise their heads when I peered over their cubicles. Our unwritten rule was never to interrupt a clicking keyboard or a scratching pencil.

My desk phone rang the second my butt connected with my chair.

"Hello, Kate Lambrose."

"Mom?"

I slapped my palm to my forehead. Why did kids ask the obvious? "Yes, dear," I said, skipping a lecture on listening skills.

"Oh. It didn't sound like you," Emma said. "You sound weird, like, scared."

Rattled for sure, and puzzled, but scared? *Not yet.* I flipped the card closed with my pencil tip.

"It's me," I said. "Same mom you've said good morning to for the last fourteen years." I studied the card while I talked and imagined RK aboard the ship in the ocean scene. *RK out at sea, huh*? "You're home from school?" I asked.

"Yup, and there's a message on the answering machine from...George."

"Your father," I reminded her, but didn't blame her for not saying the word father. Even though it had been over two years since he'd jumped the fence, the residual effects lingered.

"Yeah. Says he's planning a trip to Disneyland and wants to know if I can go too—oh, and something about wanting back a string of pearls he gave you."

I ignored the *something* about my pearls. His interest in my accessories worried me. Did he intend to wear them? "Wow, would you want to go?"

"I don't know," she said. "Is he taking Ethan too?"

"This is the first I've heard about it." It concerned me

that George hadn't discussed it with me. We agreed to talk about major plans before including Emma. Not to mention Disneyland equaled anonymous crowds, which George always feared, and it sliced my heart he couldn't have enjoyed a trip like that with me.

"He didn't say when, Mom."

"Call him back if you want or we can talk about it when I get home."

"Okay." Her voice feathered with sadness, and I wanted to reach through the phone and hug her.

"I'll see you in an hour or less. Do your homework."

"Yup."

We hung up and I turned my attention to the multiple email requests I had received in the last hour. I selected several that could result in humorous copy for my column and forwarded them to my home email. Abby's note card baited me and I read it again. The entire poem now sounded fictitious. Perhaps someone was playing games. I'm a newspaper columnist and my column is straightforward. Why obscure the request or play games?

I glanced toward Beck's office. She cradled the phone on her shoulder and typed on her keyboard. Nah, she was serious minded when it came to work. She wouldn't play games even though she had said the paper needed an interesting scoop to increase circulation.

My nose twitched and I sniffed. A delicious chocolate coffee aroma drifted in the air and something lunged at me above my sight. Instinctively, I ducked. I was gun shy when shadows hovered, since my mail flew at me from above.

"Jumpy today?" Dr. Jonathan Dohe asked. His arm hung over the cubicle edge with a Hot Joe's latte in hand and a wide smile spread across his face.

"Yes. No." On the spot quizzes made me nervous. "What are you doing staring at me?"

"Brought you a latte, but it looks like the last thing you need is more adrenaline."

"Jon-a-than," I said, which meant, *stop with the gifts, it won't win my heart.*

When I first moved to Yardman, I thumbed through the phone book for a therapist to help Emma and me work through our grief for her father, who wasn't dead, just different. It was exactly like a grieving process—maybe worse—

George still lived and wanted my jewelry. I saw Jonathan's name on the *City Scope* building marquee. I'd never turn my back on coincidence or convenience and went to speak to him. He listened to my failed fairy tale synopsis, but he declined to work with us and suggested we hook up with a female counselor. He referred us to Maryanne Everett in the next town, suggesting an out-of-town therapist kept life private. *Kids can be cruel and Emma doesn't need to deal with that gossip also*, he had said. Of course, he was right, and handsome, charming, and sexy. His nose was just crooked enough to make his features drool-worthy, not that I was interested.

My intuition pegged him as an opportunist who hid an ulterior motive when he referred us to Maryanne. I was right. About a month after I had met Jonathan, he began asking me to lunch daily, which was nice and fun and safe. Lunch segued into dinner invitations. In my mind dinner equaled date, which equaled serious, which equaled heartbreak. Thank George I wasn't on the market. So, I declined his evening outings with a bright, wide smile and claimed I was content with our friendly lunch dates. In the simplest terms, my heart was still broken from George and romance soured my palate like week old yogurt.

"Kate." He winked at me. "You're cute."

"And who needs cute?"

"I do."

"Puhhh, men."

In fifth grade, I was as cute as a baby doll. By my senior year in high school, I did have grapes growing under my training bra, which I was damn proud of and resented the doll reference. I was not an empty-headed plaything. Now forty-two, my bra was navel orange size and my long straight hair, still brunette, I cut to shoulder length. My protruding ears held my hair perfectly in place. Also, I'm no longer naive enough to believe, "you're cute" means "I love you."

"So you don't want this hot latte?"

"Don't you dare." I snatched the cup before it cleared the cube's edge.

At least once a week, Jonathan showed up with my favorite chocolate bar or a latte. In essence, his gifts said "not all men bite." Nevertheless, he was a hot latte himself. The type I had burned my mouth on in the past and withdrew from now. I easily fell in love with sexy handsome first.

"I thought so," he said. "You're making progress. The first step is to admit your addiction."

"Is this free advice or are you going to charge me?"

"What are you going to do when I find myself a steady lady that adores me?"

"Congratulate you," I said, although I'd cry for sure over the loss of his friendship and our banter. He winced and grabbed his chest, staggering back.

"Hey, look at this, would you." I picked up Abby's note card and handed it to him. "What do you think?"

He examined it front to back before he read the poem. "Interesting," he said.

"That's it?" I held out my arms, palms up, waiting for his divine insight. "No psycho babble?"

"Very cryptic," he said. "It feels embossed, but my first impression—Abby is despondent and guilty for lies either told to or about her friend Rosalyn. Seems melodramatic and I bet a youngster wrote this."

I rolled my eyes at his cryptic analysis. "Why do you think a child wrote it?"

"The switch in handwriting is a popular trend with teens, and I think an adult woman would have signed it Abigail, not Abby, however I've been known to be wrong."

Huh, that seemed reasonable.

"Refer them to me; I could use a new patient." He whipped out a business card and handed it to me, not that I needed it. I had a dozen, even magnetic ones that held take out menus on my fridge.

"Your parents were really sadistic when they named you." I studied his upper cased name. "No wonder you became a shrink."

"Or they were pragmatic."

"Yeah, right. Jonathan Dohe, just another toe tag."

"Uh, that's cruel, Kate." He laughed.

Even while he chided me, his laughter warmed me like hot cocoa after a black diamond ski run. Dimples exclaimed his smile and white teeth nuzzled his full lips. Snow blind came to mind—if I stared too long. His straight brown hair was always windblown and neatly cut above his collar. Bed head sexy, I liked that.

No worry lines creased his brow—apparently the upside

to dissecting the road map of the human psyche. Plus, his fire blue eyes probed without a word. I blinked first, breaking our eye rendezvous, and tapped the card against my palm.

"Been rock climbing lately?" he asked.

"Maybe this weekend," I said, happy for a more distant subject. "But Emma and I did truck out to the Berkshires last Saturday and hiked along the Appalachian Trail."

Rock climbing, hiking, and downhill skiing were three sports that George had introduced me to that I hadn't dismissed from my life, along with him.

"You didn't hike the whole trail, did you?"

"Hah, are you kidding? We'd still be there."

Helen Beck ambled into my peripheral space and I sat up at my desk and straightened my clutter. She was never without a chewed lollypop stick wedged between her teeth; I assumed a substitute for a cigarette. Her neck showed her age, near sixty, as well as her out dated skintight tweed business suit. I, however, admired her for wearing pretty in pink lipstick and making it work.

"Hello, Jonathan." She extended her hand. "Do you have a moment to discuss writing a feature op-ed?"

"A dear Abby column?" Jonathan winked at me.

Oh—Abby. I added the Hurry Abby poem to my inbox seconds before Beck groped for the stack.

"I'm not looking for you to reply to reader's questions," she said to Jonathan. "So, no. Perhaps a general opinion feature rationalizing angst in relationship to world events." She continued to thumb through the mail.

Her request startled me. My gaze swept from Beck to Jonathan. His wide smile wilted and his eyes rounded, as though he'd just swallowed the worm in a Tequila shot. Behind me, Dan stressed a cough. Ondrea popped up, squinting at me with her neck goose-craned over the cubicle wall. I shrugged and quickly dodged her reptilian glare.

Beck handed me the stack of mail. "This one is intriguing, Kate." She stabbed at Abby's poem with her saliva-drenched lollypop-less stick. "This might have a life span for a couple of editions. Let's move on this." She turned Jonathan toward her office and closed the door. I shook Abby's note between my fingers, ridding it of any Beck DNA.

"Kate, you better tell your boyfriend to butt out," Ondrea said. Her thumb and forefinger mimicked a gun and she jabbed at me sideways like a street thug. "He needs to stick to shrink rap."

I opened my mouth to respond, but clamped my lips back together. She was twenty-six years old, beautiful, smart, and paraded an ego to match. I couldn't find a way to defend Jonathan and still point out he wasn't my boyfriend, and I wasn't sure I wanted to.

Dan scooted his chair back against mine and whispered, "I have to agree with Ondrea. Any one of us can handle that assignment using Jonathan as a source."

In less than two seconds, my colleagues tagged me an instigator and I hadn't even moved from my chair. My mouth hung open. Jonathan didn't pose a threat. I swallowed my disbelief and said, "Yeah, but Dan, how am I responsible for what Beck does or doesn't do?"

"I don't know what to tell you, Kate." He rolled back to his desk.

I turned to my PC and glared at the bouncing screen saver. My pencil seesawed between my fingers, scoring dashes not dots. It flipped from my fingers and stabbed the side of my nose. *Jeez.*

I agreed with them, but didn't appreciate taking the heat for Beck. I welcomed Dan's commentary over Ondrea's pantomime. If Jonathan valued his life, he'd decline her offer. I sighed, picked up my notepad, and quickly jotted notes about the Hurry, Abby poem.

Abby—child or young adult, guilty, liar, and drama queen. Why would Rosalyn Kohler be at sea? Whose death severed the ties? Where are the lies buried and Abby who?

I stuffed my mail in my tote bag, shut down my PC, and stole a sideways peek at Jonathan on my way out. I was glad he was busy, glad it was Friday, and ecstatic it was May in New England and daylight lingered.

CHAPTER 3

A lawn mower sputtered from some obscure direction, and I inhaled the air ripe with fresh cut grass. The breeze spun a wet chill through the air and ruffled the spring leaves, a perfect cozy evening. A cab honked two buildings down and interrupted my commune with nature.

Main Street cluttered with commuters in a hurry to welcome the weekend, including Mack. He cut his way across the street past Gunthers Furniture store to the back parking lot. Damnit, I parked there this morning. On a good day, I was stupidly fearless and able to run from an old man or wield my ten-pound tote as a club. However, in the last hour I had been spooked over RK at sea, George wanting my pearls, Mack provoking me to flinch, and my co-workers tagging me as an instigator. I wasn't up for another conflict.

I dug my cell phone from the depths of my tote and scrolled through favorite contacts for the Pizza House, the only pizza joint in the entire two square mile suburb of Yardman. To my right and down Main Street, past the Memorial Faith Church and through the blooming dogwoods, I could see the pizza sign protrude from the building.

After I ordered a small pineapple for Emma and a small the works for me, I planted my butt down on the top step next to the building's marquee and waited for Mack to exit the alley. A dozen businesses resided in the *City Scope* building, Yardman's only hotel in 1901, lawyer offices, dentist, a dance studio, Jonathan Dohe-Therapist, and four businesses unrecognizable by their titles. *City Scope* sprawled the length of the basement, our newsroom at street level, and administrative offices on the upper floor.

Tires squealed to my right and five boys on skateboards whizzed across the street in front of a car. They jumped the sidewalk and weaved around a couple walking out of the pharmacy. Mack idled at the exit from the alley in his dust-covered black Buick. The boys swerved around his front bumper and banged on his hood.

"That'll keep it in place, old man." One of the boys laughed.

I sucked my breath in as I heard Mack's engine race. He must double pedal gas and brake with his feet or the boys would be sidewalk gravy. Apparently, he didn't care what he rammed his Buick into and I doubted the boys gave that any thought. His front bumper chrome split and peeled from multiple slams into a few too many poles. A bungee cord tied down the hood.

I bowed my head and studied my phone. My eyes strained so far up under my brows that they ached. He turned left and headed straight for me. He slowed and pulled over into the only vacant parking space directly in front of me. His tire skidded along the curb, jarring his car side to side. Five feet of sidewalk and six steps separated us. I struggled against the urge to look his way and lost the battle. His window slid down and he leaned across the seat.

"Brosy, everything all right?" he asked.

"Yup, fine." I saluted.

"You need a ride?" He lit the cigar he forever carried clamped between his teeth and it waggled when he spoke.

Still reeling from his threatening posture earlier, I troubled over his earnest attempt at helpfulness. His car looked like a death trap, and I hated when he spoke with a wet stogie pressed between his lips. "Nope." I rolled my shoulders to cut off the snaky sensation that rippled up my spine.

He saluted back and said, "Yeah, what ya say."

I didn't understand that phrase he used, but it unnerved me. I trotted to my car after he drove off. A tattered yellow nylon rope that held his back bumper in place skittered on the asphalt. I should have scored a karma point and thanked him for asking.

After I picked up the pizza, I cut through the bank parking lot and zigzagged around the Accordion Movie Theater. I drove slow and stopped at Nora's Nest storefront to admire the cute puppies in the window before I exited out on to Winter Street. Winter Street ran from the east side of Yardman, past the fire and police station, to the west side where Winter Haven Condominiums grew up overnight about two years back. Emma and I were the first of twenty families to buy and move in. We picked an end unit for the two extra windows. Our one-car garage sidled up next to our neighbor's garage. I appreciated the garage-to-garage connection, considering Emma's eclectic taste in music and my cranky neighbors.

The moment I pulled my Jeep into the garage, the raging lyrics of Linkin Park's "Crawling" throbbed my ears. Emma didn't hear me over the din as I struggled my way through the kitchen door. I schlepped like Igor from a Dracula film, left shoulder hiked up to my ear to keep my over extended tote bag from sliding down my arm. The pizzas balanced in my other hand.

"I'm home," I shouted, and step-shuffled my way to the table. I poked my elbow at her backpack to find room on the table for our pizzas.

"You're going to drop it, Mom," Emma scolded, and ran from the living room to grab the pizza.

"I could have put it on the counter, but I'd rather have my table back."

"You said, 'do your homework.'" She rolled her eyes and flipped the music off. Instead of putting items away, she stacked them neatly on the table edge and set down dinner plates.

After I soaped my hands at the sink and dried them with the dishtowel, I grabbed two sodas from the fridge. "So what's with this Disneyland trip?" I took my permanent seat at the head of the table. "Did you call your dad?"

"Yeah," she mumbled through cheese and pineapple. "He said, June sixteenth to June twentieth. Ethan has an art expo at the Anaheim Convention Center."

"Uh-huh." George was a CPA and his mental capacity to distinguish artistic greatness didn't expand past Ethan's art. He couldn't tell the subtleties between floating crap and the Taj Mahal—it all filled space. I stuffed another bite in my mouth and kept my tongue busy catching swirls of cheese.

"Dad said we would do Disneyland and then California Adventure Park one day, or SeaWorld if I wanted, while Ethan stayed at the expo."

Her head dipped forward and her dark blonde hair fell over those gorgeous blue eyes she inherited from her father. She played with her pineapple and tore the crust into bite-sized pieces. In my mind, I figured she was tearing Ethan from the equation. She wanted to go, but only with her dad.

"Well, that sounds like fun, sweetie." I smiled.

"I dunno. I'll think about it and talk to Maryanne."

That hurt. Counselor or not, I outranked Maryanne as mother. "Emma, I think your dad is trying."

"Yeah, maybe a little too hard, Mom."

"Okay." I picked up her hand and kissed her knuckles. *Next subject.* "You want to go to a movie after pizza?"

"I do, but Sammy asked me first." She tilted her head and gave me that pathetic brow bounce. "Can you drive us?"

Emma's best friend Samantha was thirteen years old. A year younger than Emma, which I prayed was a good idea instead of a year older. She lived across the street in the three-bedroom condominium grouping. We were shown at a three-bedroom model, but the kitchen was galley style, not what I wanted.

"What movie? Where? And will Sammy's parents provide the ride home?" A relaxing bubble bath and a glass of wine flitted through my mind.

"Miss Congeniality 2," she spit through her pizza. "At the Accordion, and I'll ask Sammy if her mom or dad can pick us up."

"All right," I agreed. "What time?"

She squealed her chair back out from under her and ran up the stairs to her room, yelling back, "I think it's an eight-ten movie. I'm calling Sammy now."

Again, she left me with KP; always the maid, never the queen. Ho-hum, like father, like daughter. I poured my soda down the drain, opted for a glass of wine, and settled on the couch. With at least thirty minutes to surf the Internet before driving the girls, I fired up my laptop to search for Rosalyn Kohler.

"Mom," Emma yelled down the stairs. "Sammy can't go unless you pick us up."

"Come down here so I can see your face to talk to me." A phrase my mother used years back, which meant, *my face will tell the real story*.

Emma huffed a sigh that could have blown me over and stomped down the stairs. Frowning with a smile in her voice, she explained that Sammy's parents had dinner plans, but her parents would drop the girls off at the theater if I picked them up and Sammy slept over. So much for my relaxing tub soak, then my cozy tee and bed shorts.

"Mom. What else do you have to do?"

My mouth hung open and I stared. *Huh, when did Emma become so insightful?* I doubted she understood how she just slapped me in the face with my bland life. I had nothing else to do but write my column for my Monday noon deadline.

I agreed with the arrangements and told her to behave. And she was off, bounding upstairs to her room laughing and screaming into the phone. The toilet flushed and she raced back down the stairs, kissed me, and flew out the door.

I jogged up to my room and changed into my oversized white tee and purple sweats. As if I expected my pearls to have disappeared, I checked my jewelry box. What did George intend to do with my jewelry anyway? A definite Pandora's Box I was not ready to tear open.

Instead, I redirected my energy, churning Abby's cryptic poem through my mind. I flopped on the bed like a snow angel, closed my eyes, and recited the poem.

Seeking my conscience to be set free. Find Rosalyn Kohler out at sea. Before Death severs all ties. Surface the buried lies. If I were going to uncover buried lies at sea, where would I start? Maybe from my bed, where I learned half-truths were as believable as pearls of wisdom, until someone turned on the light.

Oh my God, enough with the haunting pearls. I hopped off the bed, picked up the jewelry box that taunted me, and stuffed it under the bed. There...I may not be able to suffocate George, but I could suffocate any further remnants of him and his Indian given pearls. Back on the couch with my wine in hand and laptop ready, I picked Abby's poem from my tote and sniffed it. The Gardenia aroma had faded, but a whiff of antiseptic teased my nostrils. A familiar but elusive memory of Bactine sprayed on scraped knees rushed through my mind and skidded right out. I hated when that happened. It made me want to claw the air and grab the memory before it detached from my senses. And Abby obviously struggled with a similar conundrum. *Before Death severs all ties. Find Rosalyn Kohler out at sea.*

I typed Kohler into my search prompt, which was a bad idea as 1,023 links appeared. After back spacing, I retyped to include Rosalyn and ended up with just two hits. I clicked on the first link. In 1854, an infant immigrant named R. Kohler who originated from Hessen arrived in New Orleans aboard the ship *Talleyrand*. Interesting, but over a century old. Abby was not a child, as Jonathan suggested, but not a century old. In fact, she was older than the computer age; otherwise, she would have sent an email. A simple deduction, no Sherlock Holmes required. Besides that, her poem ragged on guilt, far more complex than something whirling around in a teenager's mind.

I clicked the second link that took me to a site that warned about pool swimming and the sucking filter at the bottom. An R. Lynn Kohler of Nova Scotia passed away without regaining consciousness Tuesday, May 13, 1975. Huh, how odd that I found this today, May 13, 2005, thirty years to the day after her death. Like I needed proof that I hadn't fallen into a time loop, I hovered my mouse over the time on my tool bar.

I kept reading the article only to be further spooked when I read her birthday, April 11, 1963, my birthday too. I slid my laptop onto the couch and stood, shaking the willies from my hands. I finished reading from a distance, as if that made it less disturbing. She was twelve when she died and forty-two if she were still alive today.

If this was the RK Abby searched for then Abby's time for absolution expired years ago. I certainly didn't want to break her heart and announce Rosalyn's death in my column. I needed to first find Abby, then break the news to her in person or at least on the phone.

CHAPTER 4

Abby's note triggered a yearning in my heart to reach out to family. I couldn't visit, but I could phone. Death severed ties once during my lifetime and robbed my chance to say goodbye when Dad died. My father, my hero and protector. With Abby's note singing in my mind, I'd take the time to chat with my family, starting with Allison, my sister.

She thrived on eerie coincidental phenomenon and loved puzzles as much as I did. When we were kids, Allison was the perfect foil for Dad's tall tales about the Bermuda Triangle, Big Foot, and the Loch Ness Monster. Allison buried her nose in books, sleuthing for clues to either prove or disprove Dad's theories. Besides, I hadn't been a very attentive older sister lately, but I vowed that would change and I could use her company right now. Emma's remark about my empty life festered in my brain.

Allison lived in Palm Springs, California with her husband Jack and their two toddlers. It was dinnertime there, but I dialed anyway.

"Kate? What's wrong?" she yelled above the warzone noises in the background.

"Why do you assume the worst? I can't call my favorite sister and say hi?"

"Your only sister—I better be your favorite." Her infectious laugh spread my grin wide.

"What's up?" she asked.

"Just wanted to—"

"NO—"

"No?" I frowned.

"NO. Jackson, don't you—"

The cat screeched and Jackson, or maybe it was Benjamin, howled in unison. "Sounds like trouble." I imagined her riding herd on my nephews and laughed. The phone clunked and heeled footfalls on a hardwood floor drum-rolled in my ear. I mashed the phone against my ear. "Kitty has claws," she said. "We don't pull him by his tail." The howling escalated and she yelled for Jack to help. A minute, maybe two, passed in silence while I waited for her to return to the phone. "I'm sorry, Kate. It's wild here —*No, the blue jackets*—we're trying to get ready— *Benjamin, do not take your shoes off*—to go out to dinner—*STOP IT, YOU TWO*—with Jack's parents."

My sister, the serious multi-tasker. If we didn't share the same DNA, I'd swear she suffered from ADHD.

"Are you sure nothing's wrong?" Allie asked again, her divided attention back on me.

"Sheesh, I just wanted to chat. I received a strange request—"

"Okay, then I'll ring you back this weekend. We'll catch up. I have to buzz off before the kids take their shoes off, again. Love you." She was gone before I had a chance to repeat the sentiment.

Huh, guess I didn't need to obsess over ignoring Allie. Her young family kept her busy and I couldn't live my life vicariously through her three thousand miles away. I dialed Matthew next, not that he'd care about Abby or Rosalyn.

He picked up on the fourth ring in a whispered rush. "What's wrong, Kate? Are you in jail?"

"That never gets old for you, does it?" His muffled chuckle tickled my ear.

Twenty years ago, he laughed too when I called him to help my then so-called boyfriend get out of jail free. Matthew did pro bono legal work back then, but now had a comfy four-man practice in Boston. My choice in men fueled Matt's big brother protective attitude and provided him constant amusement.

"You usually don't call unless you need help," he said.

"I don't need anything, and that's not true. Just checking in with my family." I sighed, perturbed that he viewed my self-sufficiency in a negative light.

"All right then, thanks for checking."

"Hey, wait a minute."

"It's Friday night, Kate."

I hated that smug tone when he pointed out the obvious. "I know what day it is—"

"Some of us have a date. You should try it."

"Then why did you pick up the phone?"

"Because you only call when—" A female giggled in the background and a hand scraped over the mouthpiece and muted his response. "Look, if you're bored, try Mom."

I growled at the dial tone buzzing in my ear. I took Matt's suggestion and dialed Mom next. At least she wouldn't cut me short. After Dad died, Mom sold the house and moved to a retirement community in Venice, Florida. The phone rang five times before the answering machine picked up with my mother's greeting. Her crazy habit of updating her outgoing message with her whereabouts played in my ear. Tonight's agenda included dinner with friends and ten-card bingo. Huh, even my widowed mother had a life. I didn't bother to leave a message. It would end with an early morning return call—well intentioned, but still a lecture—about climbing out of my hole instead of scaling cliff sides. *Join a bowling league, Kate. Get out of your solitary confinement.*

I paced around the couch into the dining room, around the table, through the kitchen, and back into the living room. The whole time with my arms and hands splayed in a make-shift pair of scales. "Work or play, work or play," I muttered.

I chose play and dialed Jonathan, hung up before I entered the seventh digit, debated, and rationalized my way right into a winning argument. I dialed again.

"Hi, Kate," he answered. "Everything okay?"

I really needed to work on my growing reputation toward the perilous. "Yeah. Perfect. What are you up to tonight? I mean, Emma's out with Sammy..." Warmth flooded my cheeks. That sounded suggestive at best. "Well, I have some time to kill. Shoot." I sighed, mentally resetting my internal START OVER button. "How'd you like to meet me for coffee?"

I expected him to chuckle at my fumbling, but if he did, I didn't hear any evidence.

"Um, I'm just getting out of the shower, but sure."

Oh, oh. I didn't need that much detail, but the visuals popped into my head just the same.

"Rubys, in fifteen minutes? I have to pick up Emma at ten from the theater."

"If you're buying."

"Good. See you then." Before I left, I wiggled into my jeans, knotted my t-shirt at my waist, and grabbed Hurry Abby's poem. I wanted an alibi for his company.

CHAPTER 5

Thirty minutes later, Jonathan and I sat across from each other in a window booth enjoying coffee and apple pie a la mode. Since the movie crowd hadn't dispersed yet, the place was nearly empty. Another forty-five minutes and the crowd would muster jockeying for position to grab the last red vinyl counter stool. The sizzling hamburgers, fried onions, and greasy fries waged an aroma war against the fresh baked pies and burnt coffee. Rubys wasn't fine dining, and certainly not fast food, but the place was squeaky clean even in the dingy yellow lighting. The table most in demand was the closest to the swinging kitchen doors and, as usual, occupied by Paulie and Rudy, the top two Yardman Sicily boy's club members, the only blight to Rubys reputation. I had heard that Rudy, Rude for short, owned Rubys and that the sign maker neglected to point out that he was dyslexic.

"So, tell me more about this feature you're going to write," I said and licked my spoon.

"Nothing sensational at all. In fact, I told Helen I didn't have the time, or for that matter, the desire, to write any articles at all."

That let me off the hook with Dan and Ondrea.

"You actually can get away with calling her Helen?" I asked, and echoed *Beck* in my mind.

"Which tells me you don't. But I respect your formality." He laughed.

I didn't see the humor, and I didn't do it for formality sake either, more like intimidation. He set down his coffee cup, slid his hand across the table, and entwined his fingers in mine.

My fingers tingled as if they were thawing over a campfire, warm and comfortable. I slipped free and patted his hand before picking up my coffee mug.

"She's my boss. If I think about her at all by first name, I follow up with her last name. Helen Beck." I couldn't stop rambling, not a good sign.

He chuckled. "You realize that you just gave away your true feelings."

"Huh?"

"You run her name so quickly together it sounds like Hell and back."

"You analyzing me?" I shook my spoon at him.

"I'm teasing you, Kate." He smiled.

Analyzing or teasing, didn't make a difference, both made me uncomfortable. I concentrated my efforts on scraping melted ice cream from my plate.

"So how well do you know, uh-*Helen*?" I smiled stupidly, proud I said her first name even while my mind punctuated it with Beck. "Is she your patient?"

"You know I can't deny or confirm that."

"I had to ask."

"Hopeful for an exposé? Gunning for her job?"

"I wouldn't turn it down," I admitted. "Just curious." Remembering the affectionate scene I witnessed earlier between Mack and Helen Beck forced me to add another sugar to my coffee.

"So, how's Mack related to Beck anyway?" I asked.

"I think he's Helen's husband's brother."

"So he's Mack Beck?" I laughed. "Or is it Malcolm or Marcus? No wonder he has a penchant for clipping names."

I expected Jonathan to ask what that meant, but he waylaid me in a different direction. "I'm glad you called. It's good for you to socialize. And with me."

"Uh-huh." I grabbed my coffee and slurped. Way too sweet now. "What's up with that guy anyway?"

"What guy?"

"Mack. He taunts me on purpose. He tried to intimidate me today."

"What are you talking about, Kate?"

"Mack, the old fart who delivers the mail. He deliberately drops my mail on my head every day."

"Why?"

"I don't know and he insists on chopping my name."

"Chopping your name?"

"Yes. It's annoying as hell."

"Just ignore him or tell him to stop harassing you."

I pondered that simple solution and cast it against the rocks with Dan's earlier suggestion, both promised failure.

He smiled at me over his coffee cup rim. "How does he chop your name?"

"He yells Brosy, Brosy at me."

Jonathan laughed, spitting his coffee into his mug. "That's cute." He held up his index finger. "And don't say who needs cute."

My eyes bugged cross-eyed and I gave him my best Elvis Presley sneer. "How's that for cute?"

"So, Elvis aka Brosy, would you join me for dinner tomorrow night? The Woodfire Inn opened their new restaurant."

I shook my finger at him. "That's not funny. It's like he hates me." I heard the invitation, but opted to ignore it.

"What's going on here, Kate? You asked me for coffee, yet you're distancing yourself. You're deflecting."

"I'm making conversation."

"Kate," Jonathan said. My name suddenly seemed ominous. His lips thinned and his eyebrow rose. "Why are we here?"

The light dimmed as I frowned at him. That was a stupid question, deserving a stupid answer, not that I had one. The simple fact was I didn't want to be alone or admit that I didn't have a life.

His blue eyes pinned me against my seat, and I struggled against my impulse to squirm. If I moved on the leather seat now, it would cause an embarrassing squeak. Maybe that would break the tension. I fidgeted, smiled wide, and apologized.

Jonathan said nothing and flipped his napkin on the table, white flagging the boxing match.

"All right," I said. "I'm sorry, I'm sorry." I fished in my tote to avoid his glare, latched on to my Hurry Abby poem, and slapped it down on the table. "Look, tag me crazy—you do anyway—I just, it's been a weird day." When he didn't make a move to take the card, I shoved it across the table. "You say it was written by a child and I Googled Rosalyn Kohler and found out she died thirty years ago today. She was twelve. She'd be my age now. Don't you think that's spooky or even coincidental that I received this note on the thirtieth anniversary of her death? And she was born on my birthday."

He sat with his arms folded across his chest and didn't answer, but I didn't stop long enough to gauge his aggravation. "Then today, I swear, I was playing nice and Mack—"

"Kate, why do you care, for Christ sakes? He's an old, sadistic man with a menial job."

"I just do. It's annoying."

"No, what's annoying is being lured out on the pretense of spending quality time together."

"There is no pretense, we *are*." I smiled.

He fished his wallet from his pants pocket, snapped it open, and tossed a ten-dollar bill on the table along with another business card.

"Jonathan—"

"This isn't a joke, Kate. I thought you were ready to move on, but you're still stuck in obsessing over things you can't control. You can't control the universe, Kate. At some point, you have to let go. Explore unknown territory."

My mouth moved like a guppy, but no words came out, and he slid across the booth. His six foot frame towered over me.

"This whole friends thing between you and me isn't working. I maintain regular office hours if you need to discuss your issues." He stabbed his index finger at his card.

"No, wait, Jonathan." I swallowed the panic rising in my throat, but before I slid across the seat, the jingle bells attached to the door tinkled and he walked past the window, never looking back.

CHAPTER 6

I woke to muffled giggles floating through the air from Emma's room. Sammy and Emma droned me to sleep last night with their constant laughter and patter of bare feet. Sometime around midnight, I exerted my parental rights and yelled *shh!* Now at 7:30 a.m., they were back at it and raced down the stairs no doubt to the kitchen for sugar cereal.

I rolled over, stretched into the middle of my queen size bed, and collided with my laptop and the collection of strewn papers. My bed pals.

Jonathan, who was now very angry with me, livid even, would have fit nicely in place of my laptop. However, he mis-interpreted my invitation last night and dismissed me be-cause I wasn't ready to replace my laptop with him.

Logically, it was time for me to move on, as his stormy words explained. George certainly didn't have a problem mov-ing on. My heart feared the unknown. The unknown equaled Jonathan. It alarmed me to share intimacy with a man who practiced insight and challenged my psyche. He'd know if I faked it.

Things just fell out of my head in funny ways. Much like the day George had told me he cared about someone else. His eyes glazed over, non-blinking at some spot in the air as he talked aloud. He was confused about it, he had said, but wasn't sure he should tell me. Had he forgotten I was in the same room? I asked him if he were practicing out loud what he would say to me, if he decided he should tell me after he got over his confusion.

His head cranked toward me; his eyes remained fixed on the air spot. With no lead in, no preparation, and in two words after a fifteen-year marriage, he said, "I'm gay."

My mouth hung open; the light dimmed as my brows met my lashes. Who, what, how? An abundance of half-finished clichés jogged through my mind. My God, how could he know that? We screwed in college and after. He kissed me this morning. We have a daughter. He's been fishing with Jack. When was the last time we made love? Not Jack. How would I tell my sister Allison? She'd blame me. It was my fault for taking him clothes shopping. He said gay, not transvestite. I laughed and my hand, trailing shadows, floated to my mouth. My fingers dug into my gummy, numb cheeks. With two words, he had doused my life's flame. Huh, I laughed last night too, not at Jonathan, but me. I gathered up my strewn, slept on papers, piled them neatly on my laptop, and promised myself I'd move on.

A whiff of burnt toast watered my eyes and I hurled off my bed as the smoke detector squealed. I bombed down the stairs two by two. The girls' squeals, now louder than the detector, launched me down the last four stairs.

"It's just smoke, Mom, just smoke, smoke, that's all." Emma met me in archway to the kitchen. "No flames."

The sputter in my chest pounded in my ears like a lawn mower running on empty. I pulled Emma into my arms and squeezed her.

"Mom, I can't breathe."

I scanned Sammy from head to toe. "Are you okay?"

She nodded her head like a dashboard critter absorbing potholes.

Not funny, but my fourteen-year-old daughter, for a moment, became the adult. I hated small appliances and flames.

After the smoke cleared and Sammy went home, Emma and I spent an hour reading my lost and found letters before we left for the mall and not for shopping. We enjoyed the novice rock climbing wall at the mall. It kept us in shape for our next vertical challenge in the White Mountains. Just when we piled in the car, George pulled in the driveway in his sapphire-silver Crossfire Coupe. The sports coupe, a recent purchase he and Ethan made, replaced his Ford Expedition. Probably because the silver flattered his eyes, or was it Ethan's blue eyes?

"Oh my God," I said, and Emma and I traded open mouth, dumbfounded uh-ohs.

"Oh, Mom, this is Dad's day, isn't it?" We both forgot it was his Saturday. "But I wanted to go to the mall, Mom. Do you think he'd go with us?"

I bit my lips together and held back my response. I understood that Emma would never quit trying to push her parents back together, but she had a better chance of winning the lottery. In her mind, she hoped he would find a switch to flip back to heterosexual. In my mind, anger lurked toward him for wasting fifteen years of my life. Somewhere along the way, I convinced myself he had planned his deception from day one.

"I don't need to go to the mall." I smiled at her. "It's okay."

She wrinkled her nose at me. George brushed past me with his arms open for an Emma hug.

"You two forgot about me today?" he asked. Emma's head ping-ponged from me to him. "Well, it looks that way, doesn't it?" I shrugged.

"We were going to the mall to climb the wall," Emma said. "Do you want to go?"

"Sure, we can do that," he said.

I shook my head no. His aviator glasses reflected twin images of me gawking at him. My eyes trailed down his American Eagle polo shirt to his pleated khakis and stopped at his leather loafers. Did he really intend to rock climb dressed as Mr. GQ? He would slide off that wall like the top scoop of a vanilla ice cream cone.

"Emma, grab the cooler and take our lunch back in the house, please."

She huffed and shuffled back through the garage and I turned back to George.

"Look. I'm your ex-wife. That is what you chose. It's not a good idea for the three of us to do anything together and give Emma false expectations."

"Sure it is, Kate."

"No." I slapped my hand against my chest repeatedly. "I'm not your BFF." I slammed the car door, swirled around, and followed Emma's path with George on my heels.

"It would be fun," he said.

"No."

"We could explain it to her."

"No." I pushed the door open into the kitchen.

Emma faced us with her hands on her hips and her eyes floating in tears. "So you're not going to the mall?"

"Not today, sweetie."

"Whatever...I don't care," she said. "All you want to do is work anyway."

"Okay, let's not get into this now," George said. "Let's go out to lunch, Emma." He brushed his hand over her hair and thumbed away her tears. Great, now I was the bad mother.

"Fine. I'm changing my clothes then, since we're not rock climbing."

"Kate, you need to split your time better." George spoke without moving his mouth, as if that would keep Emma from overhearing.

"Don't even go there with me. She's fourteen, George, in case you forgot. She spins everything her way."

"She wouldn't just say you work too much—"

"What would you know? One weekend a month doesn't qualify you as an expert." Under his scrutiny, I needed to show, tell, and prove myself. I walked into the living room where I left the correspondence Emma and I had read earlier. "And Emma sat here with me, brainstorming search tactics on the web. She actually enjoys being included in my work."

"Hey...what's this?" George picked up Abby's poem. "I know this print."

I snatched the card from his hand. "You don't know anything, George. Living with Ethan hasn't automatically given you artistic insight."

George snatched the card back. "Ha. It does when you've seen the print in its original form."

"What? What does that mean?"

"I have your attention now." George laughed. "And not that you want to hear this, but Ethan drew this. Then we produced and donated the cards to the community outreach program at Mass General Hospital."

What I didn't want to hear was how much he admired Ethan's art or about his involvement in a community program. Admiration and community gatherings were two things he never offered me. *Cheated again.*

"You're right, I don't want to hear about anything Ethan does, did, or can do." Nevertheless, I jotted a mental note to contact the Mass General Hospital. Huh, hospital, antiseptic, Bactine, all familiar aromas.

"Well, to coin Emma's phrase—whatever—enjoy your trivial pursuit."

I wanted to reach out and slap him, but Emma pounded

down the stairs and I restrained my anger.

"If you two are finished fighting, I'm ready," she said.

Neither George nor I responded. I kissed Emma, whispered sorry, and to have a good time. I watched them drive away. I could have sacrificed my pride and gone with them, at least for Emma's sake, but I wanted more from George than he could give. I even envied Emma's relationship with George. His role as her father never changed, just his role as my husband. I muttered my way into the kitchen, unzipped the cooler, emptied the contents on the table, and ate my sandwich before starting the laundry.

Maybe I did work too much, but it saved my sanity. I'd rather work and put my energy to use than trudge around the house, talk to the air, and wave my arms at an invisible ex-husband. I dialed the main number for Mass General and asked to speak to the gift shop. The nails-on-a-chalkboard voice told me that ten cards in one box with different scenes completed the Ethan Standish collection. Like I cared. I asked if the collection—using her vibrato voice—was available for purchase elsewhere. "Oh no," she said. "Mr. Standish did the artwork specifically for us."

I had introduced myself as a reporter from *City Scope News*, and as expected, she rattled on. At one point, she offered to contact Mr. Standish for me, if I wanted to interview him. Huh, a headline scrolled across my forehead. *Unknown artist and home-wrecker gayly paints landscape note cards as alms for hospital outreach program.*

I thanked her for the information, hung up, and pressed redial. This time, I asked for the patient information desk. After listening to cheerful hold music, a monotone voice greeted me. I waited for pre-recording instructions, but the voice said, "Hello?"

"Oh, I'm sorry," I said, and summarized my quest in a few short sentences before she lost interest.

"May I have the patient's last name?" she asked.

"Abby or Abigail."

"Last name."

"I don't know it."

"Room number?"

"I don't have that either." Apparently, she wasn't listening.

Two heartbeats and a sigh later, she continued, "Hospital protocol dictates that I cannot confirm or deny that an individual is a patient in this facility."

"Jeez. What are you doing? Reading from a script?"

"I apologize for the inconvenience this may or may not—"

Drones. I hung up, screwed again. Perhaps Abby was not a patient but just happened to stop by the gift shop while visiting? I'd just have to urge her to contact me when I wrote my response to her.

I wrote up fifteen responses to the twenty-six requests I received via email and post before I pondered a response to Abby. I didn't want to blurt out in my column RK might be dead. But without a more reliable search method other than me, I couldn't be sure. Joyce owned subscriptions to multiple databases she would search for me, but that would have to wait until Monday.

In the meantime, I scratched out different responses to Abby. This wasn't as easy as I expected and it brought to mind one useless clutter class forced down my throat along the way to securing my BA. Social Science-Anthropology 005, a surprisingly perfect match to my major, Journalism.

Day one lesson, the professor had instructed us to remove all items from our wallet or purse and reconstruct ourselves using only the contents.

My purse—GOD—my purse? I was certain my purse collected items I hadn't seen in months. Forgoing the use of the desk, I plopped down in the aisle and dumped my college life onto the floor. I rifled through the pile and searched for divine inspiration, *who am I?*

Several useless pencils ground down to bare wood, four tubes of lipstick, different brands—all the same shade and hardly used. A tampon, a couple of condoms—obviously I put more merit into getting laid—crumpled receipts, exactly 37 cents, nail file, nail glue, random notes to self, address book filled with first names only. I had study buddies, bed buddies, coffee or drink buddies. Rubber bands, floss, an aged piece of gum, hairbrush—with scrunches galore banded around the handle—body spray, and Tylenol. Good God, that wasn't half yet and I still had to rummage through my wallet. I aced that assignment mostly because I hid behind a barrage of quirky humorous prose, adlibbing where necessary, and I still used that purse today, now called a tote bag.

Yet with Abby's poem, nothing seemed comical or catchy. I couldn't spout adlibs when Abby's guilt suffocated her conscience. Adlibs had gotten me in trouble with Beck over the Jack Benny fiasco. The nursing home enlisted my help to find classic records for the senior mob. *Well*, I slipped in a suggestion that they join the 21st century instead of insisting on remaining thirty-nine years old as Jack Benny had. If they wanted to recapture their youth, try Elvis, and put music to their shake, rattle, and rolls down the hallways. My readers responded unfavorably. I'd rather jab my pencil in my ear before I gave Beck reason to smirk I told you so. I could just say...*call me, Abby*, but that wasn't my style. I flung Abby's note card across the room. "Ridiculous." It landed on edge against the baseboard. If I were playing tossing cards, I would have just won.

CHAPTER 7

Just as I finished stuffing my tote with my work, minus Abby's reply, George and Emma returned. She ran into the house swinging a plastic bag around in one hand and waving her other hand in the air.

"Look, Mom, look," she squealed. "Dad bought me my own cell phone."

George smiled at me—her hero now.

"I'm going to see if Sammy is home so I can show her." She hugged me and flew back out the door.

I turned to George. "You will be paying for the cell service, right?"

"Of course. I just added it to my plan. You worry too much, Kate."

"Of course, but then again, I'm the one who makes sure every day of her life is just right."

"I guess I should have talked to you about it first."

"Yeah, that would have been nice. But then again, you didn't bother to mention this Disneyland trip either."

"Oh."

"Yeah, and don't let the door slap your ass on the way out."

"Having a temper tantrum, Kate?" George bent down and picked up Abby's card.

"Oh, shut up." I hated how he pegged my bad habits and frustration.

He read the poem. "Funny," he said.

"What's funny about it? I don't see any humor in it at all."

"Look," He turned the card toward me and posed like Vanna White. "Some of the letters were written with such pressure that they are embossed on the back."

I snatched the card from him and ran my fingers over the back. "Huh, a clue."

"Be serious, Kate, but good luck with your imagination."

"Is there some reason you are so challenged by me that you have to insult me, my work, and anything else you can think of?" I really didn't challenge him, but far be it for me to admit he stomped on my achievements. His constant negative attitude hadn't changed, at least toward me.

His mouth hung open. "I was teasing you."

"Well I've had enough teasing. After awhile, it hurts."

"I didn't realize. I'm sorry and surprised."

Imagine my surprise, George, but I didn't say that. I waved my hand toward the door. "Have a good day." I plopped back on the couch with my newfound Abby clue.

"About the pearls," he said.

"What about them?" I glared at him. He had a death wish to push me further after the Disneyland trip, the cell phone, and insulting my imagination.

"Can I have them back?"

The bad girl in me wanted to heave the pearls at him, but sentiment aside, the materialist in me wanted to cling to them.

"Why? What are you going to do with them?"

"Well, it's not like you wear them."

A lame observation, but true. The last time they decorated my neck was five years ago when we took the Caribbean cruise and dressed for a formal dinner. Nevertheless, his assumption irked me.

"And I suppose *you* will?"

"God no, Kate. Why would you even ask that?" His lips pressed into a thin line, the annoyed constipated face I remembered well.

"Never mind." I waved him away. "Just tell me what you want them for."

"You have to question everything?"

"Can't you just give me a straight answer?"

He shoved his hands behind his back in the same way Emma did when caught in a lie. "They're my mother's."

"You gave me your mother's pearls?" My mouth hung open. "Did she know?"

He fidgeted and fluttered his lashes. He hadn't expected me to connect the dots from gift to theft.

"Oh my God. You stole them. Didn't she miss them?" Stupid question, his mother was flamboyant, accessorized outfits straight down to her lingerie.

"Will you give them back?" George asked.

"No." I laughed, even more resolved to hold on to them. "Buy her a new string."

"Kate. They don't mean anything to you. I'll buy you a new—"

I turned him toward the door. "If your mother hasn't missed them by now then you don't need to worry about it."

"But Kate—"

I opened the door wide and shoved him through with both hands. "Save your money, George, you'll need it for Emma's cell phone bills. Drive safe." Before he sputtered another protest, I closed the door. The pearls didn't matter to me. It mattered that he wanted to take them away.

With Emma visiting Sammy, I hurried back to inspect Abby's note. I brushed my finger over the dents, and CSI episodes flashed through my mind. They always scrutinized specks of evidence with a flashlight. I removed the lampshade, stunned by the sixty-watt glare, and held the card up to the bulb. I didn't have a working flashlight. Eleven letters in the rhyme appeared bold, traced over. Embossed on the flip side, as George pointed out. It irritated me that he noticed before I did. So caught up in deciphering the meaning in the poem and searching for any person named Rosalyn Kohler, I missed the hidden message.

I scribbled the bold letters in my notebook. K M B A C O E B L B Y and mused if each letter represented a word to create a new sentence. Like an acronym or memory jogger?

I jotted a list of words using the first five bold letters and strung them together in an idiotic sentence. *Keep my baby a criminal, know missing boy a clown.* I snickered at my weird prose.

I rearranged the letters, wrote a list of words, but none together formed a comprehensive phrase. Like, George Bush rearranged spelled, He bugs Gore. Aha! An anagrammatic puzzle. I wrote a dozen words on my notepad, careful not to reuse any letter more than once except for the b. B was bolded in three different words. My notebook now resembled a football playbook. Circles and crosshatches connected by lines.

The poem without the bolded letters pestered my subconscious like a subliminal message. I couldn't put my finger on it. Whose death? What lies? This could be my Pulitzer, before death severs all ties.

Never adept at cracking code, I needed help. A cheat, like one I used to solve my crossword puzzles. I launched my web explorer, and searched for an expert. I chose a site claiming Einstein power, typed in K M B A C O E B L B Y and clicked the solve button. Within two seconds, a suggestion flashed on the screen. *Beam by block* blinked at me—an unreasonable phrase that created no association to the poem.

I tapped my pencil and glared at my laptop. Beneath the phrase, a window popped up encouraging me to shuffle my letters again. I clicked yes. The eleven letters swirled in a mini tornado and settled into one long string, but no defined phrase this time. A B B Y B L O C K M E. I sucked in a long breath as I studied the new arrangement. The hair on my arms flared in small mounds of flesh. *Was it that simple? Abby and maybe her last name? That's clever.* Immediately, I arranged the left over letters. Abby Molbeck, Elkcomb, Lombeck. Unreasonable names, but I went searching my kitchen drawers for the phone book just the same. No such names listed in the ten pages of my hometown phone book, but I searched the web anyway. No Abby or Abigail matching any of those names, not even Belmock. I would check with Joyce on Monday about searching her databases for those names.

CHAPTER 8

Monday blurred by under rain and fog. Like a Xanax mollified maniac, I hopped from one task to another fretting over Easter eggs that never belonged to the damn bunny in the first place. George would have called it a PMS day—pardon my stupor.

Tuesday morning arrived sunny and bright like me. The weather elves had wrung out their laundry and I sloughed off my stupor. I dropped Emma off at school and raced to the newsroom. Beck always put the paper to bed every Monday at five o'clock and Tuesday morning the new edition lay folded on our desk.

It never got old for me to see my words in print. I had never lost that adrenaline rush or the self-pride, but my accomplishments saddened me too, not that I needed a weekly dose of antidepressants. I just missed my father, the braggart on my team, and his ear busting shouts of, "what are you going to do for an encore?" but at least my readers made my efforts worthwhile.

Not every lost and found request I received made worthy copy. I first considered how much space I had to work with. Then I considered the entertainment value and if my research surfaced anything prudent. I always aimed for a happy ending, a life lesson, or salvations mixed with humor.

Eighty-seven-year-old Seymour Liverpool requested my help in locating his missing drivers' license, which fluttered from the envelope when I opened his letter. On my first read through of his jittery scrawl, I read he wanted to find diver's lotion. What the heck was diver's lotion and did it moisturize skin? His last sentence explained the problem—*it looks just like this one I enclosed for your example.* In my reply, I assured him that I found it, and forwarded it on to the Department of Motor Vehicles. He could pick it up when he retested.

Lives saved.

Nicky Thomas reported a missing queen size mattress that jumped out of his pickup just South of Spring Street during a move. He hoped to have it back in his possession by the time his long-distance fiancée arrived in town. I urged him to use Gunthers Furniture coupons in this week's edition and ditch the old memory foam in favor of forming new memories with his bride-to-be. Not a saved life, but a fresh start considering last week's rain marathon. A dirty bed doesn't mean mud.

Two women, twin sisters, asked me to decipher a hand-written recipe inherited from their deceased grandmother and settle a bet. Their dispute threatened to erupt in a family feud. One sister claimed the recipe called for pepper, the other said salt. Thank goodness for Google translate, and Ling's Chinese, although I was surprised the translation turned out to be simply season to taste. I told them they were both right.

I turned in my article copies to Eugene yesterday morning before deadline and none came back for re-write, which meant he passed them off to Beck.

On Monday afternoon, Beck summoned me to her office. She held my Abby piece in her hand.

"You've got to be joking," she said.

"It's very apropos." My intuition screamed defend, defend, defend my response to Abby. "Perhaps." She drummed her fingers on the desk. "However, it has next to no humor."

"To be perfectly honest," I said, "there is nothing humorous about Abby's request."

She read it to me as if I didn't understand what I wrote. "'*Dear Abby*.' Dear Abby? To coin a phrase?"

"Yes," I said. "Ironic humor."

She shook her head and continued to read aloud.

> "'*Your poetic prose is cryptic at best*
> *And I grant you this, I thought it a test*
> *But to find your peace and end my quest*
> *Identify yourself, don't make me guess*
> *Give me a call, to discuss the rest.*'

"I'm sorry Kate." She tossed the page across her desk. "Your response is as cryptic as her request."

I grabbed the copy and scribbled below the poem. Dotted a couple of I's and crossed my T's. "How's this?" I slid it back to her.

"Instead of the poem?"

"No, in addition to."

It read, *Dear City Scope Reader, Abby's intriguing request has us all curious. If you have information about Rosalyn Kohler or Abby, please call me at the number below. Be sure to check out next week's edition.*

She shook her head again. I held up my hand. I didn't argue with Helen Beck often, but I believed in what I wrote. "If you agree there is nothing remotely humorous about her request, then consider this." Atop my soapbox pedestal now, I continued. "If we were able to contact her, we may have decided against printing her request."

She nodded. The smart-ass reporter inside me beat against the bars of my ribs and rallied to repeat her words back to her. I rolled onto tiptoes, adding an extra two inches to my height. It might not matter what I said, but I wouldn't let a Beck beat down crush me.

"As you pointed out, Abby's request is intriguing and has a life span for a couple of issues. And you know our readers will stay tuned." I waited. Her lollypop stick wiggled and twirled and bent as her jaw slid sideways. She shuffled my piece back to me. "Type it and get it back to Eugene." She waved me away as if I was a pesky gnat spoiling her vision, but I didn't mind. I won.

***

The wait was over, but not my anxiety. After my challenge yesterday, Beck could have killed my copy and wrote her own.

My copy of *City Scope News* sat flat on my desk. I said good morning three times to my co-workers, even Ondrea.

"Not," Dan grumbled, and continued to scratch out words he had just written on his pad. He always wrote on paper first, claiming it brought him closer to his muse.

"What's wrong?" I asked.

"I have to write something without implicating anyone."

"Wow, that was vague."

"Yeah."

I didn't push the issue. Dan was never vague so I assumed he didn't want to talk about it.

I flipped to page three and scanned down my column. "Yes." I punched the air. Beck let it go to print as-is.

My phone rang and everyone moaned.

"If that doesn't stop soon, I'm working from home," Ondrea said.

Promises, promises.

"Can you at least lower the ringer?" Dan asked, but didn't wait for my response. He pushed off his desk and crashed into mine, grabbed the phone, and pushed buttons until the ring faded to a distant trill.

"Maybe I should work from home," I said.

"Sorry. I'm not having a good morning," he said.

I'd hound him later about what story twisted him in a tizzy. In the meantime, a dozen or more voicemail messages demanded my attention and I wanted to follow up with Joyce. Inept at searching for missing people or the deceased, I had asked Joyce to search her multiple databases. I spent Sunday frustrated over my search efforts until I opted for grocery shopping with Emma in the rain.

"Hey, Joyce, you over there?"

"Yeah, not now, busy."

"Okay, thanks."

I carried the Hurry, Abby poem with me or pinned it to my cube wall ever since I received it. By sheer osmosis, I hoped for some secret to seep from the paper and slam me with an *aha* moment. For now, it dangled from a paper clip stuck through the cubicle fabric and I stared at it while I listened to voicemail messages.

The first ten messages from my readers either wished me luck finding Rosalyn Kohler and Abby or offered admiration about my poem. Only two people said they might have some information and left me their telephone number to call back. The next message greeted me by last name only, *Lambrose*. The voice, a hoarse whisper, pronounced it as lamb rose. I pressed the replay button and plugged my open ear with my thumb. The pitch of the voice hovered between male and female. On the third replay, I let the message continue. Traffic noise whooshed in my ear. I pictured the caller standing on the median along a busy interstate. Two or three guttural sounds scraped my eardrum. Nothing coherent until the whisper said, "*leave it go before you are gone.*"

"What?" I pressed play again. Goose bumps rippled down my arms and legs. I plugged my open ear, pressed the phone tight against my other ear, and listened to the background noise. Traffic. Then I pressed replay one more time, this time paying close attention to the grumbling voice. The words, *before you are gone* definitely threatened me, but *leave it go* was bad grammar for drop it and drop what? Drop what? Searching for RK? Abby? The other lost and found requests I responded to flitted through my mind. Alice Smedley lost her purse somewhere between Abbott's Pharmacy, the bank, Polly's Hair Salon, and home. She had five hundred dollars worth of medication in her purse and she wanted it back. Maybe it was about the diamond-studded watch left behind at the tennis club or Teacher Brown's missing toupee. None except Abby's request warranted a drop it threat. It was about Rosalyn Kohler and I knew it. My stomach kick-boxed the cereal I had eaten for breakfast back into my throat.

I pressed the save button and rolled my chair back to see if Beck was busy. A threat was important to report to her and to George too. If something happened to me, he'd have to care for Emma. I never wanted Emma in danger. One of the biggest reasons I didn't clad myself in black and investigate the underworld, not to mention I was no Nancy Drew.

My God, what quagmire had Abby sucked me in to? Beck wasn't in her office. Dan was missing. Joyce would be so upset if I told her that she'd stop searching and Ondrea—huh, maybe it was Ondrea playing a joke. It wouldn't be the first time Ondrea thought she was playing a harmless joke, which was funny until it cost Dan two hundred dollars. She had left him a voice message saying, "*I know you're covering the high school basketball game tonight—you might want to place your bet on the visiting team—it's a sure thing.*" She had disguised her voice that time. If it turned out Ondrea chose me as her next victim, what it would cost me?

Calm down, Kate. How ridiculous to suspect someone, even Ondrea, would threaten me. People would miss me or notice if I disappeared.

"Kate?" a deep voice whispered.

I whipped around, shrieking like a monkey spotting a banana. Mack stood in my space with his arm draped on the corner of my cubicle. He grinned.

"What?" I snapped, and grabbed my chest.

"You scare easy, girl." Mack laughed. "Yeah, well, I think an old buddy of mine from back in the days in Washington...."

He babbled on while I gawked. *Leave it go before you are gone* swirled in my mind. My ears listened backwards, but he said Kate and girl, not Brosy. "What?" I said again.

"I said I liked your Dear Abby poem." He sighed. "Clever that you replied with a poem too."

"Thanks." I frowned at him, perplexed by his politeness and compliments. "Why are you being cordial to me, Mack?"

"Always been, was just teasing ya," he said. "Who's this Abby that's asking about the Kohler lady?"

"I don't know."

"Well, like I said, I think I worked with a guy name Kohler. I can try to find him, but not sure if he's a relation or not."

"Yeah, sure. Okay." Still, his words misfired in my brain.

He touched my shoulder. "You okay, Kate?"

Times like this, that no matter how old I was, I wanted my hero, my father. The threat scared me, but as a forty-two-year-old divorcee with a gay ex-husband, I denied fear. Yet, when Mack rested his hand on my shoulder after complimenting me and calling me Kate, I broke down.

He took a crumpled grey hanky from his jeans pocket and swiveled Dan's chair around to sit with me. I declined the hanky.

With three or four tissues from my desk drawer, I soaked up my tears and swallowed the clog in my throat before answering his recurring question. I played the voicemail message for him.

"Awe, I wouldn't worry about it, Kate." Again, he patted my shoulder. "People that make threats do it because they don't got the guts to act."

That made sense in a weird way.

"Besides, you're never alone, right?" he asked.

"Right." I nodded. *Except when I'm not at work, hiding from Jonathan, dropping Emma at George's for the weekend, sleeping, lazing in the tub, or watching QVC.*

"Don't worry, Kate. Me and Nora will keep an eye on you."

At least for now, my mood lightened and it helped that Mack apologized for teasing me. He left and promised he would update me if he had any luck locating Frank Kohler.

CHAPTER 9

I fondled the embossed letters with my fingers, mouthed the poem again, and studied the ocean scene trying to connect the dots. My brain whisked me off on a Bahamas bound love cruise. Mr. Six-Pack waited lounge side for me with suntan lotion in one hand and a frothy pina colada his other hand.

"Hey, Kate," Joyce shouted, and kicked Mr. Six-Pack overboard as I jumped out of my dream.

"I can't find any obit on Rosalyn Kohler," she said.

I circled around to her desk. "Nothing?" I asked.

"Nope, nada." She shook her head and Aqua Net fumes tickled my nose. She must have used the entire can to keep her white-blonde hair frozen in place.

"Here, see for yourself." She scooted aside. I followed her slow scroll through the database. Her Troll doll collection crazy glued to her monitor mocked me.

"I even checked possible spelling variations," she said. "The only thing that came up was the one you found dated May thirteenth, nineteen-seventy-five, poor kid."

She minimized the obit database and opened another window that elaborated on the article I found about the twelve-year-old Rosalyn. My knees wobbled and I grabbed Ondrea's vacant chair and scooted in next to Joyce. She handed me a pink tissue.

"That's horribly sad."

"Yes, and I doubt that is the Rosalyn your Abby is looking for. No buried lies there."

Joyce clicked the article closed. I stared into the green eyes of Hijinx, Joyce's pet cat, centered on her screen.

"True," I agreed. "And you searched what? State wide?"

"Yeah. You want me to do a national database search?"

"Nah." I didn't imagine Abby would have sent her poem

to *City Scope* if it weren't pertinent to the local area.

"I'm not prepared to throw in the towel just yet, my friend." She spun a CD around on her pink glued-on nails. "I still have this microfilm database to search and at least you don't have to worry about your Rosalyn Kohler being dead, just missing so far." Her penciled in snow-blonde brows painted her face with a perpetual surprised expression. I chuckled. I must have had that exact same look on my face while listening to the phone threat.

"Excuse me." Ondrea rounded the corner. "What are you doing in my chair?"

Joyce abandoned me, turned to her monitor, and clicked away at her keyboard. "Just borrowed it." I stood up and swiveled it toward her.

"What? It's not enough that *your* boyfriend is stealing work from me, but *you* want my chair too?"

Nothing I ever said hit her gray matter, but I tried to appease her and explained why I borrowed her chair. "I was just looking over some research that Joyce did for me."

"Figures." She grabbed her chair and dusted it off before she sat down.

"What does that mean? Figures?" I slammed my fists on my hips.

She tossed her head, threw her arm over her chair, and pursed her thin lips. Her nose pointed up at me. "I read your Abby article. It sucked. I'm not surprised you can't do research for yourself."

My hand itched. Joyce's fingers ceased their rapid-fire clicking. Mentally, I counted to three and blew out a slow breath. "Perhaps, Ondrea," I said, "my talent would be better suited to write your column that merely requires reciting he said, she said."

Ondrea's mouth dropped open and I stalked away to the cafeteria and punched the air once I was out of her sight. At some point today, I'd regret my verbal slap, but for the first time, I had the last word.

Ondrea bullied the entire staff at different intervals, but I suffered the most. She circled back to me like a gambler returned to an ATM. She needed a man in her life for sure, and I should have just kept my mouth shut. Instead, I swallowed her bait as a farm raised trout and became her single opponent. I should have just slapped her.

I traipsed around the perimeter of the cafeteria shrugging the stress from my shoulders. If I didn't want to spend another weekend preparing my column for Monday morning hand in, I needed to focus.

I filled a soda cup with ice. Pulverizing and grinding ice between my teeth was not as therapeutic as crushing Ondrea, but it kept me out of jail. Halfway back to my desk, my cell rang. The display showed BRO, just what I needed. Not. My brother Matthew, always so irritatingly chipper, but I needed cheerful right now. I would also mention the threat to him just to cover my ass.

Ondrea glared at me as I slipped past. "Hey, Matt. What's up?" Short and not so sweet, but to the point, he invited me to lunch. He said he would stop by in two hours and suggested we grab a bite in the cafeteria. Wonderful, vending machine sandwiches. Unless Matthew was entertaining his next month's girlfriend, he was tighter than Ebenezer Scrooge. I'd be lucky to get a cup of coffee to go with *his* choice of half a sandwich. He ate healthful foods by the clock and I grazed on junk food hourly.

"Oh Kate!" Joyce bobbed up over her cubicle. She waved at me and her dozen or so silver bracelets chimed. "Come here. Look what I found."

"What is it?" I took the long way around so as not to invade Ondrea's space.

"Real investigation." Ondrea sniffed. "If you used your PC for more than Sudoku, you'd know that."

"Never mind her." Joyce pulled my arm. "Look at this. Rosalyn Kohler." She stabbed at the screen with a troll-topped pencil.

She found a legal notice from the original *City Scope News* microfilm dated April 1, 1965. The black on white from the negative was hard to read, but the estate of Lydia Kohler sought the last remaining relative—Rosalyn Kohler to contact Attorney Able Jackson.

"You suppose that is *my* Rosalyn Kohler's relative?" I wrote down the attorney's name and phone number listed in the notice.

"Could be. But she's dead." Joyce closed the page and toggled to her next bookmark. "But wait. Look, a month after that, a small blurb was printed in the personals."

"Can you sharpen that image at all?" I squinted.

"That's as clear as it gets. Whoever scanned this wasn't too careful."

From what we could make out, it read, *Look g for Ros ly Kohl r. Last s n ear Cat lin Isl nd i Ju 1 65. Pl se c l 2 51...... R b t M l ch.*

"Is that Catalina Island? Nineteen-sixty-five?"

"I'd say so, yes."

"Can you make out that name? You think that might say Robert Mulch?"

"It could be, but it's hard to tell if that letter is an I or an H. The print is so bad, it could even be a T or a K." She fiddled with the tool bar. "That's as crisp as it's going to get."

"Damn, another friggen game." I scratched my head and tucked my hair behind my ear. "Can you print all that for me?"

Joyce nodded and not one strand on her head wavered.

"I wonder if the police would have a missing person report."

"Cops? Oh no. Don't get me wrong, Kate. I have a lot of sources, but I don't go near cops." This time, her forever-surprised face fit with her words. She picked up her herbal tea and her bracelets sounded like the wind chimes on my back deck.

She made a fuss about blowing on the mug even though the tea was stone cold. She had a story to tell somewhere buried in her platinum hair, long beaded necklaces, and flowery skirt down to her hot pink toenails. What herb floated in her tea?

"Oh, no. Don't worry, I'll check with the police."

I left Joyce wide-eyed, grabbed the documents off the network printer, and headed back to my desk. Halfway there, I stumbled over that damn crack in the hardwood floor, rattled Dan's cubicle wall with my shoulder, looked up, and found my chair occupied. Identifying my uninvited guest was no simple feat from the backside. My mother? The age seemed right, except her girth overflowed from my chair. Polyester green pants stretched over wide hips, and a yellow windbreaker jacket drooped over narrow hunched shoulders. The color combination screamed marigold gone awry, flowering on itself. Her carefully combed out perm haloed her head in a white-gray cloud. A lifeless statue except for her head. It darted in jerky movements like a chicken hunting and pecking for food. When her hand snaked from her sleeve and she fingered my drawer open, I sprang toward her.

"Hey, excuse me." I reached over her shoulder. "I don't see a sign that says roam free." *Whoa*. Mentholated vapors burned my nostrils and stung my eyes. "Can I help you find something?" I asked, and pushed my drawer closed with my index finger, careful not to breathe deep. Borrowing my space was reasonably acceptable. Straight-out snooping crossed the line.

She snatched her hand back and clutched the red leather handbag in her lap. Her black, hawkeyed gaze fixed on me. Annoyed, but not as much as I was by her intrusion.

"You startled me, Kate." A watery glaze filled her eyes, punching my guilt button. "I...I was just looking for something to jot a note on."

"I'm sorry." I leaned over, grabbed a notepad off my shelf, and handed it to her. How quickly I advanced ranks from the office instigator to maligning the elderly. To top matters off, she clearly knew me, but her identity remained a mystery. "Have we met?"

Joyce peered over her cubicle wall and mouthed a phrase that translated in my mind as muck whiff. I nodded and pinched my nose.

"Not exactly. I'm—"

"Nora!" Beck rounded the corner. "What the hell do you think you're doing in here?" Her booming voice startled me and rattled my teeth. My head sought shelter between my shoulders.

"Ah, there you are, Helen. I've been waiting for you." Nora handed me back the notepad and rose. "You can take me to the train station now."

Nora's voice switched from sugar to spice. I blinked in surprise. My mouth dropped open. Beck's eyes narrowed.

Despite knowing the woman's name was Nora, I remained clueless, but I admired her regal performance.

"I thought I made it explicitly clear on the phone I don't have time. You'll have to wait until this afternoon." With that one proclamation, Beck turned on her heel and headed to her office.

"But I can't wait," Nora whined, and dogged Beck's steps. "I need my car now."

Beck stopped at the threshold in her doorway and swung around. Her lips clamped so tightly they disappeared into a thin line. My stance shifted to the right, ducking behind Nora's bulk. I looked back at Joyce. She swung her purse over her shoulder and tiptoed out.

"This is tedious," Beck was saying. "I have already told you. No. If you insist on continuing the conversation, you'll have to do so in here."

Nora threw me a quavering smile then squared her shoulders and marched after Beck.

Amused and curious, I glanced around trying to find anyone that could shed light on the scene. Ondrea hadn't returned and Dan was still out on assignment.

I sat down in my chair, feigned interest in the papers I still held, and rolled back enough to spy.

Nora dropped her handbag on Beck's desk and planted her hands on her hips. A linebacker posed to rush the forward or a weed ready to be whacked. I wasn't sure which cat would bite first. Beck shook her head. Nora nodded. Nora shook her head. Beck nodded. Nora turned around and pointed in my direction. Beck's head peered around Nora, and I pulled a Simon, tracking their gaze. Nothing unusual and no one interesting behind me. When I turned back, Beck pressed her phone to her ear, and my extension rang. In three words and a wave, she summoned me.

"She can take me." Nora pointed her bony finger in my face when I walked in.

Beck released her breath in a loud whoosh. "What's on your agenda today, Kate?"

"I was headed to the police station to follow up on a potential lead for my Abby story."

"See?" Nora said. "She's on her way out anyway."

Beck massaged her temples with one hand while the other hand waved at Nora like a conductor. "Please, Nora, give us a moment. Wait outside."

Nora sniffled loudly, but followed Beck's command. Sympathy for the older woman tugged my heart.

"I need you to do me a favor, Kate. Will you please taxi my sister-in-law to the West Concord train station?"

"Sister-in-law?" I spun around. Nora stood just outside the open sliding glass door peering in. Her powder-white brows arched hopefully. Beck's words didn't sound so much like a question but a plea.

"Sorry for the put out, dear. I won't be any trouble." Nora

poked her head around. The sugar laced her voice.

"Sure, I guess I could do that," I said. They both sighed in unison. Beck's phone rang and she picked it up on the first ring and turned her back on us. I considered giving Nora a hug to make up for Beck's rudeness, but worried the mentholated cloud would cement us together.

"Sister-in-law, huh?" I led the way back to my desk.

"Yes. We can choose our friends, but not our family, right?" She laughed. "Mack's wife." Huh, *muck whiff.*

"Well, it is very nice to meet you Mrs.—I'm sorry, I don't even know your last name."

"You can call me Nora, dear. Ya know, like Nora's Nest."

"Oh my God, I didn't realize that was you. I mean I didn't realize that Nora's Nest was your store." I slid my tote off my chair, grabbed my keys and the paperwork Joyce printed. "Ready?"

"Ready as Freddy." She beamed.

CHAPTER 10

Ten minutes later, we were halfway to the train station. Nora kept a steady flow of conversation running. She talked faster than she breathed. Depending on the subject that spewed from her lips, her voice shifted from a sugar sweet twang to a spicy—I am woman, hear me roar. She had multiple personalities and I cringed when she shot the bird at a semi that cut me off. *Jeez, Sybil with dementia and on crack.*

She and Mack had bought the pet store seven years ago with settlement money Mack received from a car accident that fractured his left hip and femur. At the time, they thought Mack would never walk again, and the store would provide steady income.

"Mack, bless his heart," Nora continued, "proved them all wrong. Nothing keeps my Mack down for the count. So ya see, with him having come so close to losing everything is why I don't begrudge him a little time for himself."

A little time? He only worked part-time, that left a whole lot of "little time" to fill. Why was I driving Miss Daisy and not him? "So what's he off doing when he's not delivering the mail at *City Scope,* or taking you to get your car?"

"Fishing."

I nodded. I could see Mack in hip waders standing in a fresh water stream, puffing away on his stogie alone in the backwoods while Nora struggled to find a ride. If I were in her shoes, I wouldn't be as forgiving. And I asked why she left her car at the train station.

"We forgot I drove there and Mack picked me up when I got back from Arlington."

Oh boy, the age of innocence, the full circle of life, and I didn't look forward to it. Just then, Nora swept my documents off the dashboard, the ones Joyce had printed for me. I tried to grab them, but she clutched them to her breast and

I wasn't going there.

"These have to do with your Abby column, dear? What you wanted to go to the police with?"

I nodded and shrugged, no longer offended by her nosiness. Familiar enough with my mother and her no boundaries, no filters, just dive right in attitude, I could handle Nora. She had a right to her rite of age.

"Oh my, it's really vague. I hope they don't laugh at you."

"Why would you think they'd laugh?"

The wrinkles around her eyes deepened. "For one, dear, you can hardly read it."

"That's how it was scanned."

"Well, the police aren't known to read between the lines. They want things black or white. And second..."

I turned into the train station parking lot, swung down the first aisle, and pulled over. I idled and waited for Nora to continue. She held the papers close to her nose.

"Does that say nineteen-sixty-five?"

"I think so."

"Forty years ago?"

"I know it's a long—"

"Almost half a century," she said. I almost expected her to add, *Poor Kate*. "Well, it's certainly not my business, dear."

"You think it's too old?"

"Don't you?"

"I don't know. I don't really have much else." The last thing I wanted was to walk into the Yardman PD and become a joke. Maybe she was right.

Nora patted my knee. "Something will turn up. I read your column all the time and enjoy your stories. You're very resourceful." Her eyes twinkled.

"Thank you." I smiled. She was right, still early in my investigation. I was bound to trip over something. "So where's your car?"

Nora stared out the windshield. "Oh dear. I'm not sure. It's silver."

I followed her gaze. Gosh, ten silver cars on my right and five on my left and we had three rows to cruise through. Row by row, we searched until we finally came across her 1995 Chevy Impala tucked under a weeping willow.

I pulled up behind her car and parked. When we got out, she used the seat to empty her purse and rummage for her keys mumbling "oh my" and "oh dear." I became the catch all holder for items too important to bury in the accumulating mound and was now armed with mints, rain bonnet, wallet, comb, grocery list, and rocket red lipstick—just no keys.

Her hands shook and her shoulders quivered. "I can't find my keys. I had them just this morning. I just know it."

On a hunch, I walked over to the Impala and peered in the driver's side window. Yup, the keys dangled from the ignition along with a purple rabbit's foot.

"Found them." I checked all the doors. "Locked," I said.

Nora erupted into full tears.

"It's okay." I wrapped my arm around her shoulder. "I'll call the auto club and they'll unlock it."

"That's so kind, thank you. No wonder Mack thinks so much of you."

"He does?" I circled my Jeep, dug my cell phone out of my tote, and scrolled through my contacts for Tow and Rescue. The guys I had called on once to pull me free from a snow bank.

"Oh yes, Mack talks about you all the time. Our daughter would be your age now, had she lived."

"I'm sorry," I said, and bit my lip to keep from prying. Besides, Nora would no doubt volunteer more information, and that did explain why Mack teased me. He viewed me as a living connection to his daughter. I retracted every mean thought I had directed at Mack.

While she put her purse back together, I dialed the auto club helpline. For the next twenty minutes, she quizzed me on my family. When she learned Emma was fourteen years old, she turned misty-eyed again and moaned about how she missed having grandkids. Before I could say my full name, she convinced me to let Emma help her at the pet store for five dollars an hour. I promised to bring Emma by the pet store later that afternoon for an introduction. In less than an hour, I became the surrogate daughter complete with a-rent-a grandkid. Although her fretting tried my patience, I found Nora oddly comforting filling the role of mom away from home.

"Oh my goodness." Nora's mouth hung open. She stared at me eyes wide. "Sorry for the putout, dear. I'm a complete idiot. I have a spare key tucked up under the wheel well in one of those fancy magnetic boxes."

I would have called Tow and Rescue to cancel, but the tow truck just pulled in behind me. Nora exited my Jeep, red handbag clutched to her chest and her nylon windbreaker rustling at her sides. She fetched the key box and waved at me. The tow truck driver slouched up to my window.

"What seems to be the trouble, ma'am?" The embroidered swatch on his jacket read Ace.

"Apparently, no trouble at all." I laughed as Nora gunned her engine, but then drove off, leaving me to pay for services not rendered.

CHAPTER 11

I had just enough time to swing into the police station before Matthew beat me to the office. Unfortunately, the information Joyce printed earlier inadvertently walked away stuffed inside Nora's red purse. No matter, I knew the year and the place and, of course, it was all about Rosalyn Kohler.

The young officer riding desk jockey in the lobby wore a nametag pinned to his shirt pocket.

"Officer Gleason," I said. "My name is Kate—"

His phone rang and he snapped his hand up in a traffic stop wave and pointed me to a bench while he took his phone call. I huffed, checked my watch, and took my seat.

The potted Fichus tree next to the bench dropped a few leaves as I plopped down beside it. Hopefully, they offered resident jailbirds food more regularly than they watered their plants. Unashamed, I eavesdropped on Gleason's conversation, not that I could help but overhear his megaphone voice. His posture changed, suggesting his superior snapped orders and from what I gathered, it pertained to the arrangements for a small motorcade for Selectman Batley's funeral. Good information I could pass on to Joyce.

Finally, Gleason hung up and I leapt off the bench before he took another call.

"Hi," I said, and slapped my business card on the counter.

He studied it before looking up at me with such a deep frown that I wanted to steam it away, at least figuratively; I don't do the ironing thing. I'm a wash and wear woman.

"Can I help you?" He took the card and wrote my name, the date, and time into a logbook. I wondered why the logbook was chained to the desk, especially a police desk.

"I hope so. I need to research missing person reports. You know, for Rosalyn Kohler."

"Who's that?" He handed me back my business card.

"Do you read the *City Scope News*?" I asked, surprised that I found one person in town who didn't want to know the scoop. Then again, with a quick review of his desk, I saw Gleason's reading habits ran along the lines of Rifle magazines and a dog-eared copy of last year's *Sports Illustrated* swimsuit edition.

"Nope. Is Rosa Cole the missing person?"

"No. Rosalyn Kohler."

He turned to his keyboard and punched a few keys. "You're reporting her missing? Has it been over twenty-four hours?"

"No. Someone else did. And yes, it's been well over twenty-four hours."

"That's, K O H L E R?" He typed. "Like the faucet company?"

"Yes. Rosalyn, and no relation." At least he knew how to spell so I forgave him for not including *City Scope* in his reading choices. I leaned over the desk to peer at his monitor.

"Back." He held up his hand.

Jeez. I'm the one with information, here.

"No one by that name. Who made the report?" he asked.

"Um, I'm not sure. The note was faded."

"There's a note involved? A ransom note?"

"No, no. Nothing like that." Did his hand just unlatch the hammer strap on his holstered gun? I gulped.

"May I see this note you have?"

His head to toe assessment of me, committing me to memory to join a future line up, worried me.

"I-I don't have it. I did. But Nora, this little old lady, took it when she couldn't find her car keys."

"The Kohler lady's keys?" His eyes squinted.

"Oh my God." I buried my face in my hands. "Let's start over."

"Why not, starting with your driver's license, please." He held out his hand.

Ah, Jeez. Had I paid those parking fines? Matthew would split his pants laughing if I called him to post bail. I placed my tote on the counter and rooted for my wallet.

"If I could explain—"

"Careful."

I pulled my wallet out with two fingers. "See there was a

personal ad placed in the *City Scope News* back in nineteen-sixty-five. Someone by the name of Robert or Richard Mulch placed the ad looking for her. I'm trying to find out if a formal missing person report was ever filed."

Gleason's mouth dropped open.

"Don't you read the paper?" I asked. "Or at least the IN SIGHT column?"

He shook his head.

"If you did, you'd understand all this." I snatched my license back and gave him one of George's infamous *I can't believe you're clueless* headshakes. I punctuated my rendition with a loud sigh.

"Let me get this straight. You're looking for a report from—"

"Sometime in June or July nineteen-sixty-five."

"And you do understand that back in nineteen-sixty-five we didn't have a computer never mind a missing person's database." He laughed.

Huh, Nora was right, damnit. Heat flushed my cheeks and I tried to keep my voice from squeaking. "So, you have no records, at all, from that year?"

Now it was his turn to shake his head. "You'll have to make an appointment with the House Mouse. He has to arrange to retrieve those cold paper records from the offsite depot."

"House Mouse?"

"Yeah, Officer Earl."

Thank God, he didn't say Mickey, but that still didn't explain the jargon. He gave me Officer Earl's card and told me to call him. I turned with my tail between my legs and scampered out.

CHAPTER 12

Matt was already at the newsroom waiting for me. He buffered the doorway. Arms folded across his chest, and his megawatt smile lit the room. I swallowed hard. Oh my God, he was flirting with her...Ondrea. She twirled her hair, touched his arm, and laughed at whatever lame come-on he used. Not in my lifetime. Dread kicked up my pulse.

"Matthew." I snapped out his name in one syllable. My voice bounced off the brick walls. His eyes shot to me and his lazy smile spread across his lips, the same smile that melted my girlfriends' hearts when we were teenagers. When our father died, Matt became the voice of reason for Allison and me. Allison was thirteen then and I was sixteen. Matt jumped from eighteen into father figure overnight. Now it was my turn to do him a favor and voice reason and caution.

"So, are you ready?" I grabbed his arm and pulled him away from Ondrea.

"Hey, babe." He kissed my cheek.

Ondrea's smile froze and the papers crunched between her clenched fingers. My inner little girl jumped up and down and batted my eyelashes at her. I reveled in her irritation.

"Ready for lunch?" I asked.

"In a minute." He dragged his arm free from my snake wrap. "I was just telling Ondrea how much I enjoyed her piece on funding Yardman High's hockey team."

Oh my God. The hockey article? The one I complained wasted column space.

"That's sweet," Ondrea and I chimed in stereo. We grimaced at each other, surprised identical words came from our mouths.

"Hey, Kate!" Dan hollered from across the room. "Your phone is ringing off the hook."

"Yeah, okay." I shot him a dismissive wave.

"That's not cool, Kate," Ondrea said.

"I've got voicemail and I'm starving." I hooked my arm around Matt's. "Let's go."

"Uh, Kate." Ondrea pointed over my shoulder. "Pick which boyfriend you're going to lunch with, Matthew or Dr. Shrink Rap."

Matt and I nearly bumped noses turning around. My stomach flip-flopped and not because I was craving food.

"Afternoon, Kate, Ondrea." Jonathan nodded and looked to Matt. He offered a gentleman's hand to him. They introduced themselves by first name only.

"Attorney Matthew?" Jonathan connected the missing dots immediately. "Kate's brother?"

I had mentioned Jonathan to Matt and talked endlessly about Matt to Jonathan, but never intended them to meet. I preferred keeping them anonymous.

"Your brother?" Ondrea's lips mimicked.

Jeez, was the universe conspiring against me?

"Dr. Dohe?" They nodded to each other.

Everyone looked at me and I couldn't decide to fold my arms or stuff my hands in my pants pockets or leave my hands fisted on my hips. Now would be a good time for a fire drill.

"Huh, the last time I talked to you, I watched your backside walk away," I said to Jonathan.

"Two day conference. Come to lunch with me," he said. "I need to tell you something."

"Matt and I were just headed to lunch."

Matt pushed me toward Jonathan. "No problem, Kate. I'll have lunch with Ondrea."

Ondrea leaped at the opportunity. "I'll get my purse."

"She's half your age, Matt, and I don't need her entwined in my life."

"Its lunch, Kate, not marriage. Get over it," Matt said. "Besides, the doc obviously has something important to talk to you about."

Ondrea returned. Matt extended his arm and escorted her out. I blew out a sharp breath, two more backsides retreating.

"Come on." Jonathan reached for me. "I'll buy you a latte to punctuate your stress."

"Don't analyze me." I stormed back to my desk. "What can I do for you?" Still wounded by his brisk exit from Rubys last Friday, my cold shoulder chilled even me. I had missed him these past few days, and hearing he'd been away at a conference erased my anger but heightened my guilt.

"Your phone has been ringing off the hook, Kate, enough already," Dan said, and left.

"Sheesh. That's what voicemail is for," I called after Dan. It was unlike him to be in a snit. "I don't understand the big deal about letting a couple calls go to voicemail," I said.

Uneasy and aware my friendship with Jonathan was splintered by my own doing, I shuffled papers and mulled over how to react or what to say.

"Kate. I owe you an apology."

"Huh?" I dropped into my chair and gazed up at him.

"I overreacted the other night, and I'm sorry. I've thought about this a lot."

"Jonathan—"

He held up his hand. "We're good together, as friends." He smiled. "I can accept we're not on the same page when it comes to anything else. I won't make false assumptions again. So, what do you say? Can you forgive me?" He extended his hand.

He smiled. I smiled. He meant what he said, that I could count on. I took his hand and rose to my feet. "No hard feelings."

Since I didn't intend to join the dating game, and controlled the situation, I allowed a little self-torture. I hugged him and sealed our pact. Oh, why do men have to smell so sexy?

My phone rang again. This time, I answered. "Kate Lambrose," I announced.

"Sadie Arnold here, Kate," the woman said as if we were old pals.

Sadie went on to explain how she managed the River Plaza apartments in Hudson. She had read Abby's poem in the paper and thought she might have some information. Sadie recently rented an apartment to a Rosa L. Kohl. She figured, even if the name didn't match, it was similar enough to call me.

"Do you have a phone number for her?" I asked.

"If she got herself a phone in there, I won't know, but her bug is parked out front in her space, so I'm guessing she's at home, unless she took off for a walk. She does that at least once a day, ya know—a fast walk with those small weights in hand. You've seen those, right?"

Yikes. I feared asking another question, but as it turned out, I didn't have to. Sadie was sure the girl wasn't going any place until later when she left for her job.

I thanked her and told her I'd stop by. A short ride for a long shot, but any good reporter followed up on the smallest lead.

I rain checked lunch with Jonathan. He understood, but coaxed me to join him for dinner, testing my new foothold on the *just friends* theory. George had made plans to have Emma for the weekend, so I agreed to a Friday night out.

I left Jonathan with a grin pasted on his face, hightailed it out the door, and ran head-on into Beck.

"Kate, thank you for taking Nora off my hands."

I walked backwards. "Oh, sure. In fact, it might have secured a job for Emma at the pet store."

"Oh. Elaborate."

When would I learn to shut my mouth? "Nothing more to tell." I walked backwards through the door. "I'm off to Hudson to do an interview."

CHAPTER 13

An hour later, I pulled into a guest parking space at River Plaza Apartments. The neighborhood seemed quiet. Ever-greens clustered and towered around the five brick buildings. I followed the red arrow to the rental office. Sadie Arnold, a large African American woman with dyed blonde hair and harlequin glasses greeted me.

"Mrs. Arnold? Hi. I'm Kate—"

"It's Sadie and I know who you are." She smiled. "I read your column every week, recognize you from your picture. Not often we get us a celebrity here." She shook my hand as if she pumped a jack handle.

"Hardly a celebrity, but thanks." From the pile on her desk, the woman also read every tabloid available at the gro-cery store, so I wasn't quite sure the celebrity title was com-plimentary.

"I knew you'd be interested. See, I'm always on the look out to help, and when I read your piece, I couldn't help think that I may actually know this person you're looking for. Well, not exactly know. This girl basically tends to keep to herself. Kind of a paranoid girl. But see, that got me to thinking too. I imagine if someone was looking for me, it might make me paranoid too, and I'd be chopping up my name so I was not to be found."

She sucked in a long breath, filling her bellows. She des-perately needed more conversation than I was prepared to offer. I should have brought Nora with me. "That makes sense to me," I agreed. "How long ago was it that you rented her an apartment?"

Sadie turned to a metal file cabinet behind her and opened the middle drawer. "Let me see. She's in the seven-ten build-ing. That's the one just to the left when you step outside." She nodded in the direction while she pored through her files. "Ah, unit B. Here she is." She pirouetted and faced me. Her right hand fanned the file, and her left hand adjusted her glasses up and down her long nose. "Now, mind you, I can't show you the actual application. But small minor details won't hurt."

I dug in my tote and pulled out my notepad and pen. "Uh huh," I said, although I believed in the reporter's creed and never revealed a source.

"See here, she moved in about three months ago. Said she previously lived in Boston. She's not married." Her stern gaze peered at me over her glasses. "At least in the legal sense, if you know what I mean, and according to her application, of course."

"How old is she?"

"Um, I'd say mid-twenties. Got that baby face still."

I raised my brows and Sadie chuckled. "That's from memory, not the application."

"Of course." I laughed with her.

"She works the swing shift at Bob's. Always pays her rent on the first. In cash too."

"Huh. Well, I'll go on over and knock on her door."

"You go on and do that," Sadie said. She waved her arms, shooing me out. "Mind you stop back in here when you're done. Fill me in on whether I was helpful for your next CSN article."

"CSN?"

"Yeah, *City Scope News*." She giggled.

I thanked her and headed over to the next building.

Stairways at each end zigzagged up three flights and the downstairs small patios jutted out beyond the landing overhead.

Rosa Lynn Kohl's unit was the second apartment on the second floor. I knocked. My stomach somersaulted. I wiped my sweaty palm on my slacks and waited. Masking tape with the occupant's name and a little stenciled heart stuck to the door beneath the unit letter *B*.

Footsteps, then the door popped open the length of the security chain and cigarette smoke rolled around the doorjamb. I peered through the gap and spied a bulbous nose, and one dark brown eye smudged with chocolate mascara.

"Yeah?" she said.

"I'm Kate Lambrose, from *City Scope*—"

"I don't want the paper." She slammed the door.

I knocked again. "Look. I'm not selling subscriptions." No answer. I knocked again. "You're Rosa Kohl, right?"

The chain yanked and the door flew open. "What about it?"

My eyes met a well-endowed bust restrained by the thinnest tank top material. I tilted my head back and peered up the flaring nostrils of the largest woman I had ever encountered. "You wouldn't happen to uh..." I swallowed hard. Insanity equaled asking an angry giant if she used an alias. "Use the name Rosalyn Kohler?" She took a step towards me. Her bare, flat feet slapped the concrete deck, and I stepped back to avoid a nipple in the eye.

"Does it say Rosalyn Kohler?" She smacked the door where the tape held fast.

I flinched. "Do you know anyone by the name of Abby?" No time to explain my crusade, I valued my life.

"What are you, a cop?"

I shook my head and back stepped as she took another step toward me. My butt bumped against the balcony rail.

"FBI? CIA? ICE?" She fired initials at me.

"CSN reporter." I managed to get my mouth working again.

Obviously, she had buried lies, but not out at sea and she was not my Rosalyn Kohler, thank God. The Amazon woman scared me gray, especially after she threatened to drop kick me over the railing. *Baby face? Maybe if her daddy went by the name Jolly Green. Paranoid? Absolutely, and definitely in need of anger management classes.* I beat feet down the steps. Next stop, Abbot's pharmacy for Summer Brunette hair dye to wash away my gray.

My knees were still shaking when I stopped at the rental office and thanked Sadie Arnold. She was sorry her lead hadn't panned out, but thought she might have info on the Alien Baby headline.

On the drive back from Hudson, I compartmentalized all my facts, which wasn't much. After my run in with Rosa Lynn Kohl, my imagination ran wild and tangled with the words from my phone threat. "Leave it go before you're gone." Giant woman's paranoia infected me, and I spun conspiracy plots in my head. Maybe Sadie Arnold's tip had merit. Maybe Rosa Lynn Kohl really was Rosalyn Kohler and somehow tied to my phone threat in ways I hadn't suspected. I checked my rearview mirror repeatedly during the ride back to Yardman, as if I could spot a tail. Just to be certain, I skipped the first exit off the highway and opted for the second. A slight detour and it put me on the south end of Yardman. I vowed to watch fewer murder mysteries.

CHAPTER 14

I arrived at City Scope at quarter to five after seesawing between going straight home or back to the office. Checking my afternoon mail delivery for an Abby reply won over a soak in the tub with a glass of wine. If I didn't have Pulitzer on my mind, I would have missed everyone filing back into the building.

Fire Chief Ramsey and Beck stood curbside, chatting. I slowed my pace, enough to eavesdrop, but kept far enough away not to get pulled into their conversation. I knelt down and pretended to tie my sneaker.

"Every time that alarm rings, Helen, we have no choice but to respond," Ramsey said.

"I understand the Department's prudence, chief, and appreciate the dedicated response. However, we do notify the department immediately once we ascertain it is a false alarm," Beck responded.

Ramsey scribbled on some papers attached to a clipboard and shook his head at Beck. Same headshake I received from George when I'd made a logical point he considered irrational. At that moment, I sympathized with Beck even as I understood the chief's point. "Your husband owns the building, Helen. Either get the fire alarm system fixed or the next time you'll be fined. You're wasting my resources." He ripped the sheet free from the clipboard and handed it to her. "This is your written warning to comply, again."

I retied my shoestring in another knot and stood up. Aha, I had the scoop on the funky fire alarm and Beck fit the *who* responsible to fix it. Now only to uncover *when*, and *why* the delay.

Helen took the note. Her lips compressed tightly and the lines around her mouth deepened. She stormed up the steps ahead of me and Ramsey nodded as we passed each other.

I heaved my tote on my desk and slumped into my chair. Dan and Simon were already gone for the day and Ondrea chatted with Eugene in his office. Joyce must have been in the ladies room and Beck screamed at someone on the phone. I suspected it was about the fire alarm.

I snapped the rubber band off my mail and flipped through ten pieces, all letter-size envelopes, and none from Abby. All had return addresses except one from G. Lambrose. I tore into that one. George would rather use the phone than write a letter, unless of course he was crunching numbers and sent me Emma's phone bill. Even when we were dating, he never wrote more than I love you on a napkin. I blew out a long breath. Gosh, what was it going to cost me, or was it something more serious?

Dear Insightful Kate, I read. *I'm trusting you to help me recover a pearl necklace before you know who asks me again if I've seen them. Lives are at stake, either yours or mine, depending on how the story unfolds. You know I love ya, even though Mother never did. Hugs, George. PS: Sorry for picking on you and for not discussing Disneyland or the cell phone. I promise to remember. —Love, GL.*

"Oh pleaseeee." I laughed aloud and crumpled his letter, tossing it into the trash bucket. It would be justice if I just packed up the pearls and mailed them to his mother with a thank you note for the loan.

Next, I checked voicemail. Only two messages waited, one from Mrs. Grant, Emma's teacher. She wanted to meet with me Friday morning. Emma must have done something either spectacular or horribly wrong for Mrs. Grant to request a conference. I couldn't recall the last time one of Emma's teachers requested a meeting before the quarterly meet and greet progress report. Huh.

The other call came from a woman who identified herself as Bea. She worked for Elderly Assist Gardens, a retirement home in Arlington. She claimed they had a resident named Abby a few years back, but she couldn't recall the last name. Although Abby was no longer a guest, Bea did not want to divulge additional information and risk compromising patient confidentiality. Knowing a woman named Abby wasn't enough of a lead, but then Bea stated the Abby she knew kept journals filled with poetry. She ended her message by rattling off her phone number and gave me a time to reach her on Sunday.

"That's just great." I groaned. Twiddling my thumbs waiting patiently was not one of my greatest assets. And the wonderment of it all plotted nightmares in my mind.

CHAPTER 15

By the time I pulled into my garage, I had smashed my parental hat on top of my reporter hat. No way did I intend to wait for Friday to find out why Mrs. Grant wanted to meet with me. I headed to the source, Emma.

I dropped my tote on the kitchen table, barely missing a brown limp banana peel and a plastic spoon with peanut butter stuck to it. Both went in the trash off the tips of my fingers. "Emma, you need to clean..." I glanced toward the living room. No Emma, no blaring stereo, or the television. I cocked my head and listened then followed the giggles drifting down the stairs from Emma's room. Hearing only Emma's voice meant she was chattering away on her cell. Most likely to Sammy, who lived close enough to read a sign tacked on our front door. *Wait until George gets her first bill*. I inched her door open with my palm. When she saw me, she cut Sammy off in a serious tone and announced she was off to meet her new boss.

"We're not going," I said, dropping down to sit next to her on her bed.

"Why not?"

"I'm too tired and hungry."

"Well, I'm not hungry."

"I figured that when I found the banana peel and peanut butter. We can go tomorrow."

"Why?" She stomped her foot.

"Emma, it's not like you're going to start work tonight at five-thirty anyway." She flopped backwards on her bed, grunted, and crossed her arms in a huff.

"I'm sorry, sweetie, really I am. And I have something to talk to you about."

"What?" She pouted. The only reason she still spoke to me was that I could still say no tomorrow.

"Mrs. Grant left me a message to come see her on Friday. Do you happen to know why?"

She shook her head then pushed herself up in her bed and leaned against the wall.

"Are you sure?" I asked. "I hate surprises, Emma, so if there is something I should know, please clue me in."

"Mom...I don't know why she'd call you, honest."

Downstairs, the doorbell chimed. "Sammy?" I asked her.

"I doubt it. She's grounded."

I trotted back down the stairs and swung the door open. Matthew stood holding a pizza in hand. I stared at him with my mouth open. "What are you doing here?" *Oh no, the age of innocence has snuck up on me. Did I forget I had invited him?*

"Nice greeting, sis." He walked around me and headed for the kitchen.

"I meant, was I expecting you?"

"No."

"Is Mom okay?" I asked.

He nodded. "I assume so."

"And Allison is okay?"

"As far as I know, she's okay too."

"Then what's up?"

"Nothing. Was in town and thought I'd pick up a pizza and say hi."

I frowned at him. Matt never dropped by. He penciled appointments in his daily planner to grocery shop.

I turned back to the stairs and hollered, "Emma, your Uncle Matt is here with pizza."

She bombed down the stairs and I fished out two wineglasses and the half a bottle of Pinot Noir I had leftover in the refrigerator.

"Hey, Uncle Matt." Emma gave him a hug. "What are you doing here?"

"What is it with you two? Can't a guy visit?"

Emma shrugged her shoulders. "Mom doesn't think so. She says I'm not old enough to have boys over and she doesn't date. You don't really count, though."

"Gee, thanks." Matt laughed.

My daughter, loose-lipped and tactful.

"Oh, and guess what? I got a job."

"You did?"

"Yeah, at the pet store. Mom was supposed to take me there tonight to meet my boss, but she's too tired." She rolled her eyes.

He raised his brows at me. "Did I interrupt you two going out?"

I shook my head. "Too tired. We'll go tomorrow."

We ate the hot pizza straight from the box, using paper towels as makeshift plates. "So...what brings you to Yardman all the way from Boston?" I asked.

He sighed. "I planned to take Ondrea out to dinner."

"Oh God."

"Now see, that's the attitude and reason why I'm consoling myself eating a greasy pizza with my sister rather than prime rib with her," he said.

"What's that mean?"

"She said yes, but then when I arrived to pick her up, she changed her mind. Your fault, I might add."

"Me? I doubt it." *She's probably playing hard to get.*

"Yeah, you. She said she didn't see any sense in us dating when you despise her. That it wouldn't make for a good relationship between us."

"Well if you ask me, that's pretty damn presumptuous for her to assume you two could have a relationship."

"Mom."

"What?" They both stared at me.

"You can't decide who he likes," Emma said.

Matt patted Emma on the shoulder. "Thanks, sweetie," he said.

"Well, first, she is too young for you and second, it's not me that despises her; it's she that despises me. She's rude and insulting."

"How old is she?" Emma asked.

"Never mind," I said.

"She's twenty-eight." Matt answered.

"No, she's not. She's twenty-six." Subtracting the two extra years was petty, but I used it as ammunition to build my case. Rude, insulting, and now a liar.

"How old are you, Uncle Matt?"

He leaned over and whispered, "Forty-five."

"Wow," Emma said. "You're older than my dad."

Matt and I laughed.

"So, you're like nineteen years older than she is," Emma

said.

Huh, so she wasn't having any difficulty with math or word problems, for sure.

"Older boys are so cool."

My mouth snapped shut and I glared at Matthew. *Thanks a lot.* I wanted to wipe the sheepish grin right off his face. "Are you done yet?" I asked Emma.

She flipped open the pizza box and ate a stray pepperoni, the only crumb left in the box, and nodded.

"Good. You have clean up duty," I reminded her.

Emma mumbled something about being a slave as she stood up, grabbed the empty box, used paper towels, and tossed them into the trash. Before vanishing back upstairs to her room, she threw her arms around Matt's shoulders and thanked him for the pizza.

"Oh, and good luck with your girlfriend," she called from the stairs.

Matt broke out in a howl, slapping the table with his hands. "You cloned yourself, Kate."

"I don't see what's so amusing." I scowled.

"You would if you could see your face. I thought you were going to have a stroke when she said older boys are cool."

"Yeah, well, I don't want to talk about it or even think about it. She's fourteen."

Matt grinned. "She's just like you were at that age."

I almost spewed my wine.

"Remember? You had a crush on my bud Alan. We'd be playing catch in the backyard and you'd come out in a bikini to tan yourself."

Pitiful, but true. At fourteen, I resembled a two-by-four, ill equipped to catch the eye of a sixteen-year-old.

"Those days are over." I waved my hand.

"Going for the younger ones these days, too, huh?"

"No."

"The doc's younger than you."

"No, he's not." *Is he?*

Matt raised his eyebrows.

I sipped my wine, trying to appear unfazed. "Well, even if he is, it doesn't matter. We're just good friends."

"Uh huh."

"We are."

"Oh, in other words, you haven't taken him out for a test

drive. Still window shopping?"

"Let's not discuss me, let's get back to you and Ondrea. My God, Matt, I'm confused. I thought you were a confirmed bachelor and here you are pouting like when Lucy..." I snapped my fingers to conjure up her last name. "What's her name—in high school—the girl that turned you down for prom."

"You would bring her up." He shook his finger at me.

"You started it." Alan and Lucy had hooked up in high school, and both Matthew and I had been crushed. Later, they married, and as far as I knew, they were still married.

"Alan still keeps in touch. Sends me a Christmas card every year, those family photo ones. They have four kids—two boys and two girls."

I shrugged, even though I wanted to ask if Alan was still as sexy as I remembered. Matthew leaned across the table and studied my face.

"What?" I asked.

"Gauging your curiosity level." He smirked. "About a nine."

"No."

"Ten then?" He laughed. "Truth or dare?"

"Nooo." I shoved his shoulder and he clucked and flapped his elbows at me. "Fine. Dare," I said, hoping he would let me off the hook about any Alan questions.

His eyes twinkled. "Call the doc. Tell him you want a road test. Tell him you want to show him the candy store."

"Oh my God, *no*." My ears heated and I flipped my hair out from behind them. "Truth then."

"You're jealous of Ondrea."

"That's not true." I crossed my arms over my chest.

"Threatened then?"

"Pfft." I took a healthy swallow and drained my wine-glass. *Game on.* "Truth or dare?"

Matthew leaned back against the chair comfortably. "Truth."

"You're only interested in Ondrea for the, uh, how'd you put it? Test drive possibilities?"

"False." He looked me square in the eye.

My turn, I leaned across the table and scrutinized his face. "You're serious?" *Oh my God, he is serious.* "I think you've had too much to drink."

"I'm not getting any younger. It's time I settled down or the Stanton name will die with me."

"Matt, why would you say that? You're not going to die. Are you?"

"I'm not psychic, are you? But what woman my age wants to have kids? Would you?"

I thought about that for a whole two seconds before my mind scream *no*. Matt had my mind spinning in wonderland. I wondered if Jonathan wanted kids some day and then wondered why I even chose to throw Jonathan into the mix. Jonathan and I were just friends. The only candy I offered was stashed in my desk drawer.

"No, I don't want any more kids," I said to Matt. "I'm too old to start over."

"Exactly my point."

"You are serious." I gawked at him, not believing we were having this conversation. It never occurred to me he obsessed over his internal clock winding down, but it should have. He probably had a date circled on his calendar for pending nuptials and was just looking for the name to fill in the calendar block. "Okay, so let's say I understand for one minute why you want to get involved with someone younger. Does it have to be her?" I shook my head.

"I like her."

"You had one lunch date with her."

"She's smart, funny, interesting, and pretty. We didn't struggle once for something to talk about. She knows all about fishing and hunting and—"

"Wait." I held up my hand. "Don't tell me she owns a gun."

"No. Rifles."

"Oh my God." Great, Ondrea on a rooftop getting ready to pick me off as I showed up for work.

"What is wrong with you, Kate?" He shook his finger at me. "She fascinates me. She'll never be as boring as your doc."

"Jonathan is not boring."

"Sure. From what you said, all he ever does is invite you to dinner and even that has you putting on the brakes. Boring." He rolled his eyes.

"That's my choice."

"Right. But if he invited you out to a show or concert, you would have a harder choice to make."

Maybe. Why hadn't Jonathan done that, and what answer

would I give if he offered more choices? Maybe Jonathan was a loner, like George, and preferred solo activities instead of crowds. Huh, the reason I kept him at arm's length was so I wouldn't end up stuck being someone's all when forever was fictitious. Although, I did enjoy ogling him. On a tachometer scale, he revved my engine a healthy three, not bad, but could I do better?

"Never mind, back to you and Ondrea," I said. "What do you want me to do, give her my blessing to date my brother?"

"That's a start."

"Be serious. She could care less."

"Well, see, Kate, that's you not looking past your own nose." He stood up and rinsed his glass at the kitchen sink. "She obviously is concerned about it, enough to not even want to bother to find out if we are compatible or not."

"Fine, I'll say something to her tomorrow." *Like drop dead.* "Sheesh. I promise."

I walked Matthew out to his car, surprised and disturbed over our conversation. I locked up the house, trudged up-stairs to marinate in the tub and mull the whole thing over again. I'd rather cut my tongue out than give Ondrea a thumbs up to date Matt. My brain went full circle until I worked myself into anger. *How dare she not give my brother a chance?*

By the time I climbed into bed, I reasoned if I woke up tomorrow, I had no other choice but to hint to Ondrea I could care less if she went out with Matt. As I drifted off to sleep, I remembered I should have mentioned to Matt the phone threat I received. If I died tonight, he'd think I did it to avoid keeping my promise.

CHAPTER 16

Before eight o'clock the following morning, Nora had bombarded me with five voicemail messages each longer than the previous. She babbled on about how in her day, she was taught to keep a commitment, and hadn't my mother possessed the good sense to teach me common courtesy? It was my fault. I had stood her up last night and was even too tired to call and cancel. Emma's disappointment waned after Uncle Matt and pizza, but I promised to take her today. My day was full of promises.

Finally, Ondrea showed up, not the brightest moment in my day, but I had to fulfill my second promise. Granting her straight out permission to date my brother would give her the upper hand and that scared me. I tried to practice what I could say to her, but nothing came to mind. I would max out my adlib skills today for sure.

"Ondrea, you have a minute?" I asked, fondling my coffee mug and heading to the cafeteria. She hummed a reply, but followed me.

"What do want, Kate?"

I turned and faced her, gripping my cup, my prop, something to do with my hands other than slap her. Oh how awkward and embarrassing, but a promise was a promise.

"Just so you know, my brother is a grown man and I have no say about who he dates. We don't interfere in each other's lives that way." That was very mature of me, even though my voice quivered.

"Wow. I thought you wanted to pilfer my vanilla creamer, but here you are negotiating for your brother."

"Pilfer—negotiate? I—"

Her eyes widened and her lips twitched. "You *what*, Kate?"

I bit the inside of my cheek and clamped my free hand

tightly to my thigh. If I slapped her now, I couldn't count on Matthew bailing me out and with my luck, the two of them would bond while I rotted in jail. I took a deep breath and smiled. "I just wanted to let you know, I can accept my brother dating you."

Ondrea tossed her hair over her shoulder and laughed. "Seriously, Kate, are you giving me your permission to date your brother?"

"Yes, no...I mean, it doesn't affect me one way or the other." My ears burned hot.

"What makes you think I need your permission or that I even care how it affects you?"

"Matt said that you changed your mind because of me."

"Oh, that." She snorted. "It was as good of an excuse as anything." She twirled and headed back to her desk.

"What does that mean?" I stomped after her and almost ran into her backside when she stopped short.

"It means he's not my type. Now, if you'll excuse me, unlike you, I have an actual article to write."

She sashayed around the corner and back to her desk. Shocked speechless, it took me a full five seconds to recover before I scrambled after her.

"What's wrong with my brother?"

"Other than being too old, he's obviously a tattler."

I ignored that. This wasn't going at all like I expected. I intended to say my piece and be on my way. However, Ondrea's ego sucked the air out of my self-inflated ego. I needed a new strategy, and not just one to make Matthew happy, but to get my ego out from under her foot.

"This is silly, Ondrea." I sighed. "You're right."

Slowly, she slanted her eyes away from the monitor and her gaze slid over me. "I'm right about what?"

"First, there's nothing wrong with Matt. He's intelligent, a senior partner in his law firm, financially stable, not hard on the eyes, and looking for a serious relationship. It's just that you're too young for him." I saw the twinkle in her eyes and continued. "Stupid me. What was I thinking? And I suppose in a few years, you'll mature enough to want those things Matthew has to offer." I sauntered back to my cubicle, propelled by her loud hiss.

Matthew would either kill me or be proud of me, but either way, he'd have to at least forgive me. We were family.

I wasted the morning tracing down the attorney offices responsible for the estate of Lydia Kohler only to find out they packed up and moved. The law firm was now part of a large conglomerate with corporate headquarters in Arizona.

By one o'clock, I had finally reached a live person who assured me I'd receive a return phone call, but cautioned it might take a day or two. I gave the woman my cell number.

My day just seemed useless. Even Officer Earl, the house mouse, busted my hopes by telling me he doubted there were any cold papers from that era. And he said era as if it were another dimension, but he'd stop by the depot later and let me know. At least he understood what to look for, unlike Gleason, and asked if Abby had contacted me yet.

"No, not yet, but I'm hopeful." My hopes were dwindling fast.

"I enjoy a good mystery," he said.

"Oh yeah? Well I'm still mystified by the phrase house mouse."

He laughed, which brightened my senses. His laugh rolled like a spinning coin into a soft hum, warm and contagious, not to mention inviting.

"House mouse refers to the police officer that rarely leaves the building," he said.

"Oh." I expected an amusing story, not a definition. "So, is Earl your first name or last?" My God, I was flirting. I slapped my hand from twirling my hair.

"Last, first name is Michael." A radio chirped in the background. "Got to run, Kate," he said, and hung up. Disappointed but relieved, I hung up. My flirting skills had abandoned me anyway and he left me breathless from listening to him breathe his name into my ear. He even made Kate sound sexy, which heightened my imagination. I was panting, Michael Earl, Michael Earl.

Then Jonathan called to invite Emma and me to dinner. Predictable, as Matt said, and oh so boring. I hemmed and hawed then changed it up a little and finally agreed, but at my house. Damned if I didn't start with the panting again, but this time, I tried Jonathan Dohe, then George Lambrose. Neither echoed that sexy breathless moan like Michael Earl had.

Mack showed up empty-handed. "No mail, Kate."

That was unusual and I made him look again. Although Abby would not have had time between seeing my column to mailing a response, I did at least expect a phone call.

However, the phone call I least expected came from Emma who found new independence with her cell phone and rang me between her fifth and sixth period. She stated if she was old enough to work, she was old enough to walk the two blocks to Nora's Nest without me. I agreed.

"Really?" she said. Apparently, she hadn't expected me to agree so easily.

"Sure." I laughed. "I'll pick you up at six."

"Cool. Thanks, Mom."

"You're welcome. But I have a question for you. Would you mind if I invited Jonathan over? Nothing fancy, just some fast food."

"Yeah, whatever. Got to go. That's the bell. Love you."

Huh. I laughed. I was just as surprised by her indifference as she was of mine.

My phone rang again just as I hung up with Emma. It was Matt.

I had done what he asked and talked to Ondrea, but the outcome sucked and I hated delivering bad news.

"Kate, just wanted to say thanks."

"Well, uh, I wouldn't be so quick to—"

"We have dinner plans tonight, so thanks again." He laughed.

"Wait. Who has dinner plans tonight?"

"Ondrea and me. She just called and agreed to dinner."

"What?"

"Kate, I have to go. Talk to you later." He hung up.

I shook my head, trying to understand what happened. Clearly, she had said he was too old, not her type, and a tattler. Then the light went on. She turned everything around on me so that I ended up serving up my brother to her on a platter. Oh boy, I hope he knew what he was doing.

CHAPTER 17

Five minutes before six, I left work. I could have walked to Nora's Nest, but to keep from doubling back, I drove and grabbed a parking spot across from the storefront. The yellow Lab puppies I ogled earlier were gone from the display window, but I peered inside anyway. Emma's first work experience and I wanted to spy on her, but no one staffed the checkout counter and nobody wandered in the aisles. I pushed through the door and triggered the electronic eye. Winchester chimes trilled above the door, and then a squawk and flap of wings lunged at me. I ducked.

"Watch out, Mom." Emma popped up from behind the counter. "Don't let him get out."

The yellow-green parrot circled over my head, thwacked against the glass, and scrambled for footing. Finding none, it swooped back toward Emma. She ducked in time to dodge its beating wings and the bird u-turned to avoid the wall. It made one last frantic circle and perched on the top shelf in the middle aisle.

"What the heck is going on?" I shouted above the ruckus. Crouching low, I scooted along the perimeter without taking my eyes off the parrot, and made my way to Emma. The bird stretched its wings and walked a semi-circle, keeping one eye trained on me. Its head bobbed left and right. Its dither reminded me of how Nora appeared when I first spotted her at my desk.

"The bird got out."

"I can see that. Where's Nora?" I asked. The bird mimicked, "*No rah, O dear.*"

"She went to make the bank deposit. Oh Mom, we have to catch him before she comes back. Every time I stand up, he swoops at me." Her blue eyes shimmered on the verge of tears.

"We can do this," I said. "Get a cat."

"Not funny," she said, but laughed.

I grabbed the two butterfly nets hanging behind the counter and handed one to Emma. "You go that way and I'll go this way."

We exited opposite ends of the counter, nets raised. The bird took off, feathers flapping, and angry screeches circled about us. Emma rushed forward. The bird dodged, knocked items off a display, circled back around, and dive-bombed toward me. I raised my net and ducked at the same time. The front door chime dinged barely audible above the barking dog chorus and the parrot's panicked cry. My net came up empty and I prayed the bird didn't escape out the door.

"What on earth?" Nora said. Her eyes darted between Emma and me. The parrot circled high above our reach one last time and landed on Nora's shoulder. "Silly bird." She clucked and it nuzzled against her cheek.

"No rah, No rah."

"I'm so sorry," Emma said. "I don't know how he got out."

"Not to worry, dear. Mackie is a bit of an escape artist." She clucked to the bird, "Naughty bird, aren't you?"

"O dear, O dear." The bird squawked.

I took the net from Emma's hand and returned them to the hook on the wall. "Mackie? Did you name him after your husband?" I snickered.

"You didn't think you'd catch him with those nets, did you?" Nora offered the bird her arm as a perch.

"It was Mom's idea." Emma threw me under the bus.

Nora's stern, crinkled face insulted my ingenuity. "What's wrong with using a net?" He seemed more like an attack bird than an escape artist and I liked having two eyes and an un-scarred face.

"He could have broken a wing, Kate. Best you stick with writing words." She tucked Mackie back in his cage and draped a blanket over it. "Next time he gets out, Emma, don't be afraid. If you stand still, he'll land right on your shoulder, dear."

"Cool." Emma grinned.

"Just don't rush him."

"Probably would have been a good idea to tell her that before you left her alone," I said. The last time I saw that how-stupid-could-you-be? mother look, I was twelve explaining why I filled the dishwasher with Dawn dish soap. What did I know about birds? A net was a great idea.

I picked up the few items that tumbled off the display and returned them to the shelf. "Get your backpack, Emma. We have to go."

"You're not mad at me, Kate, are you? I'm sorry." Nora's eyes watered. "You're right, dear, I should have known better."

"No. I'm not mad. It's fine."

"You'll let Emma come back, won't you?" Her lip quivered.

"Please, Mom. It wasn't her fault." Emma's brows crept up her forehead. She stood next to Nora. They posed a united front, trapping me against their emotional wall.

"Yes." I sighed, and they both cheered and hugged each other. "Tomorrow. But if you're going to do this, you have to keep your grades up."

"Done." Emma grinned.

"And you—" I squinted at Nora.

"Don't worry. I'm sorry for the put out, dear." Nora smiled.

In the last two days, she had said that at least three times. Her *put out* phrase was as peculiar as Mack's *what ya say* expression, except hers asked forgiveness and his said he didn't give a shit.

"How about we go out to dinner?" Nora suggested. "We can have chicken. Make you feel better eating some drumsticks after being terrorized by Mackie."

Emma and I scrunched up our noses at each other. "Uh, another time maybe. We're having company tonight," I said.

"Oh. That sounds like fun. I'll lock up and come with you." She bounded off with determination back in her step.

"No, Nora." Argh.

She headed to the counter to retrieve keys and purse. "Oh come on, Mom. She's a little lonely," Emma whispered.

"No, Emma." I shook my head. "Nora. We have to go."

"I'm coming."

"I'm sorry, but—"

"Oh, I see." She fished a tissue out of her bra and sniffled into it. "I'm not invited."

"It's just—" Great, more tears. "It's a business meeting. It'd be awkward. I'm sure you understand." Why did I lie to top it off?

"I'll be fine. I'm sure I have some crackers around to snack on."

I pulled Emma toward the door. "Okay then. We'll do it another time."

Once back in the Jeep, Emma heaved a massive sigh and spit my words at me. "Aren't you supposed to respect your elders? That was plain mean. You made her cry twice and I can't believe you're gonna let her eat crackers for dinner."

I didn't have the energy or the patience to explain how the over sixty crowd practiced the fine art of manipulation. I reached for my seatbelt and brushed my hand against something wet and sticky on my shoulder. "Well, if it makes you feel better, there are consequences to every action. Karmic law."

"What that does mean?"

"Mackie pooped on me."

My cell phone rang deep in my tote. Emma reached in and grabbed it for me. "Say's restricted number. What's that mean?" she asked.

"Paranoia." I snagged it from her hand. "Just means it's a blocked number."

She huffed and folded her arms across her chest. "Nora would have explained without the sarcasm."

I scowled at Emma. My displeasure with Nora didn't mix well with my daughter spouting accolades about her.

I flipped open my phone. "Nora didn't get pooped on."

"Excuse me?" My caller asked. "Is this Kate Lambrose?"

"Yes, uh sorry," I said. Emma giggled.

"This is Attorney Able Jackson's office. Please hold for Mr. Jackson."

"Quick. Get my notepad and pen." I pointed at my tote and turned on the dome light.

"Who is it?" Emma asked.

"Hopefully a lead on my Abby Story." She handed me a broken pencil and a crinkled grocery receipt.

"Oh, that," she said with her nose crinkled. "Nora says—"

I pointed at her and narrowed my mother stare into the I-dare-you-to-say-another-word warning.

"Ms. Lambrose, I understand you're interested in the estate of Lydia Kohler." A silky smooth baritone voice tickled my ear. "I haven't heard that name in forty years."

It surprised me he could remember any name after four decades and I said as much.

He chuckled and went on to explain he was Jackson Junior, who interned for his father's practice forty years ago, five years after Lydia Kohler's death. I did the math in my head and calculated his age between sixty and sixty-five years old.

"It's not a common name to forget," he said.

"Was she rich? Lydia Kohler, that is."

Mr. Jackson laughed. "Well, that's subjective, isn't it? One man's buggy is another man's chariot."

I rolled my eyes at his lame attempt at humor and drew circles on the grocery receipt. "So what happens to un-claimed inheritance? Will it go to the state?" I had no clue about inheritance rules or regulations, but it sounded good.

"No, on the contrary. The state received the appropriate taxes. My father, Jackson Senior, placed the estate's effects in a safe deposit box. Rosalyn Kohler, whatever her reasons, never came forward."

"So you have stuff gathering dust. Will it just stay in a safe deposit box? Are you still actively looking for Rosalyn Kohler?"

"Yes to the first question, at least until the rental cost of the safe deposit box exceeds the value of the items. And no to your second question. The firm has done its due diligence and will remain the depository until the value becomes a li-ability and the maintenance then incurs a cost, at which time they will be auctioned off."

Double talk, he answered both my questions with the same answer. At the inflation rate, whatever value Lydia Koh-ler's personal effects totaled, Mr. Jackson's law firm stood to make a bundle.

"Did a woman named Abby or Abigail ever come up, maybe not so much in Lydia Kohler's estate but in your search for Rosalyn Kohler?"

"Our due diligence did not consist of an active search, Ms. Lambrose. Our responsibility ended at placing notice in the newspaper."

"How many newspapers?"

"One."

City Scope. "Why the *City Scope* newspaper?"

"Last known city address for Rosalyn Kohler." He sighed. "All measures and safeguards to the estate were dictated in Lydia Kohler's final will and testament. Our diligence is to protect what assets are left until an heir claims them. And, if an heir is out there but doesn't wish to be found, that's not my firm's concern."

Huh. Another reason for me to find Rosalyn Kohler.

"So Rosalyn Kohler lived here in Yardman? Do you happen to have that address?"

"No to both your questions. That newspaper covered the circulation area for her last known city address."

I'd bet a week's pay he was looking at the last known city address while he snapped off his words.

"Can I ask what's in the safe deposit box?"

"You can ask, but unless you are the heir—I cannot disclose that."

Whatever, it didn't hurt to ask. I thanked him for his time, and he wished me luck, although he seemed more amused than sincere. A figurative clock ticked down to the twelfth hour and Abby's poem floated through my thoughts. *Surface the buried lies, before death severs all ties.*

I smoothed out the grocery receipt. Dots, dashes, and paisley designs circled the words *last known city address*, a dead end. Rosalyn Kohler's name never surfaced in any town listings Joyce and I had searched.

"Are we going to eat sometime this year?" Emma asked. "'Cause I'd have chicken with Nora."

I handed her my pen, and cell, flicked the dome light off, and put the Jeep into gear. Her independent streak stirred the surly teenager. If working with Nora meant she would challenge me at every turn, I might rethink this. For now, I would let it ride.

***

I pulled into Rubys' parking lot, handed Emma two twenties, and sent her inside to pick up our to-go order—three All American Specials—cheeseburgers, fries, chocolate shakes, and half an apple pie. My mistake was telling her to hurry, we were running late. Next time, I'd suggest she exit the car slowly and not worry if the food refroze while she lollygagged back to the car. I sped out the alley, up the hill, and out on to Winter Street.

I expected to see Jonathan waiting in my driveway when we pulled in and it concerned me that he wasn't. He was always on time or early. Huh, did that make Jonathan boring or dependable?

I put his shake in the freezer and our food in the microwave to hold any heat that remained. While Emma sat down to eat, I tossed my pooped-on shirt into the laundry and ran upstairs to grab a clean one.

"You're phone is ringing. Again," Emma hollered.

"Who is it?"

"Says Jonathan."

"Answer it, please." No way could I make it down the stairs in time without breaking my leg, but I tried anyway.

As I rounded the corner, Emma held the flipped open phone above her head and concentrated on swirling her fries in ketchup. Another dismissive body language attitude.

"Hey. Your food is getting cold. Where are you?" I asked.

"On my way to Connecticut," Jonathan said. "I'm sorry I have to cancel on you."

The strain in his voice bled through the phone, talking with his teeth clamped tight as he always did when he talked about his parents. His destination explained his tension. His parents lived in Connecticut, but his relationship with his father had become estranged years ago. He continued to make monthly calls to his mother, but he hadn't visited in ten years. I couldn't pretend to understand how difficult it was for him and his mother. My father and I had been best friends and I still missed him. Had death not stolen him, nothing would have separated us. My heart broke for Jonathan every time he mentioned his mother. And my anger rose every time he swore his father refused to talk to him.

"What's wrong?" I asked.

"My mother asked me to visit."

"And your father agreed?"

He was silent for a moment and I could hear Rascal Flatts, his favorite CD, playing.

"Jonathan?"

"At this point, I don't think it matters what my father wants. Her dementia has reached the stage of—she's frightened. It matters what she wants, and what I need to do, not what my father wants." He had his in-charge voice in high gear, the voice men use when they know for sure what they are saying is a hundred percent correct.

"Are you okay?" A dumb question to ask, but I was saying I cared.

"Of course," he said. "And Kate, we're still on for Friday."

"Absolutely." I smiled and hoped it came across on the

phone. "Call me later if the drive gets long and you want to talk."

He thanked me, and I hung up awkward with volumes left unsaid. I removed the dinners from the microwave and put Jonathan's Styrofoam container in the fridge. Most likely, I'd throw it away at some point tomorrow. Reheated dinners from Rubys lost appeal, and I had already lost my appetite. Part from disappointment, but more from knowing Jonathan's efforts would go unwanted. The last time he saw his father, their tempers soared and Jonathan walked away with a broken nose. Ten years ago, Jonathan's fraternal twin brother, Thomas, died of a drug overdose. As unreasonable as it sounded, his father blamed Jonathan. According to his father, Jonathan should have recognized the addiction symptoms in his twin. He should have done something, anything to fix his brother. He attended the best university, aced his clinical exams, had written a paper published in the *Journal of American Medicine Association,* but ignored what was happening within his own family, according to his father. Jonathan shouldered the blame because he said he shouldn't have missed the signs.

CHAPTER 18

Two days since *City Scope* hit the stands with Abby's poem and my response. The interest generated kept my phone lines ringing until I couldn't tolerate the ringer any longer. Even the grocery clerk at Market Rite wanted to know if I had found Rosalyn or Abby. Secretly, I enjoyed the notoriety. I, however, feared failure.

The embossed letters haunted me—words cluttered my pillow and sprayed from my shower. I scribbled and scratched tons of words on my desk calendar blotter, so much that the days and dates vanished. My elbows had graphite bruises from leaning against it; plus, I ruined my favorite white sweater.

I set up a whiteboard between my cubicle and Simon's. With Simon out today, he wouldn't mind if I encroached on his space. In red, I printed Abby's embossed letters across the top of the whiteboard. From memory, I wrote K M B A C O E B L B Y.

In black, I wrote down my "keeper" words. Abby, Block, Me, Came, Come, Cake, Me, By, My, Back, Black, Be, Bake. Finally, yet importantly, I wrote down the four potential last names I created. Molbeck, Elkcomb, Lombeck, Belmock.

Now and then, I rolled my chair back a few inches to peek at the board or add another word. Joyce stopped by my desk and reviewed my progress. She took a stab at adding to my collection and wrote bake, cake, Beck, and blob. I laughed at her stunned *oh my God* face when she realized she associated our boss to a blob. Bake and cake seemed more aligned with my sweet tooth than solving a mystery and I erased Beck and blob before Ondrea tattled. Dan tried his hand at code cracking and added his choice words. Bomb. Mob. Mole. Lake. Huh, what did he know that I didn't? All threatening words, but I welcomed his additions. Until I cracked the code, no suggestion was wrong or right. Ondrea added her two cents and drew a cartoon gallows complete with a hanging stick figure. A bubble circled my name and pointed back to the hanged man. Even I laughed. It did resemble a poorly played hangman game.

At two o'clock, my concentration slipped. I skipped lunch and my hot latte. My eyes stung from reading email, re-searching, and writing responses for my column. Determined to meet my Monday deadline by the end of today translated to no homework.

The familiar flicker of lights announced Mack's ascent in the elevator.

"Kate, Joyce, Simon, and Beck," Mack hollered.

I smiled. No more Brosy, Brosy. Even the squeaky cart didn't faze me. Rather than popping from my desk like a jack-in-the-box, I contained my excitement and waited for him to round the corner to my desk. Rubber-banded mail stacks kerplunked on desks and marked his progress.

"Here you go, Kate." He politely handed me my mail.

"Thank you, Mack." Finally, adopted and honored by his simple handoff. My toothy grin spread across my face as I ascended from the ranks of peasantry in Mack's eyes. I ripped the rubber band off the letters. None of the addressed envelopes looked similar to Abby's writing.

"I wanted to tell ya about that Frank Kohler I told ya about the other day, Kate," Mack said.

I put down my mail and turned to him. "That's right, I almost forgot about it." After the information Joyce and I dug up, his contribution seemed small, not to mention he'd scared me on top of my threatening phone call.

"The guy is in a nursing home out in California and Rosa-lyn was his sister. But last he knew, and this is second hand info from some nurse there because the guy can't hear over the phone, she moved to France or England."

"California again, huh."

"What ya say?" Mack asked.

I told him about the personal article Joyce uncovered that we couldn't read well.

"Someone named Robert or Richard Mulch placed an ad looking for Rosalyn Kohler in nineteen-sixty-five, I believe."

"Oh ya that," he said. "Nora told me you were going to the police with that."

"Well, I did, but haven't heard back yet."

"Yeah, what ya say."

He traced his finger over the letters on the whiteboard, inadvertently erasing them.

"What are you doing?" I grabbed my marker and rewrote the letters.

His stogie wiggled as he chomped on it. "What's this?" he asked.

"A clue I think Abby hid in her poem." I shuffled through the mail again. Nothing jumped out at me, no unusual shaped envelope, no Abby handwriting.

"What ya say," he grumbled.

"Anything Abby-ish?" Joyce asked. She scaled her desk to peer over her cubicle into mine.

I shook my head no and grabbed my letter opener. "Not yet."

"You're gullible, Brosy," Mack said. "Follow yourself right off a cliff."

Brosy? How'd we get back to that, never mind the insult? I frowned at him, but his attention riveted on my whiteboard. He smiled his half-lipped snarl and his teeth kneaded the stinky cigar stump.

"That's not very nice." Joyce defended me. Mack studied the capital red letters.

"Mind your own folly, Joyce. Kate and I are friends. She knows I don't mean harm." He turned to me and smiled. "Don't ya, Kate?"

Did I? "What exactly do you mean, Mack?" Even if I chalked up the Brosy to teasing, *follow myself off a cliff* bruised my pride.

"Ah, well." He stared over my shoulder at the original Hurry, Abby poem pinned on my cubicle wall. "You're looking for a tree in the forest."

"Huh?"

"All them letters are important and somehow you figure you got the right ones? Why are the others half-capital half-small?"

I squinted at the card and I tried to see it from Mack's viewpoint. He chuckled and forced his cart through the aisle. The left front wheel smacked against my whiteboard and tipped it over. The edge came down hard on my shoulder.

"You okay, Kate?" he asked, and rubbed my shoulder.

"Fine," I lied, although I would sport a pretty bruise

across my upper arm by morning.

Mack grunted as he bent and righted the board. He slid it toward me. "Might not be the best place for this."

"Probably not," I agreed as he rolled down the aisle headed to Beck's office. I tore Abby's poem from the paper clip. Had I chosen the wrong letters? Was he right? Was I gullible?

In hindsight, sixteen years ago—Emma's lifetime and then some—a soft touch gullible girl described me. Especially after I found out my boyfriend plied his trade as an armed robber and stole all my money. I swore off dating. At least until my college roommate railroaded me to join her at a frat party, where I met George.

"Kate. This is George," my roommate had said, then spun me around and added a stern warning whispered in my ear. "Make nice."

"Hi," he said. His grin spread ear to ear.

No tall, dark, or handsome and he didn't look dangerous. Not the type that usually drew my attention, but my traitorous heart skittered an extra beat. Dark wavy blond hair fell across his forehead, teasing me to push it back in place.

"George Lambrose." He extended his hand. I hesitated. So often, when I shook hands with strangers, I cringed at the foreign gummy texture against my skin, but not that time. His strong hand swallowed up my own unusually large palm. I held on a moment longer than expected, enjoying his firm grip and his palm resting against mine.

"Kate Stanton," I said, and twirled my split ends.

He leaned in close to my right, reaching around me, and I jumped at has forwardness.

"I'm not a caveman, Ms. Stanton. Besides, we just met." He chuckled and smiled and his eyes smiled too. Huh, those eyes, his ears, and my toothy grin would make pretty handsome children. Oh my, why was I thinking children?

"See?" He snatched a beer from the tableside cooler behind me, twisted the cap, and offered it to me.

He was sexy and charming and his playful humor made talking to him easy. Throughout the evening, I spilled my guts to him about my last relationship and he listened without comment or criticism. By the time the party ended, we had taken turns confessing truths about our lives and shared visions of where we wanted to be in the future.

"I think you should go out with me," George said.

"I don't think that's a good idea." I liked him, but was gun-shy.

"Sure it is, Kate."

"No, I don't think so."

"Yes," he said, and stepped closer with conviction.

"No, I told you—" And then he kissed me and I found my *one*.

All my previous relationships were shams. Like movie clips and photo collages, memories strung together. George and I dancing in the kitchen while making homemade spaghetti sauce. Camping, snuggled together in a sleeping bag, making love under the stars. Walking down the aisle and George smiling, taking my hand from my brother as he pulled me forward to stand beside him at the altar. Buying our first bed, first car, first home together. George filled with emotion, quietly spilling tears when he held Emma in the delivery room. We grinned like fools when we finished each other's sentences and he knew how to console me with a quiet hug. I would fall for him all over again if I didn't already know how the story ended.

I covered my face with a pink tissue and swiped my eyes. I hated him for sweeping our life and love into a dust pile. I hated that he still looked at me with love in his eyes while he loved someone else. I hated that he moved on to another life so easily when I continued to stumble around in the past, dwelling on my stolen happily-ever-after. More than that, I hated that I still loved George with the intensity and depth that a woman loves a man.

My anger kept my pain trapped and destroyed my trust to venture into another relationship, which was easier to accept than change. Change wasn't as easy as Jonathan suggested.

Clearly, I could see what it cost George to make his decision. After grieving for one year, eleven months, three weeks, and four days, I struggled to transition from disbelief into acceptance. As angry as his confession made me, I still loved him for having the courage to live his life as he felt he should. He loved me enough to let me go. I just had never cried for him.

I balled up the tissue and tossed it in the trash. Time to turn a page in my book and believe our love still flowed from our hearts, but in different degrees. But I'd keep the pearls. We would forever be strung together.

CHAPTER 19

Friday morning, I woke from a restless night drenched in sweat and twisted in my comforter. The alarm on my clock radio became a fire alarm in my final dream. During the night, my psyche created a remake of *Attack of the 50-Foot Woman*. And even larger than life Rosa Kohl chased me through the streets of Yardman, opening up rooftops as easily as popping the seal off Tupperware bowls. I darted through a backyard, scaled a wall, and jogged around a corner where three houses huddled in a cul-de-sac. At the beige house, Jonathan waved from the doorway. At the second house, the purple one, George grinned, but George's face morphed between his and Ethan's face spinning on a slot machine reel. The third house, my house but not my house and covered in green feathers, Mack and Nora stood on the threshold in my bizarre dream home. Mack hollered Brosy, Brosy. Nora clutched a squawking parrot to her chest. I ran toward my surrogate parents, fleeing not only Giant woman but also my screwed up relationships. In my living room but not my living room, Mack and Nora played solitaire with a deck of Tarot cards, oblivious to my panic.

I raced the stairs and hid in the loft among Emma's abandoned dolls. The walls dissolved into glass. Mack stood in the grass below with his mail cart overturned. Giant Rosa squashed him with one truck-sized flatfoot, ripped the roof off my condo, and howled with laughter. "*Leave it—*" Mack's dead voice rose around me. Rosa Kohl lit a cigarette and blew smoke out in hurricane force around me. The air settled and she dropped the still glowing match into the room. "*And now you're gone.*"

I drowned the images left behind from my dream with a lukewarm shower and hot coffee. In my nightmare world, Mack transformed into my hero. He tried to save me from the 50-foot woman. Despite my broken relationships, I salvaged one. Mack and I were allies, a new braggart since my father died. Nora, however, became my private watch commissioner dictating what I should or shouldn't do via Emma.

I was running late and pulled the plug to the coffeemaker, not trusting the automatic off switch. Before meeting with Emma's teacher, I wanted to hand in my copy to Eugene. That would give me the entire day to rewrite if needed. I didn't want to spend my entire weekend working. *City Scope* was on the way to Emma's school, but my child reacted as if I intended to drop her off in Antarctica, alone.

"Come on, Emma," I hollered, and grabbed her sack lunch, my tote, and keys off the table.

"Whyyy?" She stomped her foot on the top stair. "Why can't you just drop me off first?"

"Because I don't know how long I'll be with your teacher."

She huffed and trudged down the stairs, dressed in black from head to toe. Her book bag dragged behind her and thumped on every step. I didn't have time to send her back to change and chose to pick my battles even if it meant Goth.

"Why can't I stay home today? That way I have all day to pack to go to Dad's tonight."

"You're going for the weekend, not a month. What's to pack?"

"I never get a day off," she whined out the door.

"Except spring break, winter break, three months in the summer, and holidays." I rattled off a list as I locked the door behind us. She tossed her book bag in the backseat and settled in the front, arms crossed around her chest. Surely, surly, not that she smiled and sprouted sunflowers every day, but mother's intuition whispered pity pooled inside Emma's head more than wanting a day off from school. I'd find out soon enough during my meeting with Mrs. Grant.

I started the Jeep and reached across the seat, sticking my hand on her forehead. She indulged me, flopped her head against the headrest, and rolled her eyes. "I'm not sick, Mom. I just want to stay home."

I nodded and patted her knee. "I know, sweetie. I feel the same way sometimes." I put the Jeep into gear and backed down the driveway. Even if she was ill, she wouldn't admit it, since I would cancel the weekend with her father.

I swung into the fifteen-minute parking spaces outside *City Scope*, which cost me a pretty penny in parking tickets in the month.

"I'll be right back," I promised Emma.

As I exited my car, Ondrea walked up the sidewalk. "Must be an advantage to have an attorney as a brother."

"Huh?"

"Or do you feel it's your personal duty to support the Yardman police budget with parking fines?" She laughed.

"Oh—" I hunted east and west for Phyllis, the meter maid. At five minutes to eight, and not yet on duty, she couldn't legally chalk tires. "I have time."

Ondrea reached the door before me and held it open. "So, Kate. Has your brother ever been in a serious relationship?"

"Don't you think he is a little old for you, Ondrea?"

"Age is relative or irrelevant," she said, and skipped off to her desk.

I dropped my tote on my desk. As I fished out the file with my responses, Dan arrived.

"Morning," he said. "Better move your car, Kate. Phyllis is down the street."

"I'm not staying." The light on my phone blinked. More voice messages waited for my attention. I erased the first message from a private investigator who promised to help me find my missing person for a small fee. And dumped the second message from an automated telemarketer. I hung up before the saved threatening message replayed.

"I'm just saying, she's tagged your Jeep, and will be heading back soon."

I checked the clock. I had six minutes before she ticketed me. "I swear that woman just looks for my car around town."

Dan laughed. "You're her meal ticket. Keep her employed."

"Not today," I said. "Do me a favor? When Eugene gets in, tell him I'll be back before ten. I have to meet with Emma's teacher. My copy is in his inbox."

"Sure."

"Thanks." I grabbed my tote and headed toward the door. Joyce pushed through the left side of the double glass doors as I spun through the right side.

"Phyllis is just—"

"I know. I know." I cut her off and raced out to my Jeep.

"Hurry," Emma called from the Jeep window. The golf cart Phyllis drove puttered two cars down from where I parked. I sprinted ahead, hopped behind the wheel, and managed a friendly wave out the window as I pulled away from the curb.

CHAPTER 20

Five minutes later, I parked in the Boys and Girls Club lot across from the school. Emma darted off to catch up with friends, and I headed to the school office like a dutiful parent.

The women in the front office grilled me and demanded spoiler information about Abby. Everyone I bumped into bobbed up and down excited and couldn't wait until Tuesday to find out the next installment of my Abby saga. My column became the Yardman soap opera that every one gossiped about and spun their own tales. Beck could have made a mint if she put out a Special Edition. The problem, though, I was still empty-handed when it came to solving this particular lost and found.

Mrs. Grant breezed in to my rescue. She reminded me of Rose in the *Golden Girls*, blonde and cheerful, but savvy like Dorothy. "Thank you for coming in early." She opened the waist high swinging door and led me through the office.

"I have to admit, I'm concerned, and glad I didn't have to wait all day." After waiting two days, a few more hours would have killed the cat for sure.

"It's nothing drastic to ring alarm bells, Kate. You're not raising Lizzie Borden." I sighed a long whistle and excused Emma's Goth black attire. We walked two classrooms down the hall to her homeroom. I sucked in the scent of pencils, books, and chalk dust, which outranked a new car smell. What the hell did I know? I drove a five-year-old Jeep. I glanced along the walls covered with student's papers, scouting for Emma's work, but found none.

"I don't see any of Emma's work on your wall of fame," I said.

"That's what I wanted to talk to you about."

I sat at the student desks in the front row and center. The coffee I drank earlier now burned a hole in my stomach.

Emma was a smart kid, insightful, sometimes beyond her years. Why was Emma's work unfit for wall mounting? "I don't understand. She does her homework."

"She's an excellent student, Kate," she assured me and shuffled through tattered notebook papers.

A shelf loaded with the classics hung directly behind her desk and I spotted my favorites, *The Wind in the Willows, The Black Stallion, The Adventures of Sherlock Holmes*. Books I saw on Emma's nightstand also.

"She didn't want to come to school today," I said.

"Well, I think I know the reason." She pulled two sheets from her folder and handed them to me. Emma's curly-q cursive sprawled across the page. "The first is a poem. A Diamante. Are you familiar with the term?"

"I think so," I said. "It's been many years, but don't the first three and a half lines relate to one subject and the second three and a half lines relate to an opposing or complementary subject, and it's in the shape of a diamond?"

"Correct." She awarded me with a pleased teacher smile.

I grinned, sat up straighter in my chair, and expected a star placed on my forehead.

"The second paper is an essay," she said. "I asked the class to write about something that changed them from the inside out. When I assigned the task, I didn't tell the children they would have to read it aloud. I hoped it would encourage them to write from their hearts, uncensored. When I gathered the papers, I told them they'd have to share them with the class."

"That's cruel," I said. "Letting them pour their hearts out to someone trusting then pull the rug out?" Huh, so that's why Emma wanted to stay home today.

Mrs. Grant flushed. "You're right. I didn't see it that way though until I read Emma's piece. I plan to announce today that the children can shred their essays after grading. However, I think you should read Emma's paper. I think it's important, and meant for you and your ex-husband."

My chest hollowed and I gulped down my breath. The papers shook in my hands as I tried to focus on the words. Mrs. Grant stepped to the back of the room to write on the chalkboard. I read the Diamante first:

Father

Forever, Mine
Guiding, loving, Laughing
Strong, separate, constant, distant
Crying, loving, helping
Always Loved
Mother

Her father and me at opposing angles joined by the word loving but forever separated. My breath stuttered in a shaky inhale strangled by the lump in my throat. I needed a dam for my eyes to clog the tears that trailed down my cheeks and splashed on her words. I read it again and my heart clutched my ribs, bruising me from the inside out as I absorbed my only child's anguish.

I turned to the essay, simply titled, *An Uncelebrated Hero.* The title alone hitched my breath as I struggled to breathe through my stuffy nose. Her handwritten words blurred under my tears. The story reminisced how she and her father built tent cities in the living room when chicken pox kept her from friends, how they giggled at Saturday morning cartoons, and how he slew dragons and protected her imaginary castle. She painted her turmoil with words I didn't know she knew. Her fairytale had a faulted hero, and a new happily-ever-after was rewritten without her say. She recorded the transition of her journey, her inner struggle to accept him, her reflections, self-awareness, and how she learned her right to hate and love. Understanding her father's courage to be true and different but remain as always her father was her celebration. I had no saliva left to swallow when I finished reading the last word.

I grabbed some tissues off Mrs. Grant's desk, blotted the essay and my face. She came and stood next to me speaking softly. "You didn't know she wrote this, did you?"

"No." I smoothed the papers across the desk, caressing away her pain.

"She's very talented, Kate. I dare say, I cried also. And she'll follow her mother's footsteps and be a magnificent writer," Mrs. Grant said.

The last thing I wanted Emma to do was follow my example, but the talent part was true. Emma had a gift that left every bone in my body rattled. Proud and humbled, but ashamed I hadn't done more to bridge the gap between Ethan and George and Emma and me. The truth knocked me upside my head by the written words of my fourteen-year-old Einstein.

"I'm glad you rethought asking them to read their work aloud."

"Agreed." Mrs. Grant smiled. "That's your copy. I'll give Emma the originals for safe keeping."

"Thank you." I folded them, slipped them inside my tote, and turned to leave. "And thank you for calling me."

I had made it to the door when Mrs. Grant called me back.

"Kate. I almost forgot. I wanted to ask you about Abby. Have you found Rosalyn Kohler yet?"

"Not yet. But I have a few leads to follow." After her kindness, I couldn't put her off like I did to the ladies in the school office and tell her she'd have to wait for Tuesday's edition.

"Oh. Then maybe I have something to offer."

I dropped my hand from the door and scrounged in my tote for my notepad and pen while she talked.

"It's just such a small world, Kate. I don't know if it's relevant, but I took a class given by a Professor R. Kohler when I attended college. I can't even be certain if it's the same person you're looking for."

"When was this?"

"Nineteen-fifty-nine. No, sixty, I think. I took a few continuing education courses at Long Beach State College."

"California?"

Mrs. Grant laughed. "I know. It's a long shot. I'm sorry, Kate. I can't help but want to jump on the bandwagon along with everyone else. I suppose it was a different Rosalyn Kohler. My mother used to say there's more than one black and white cow in the pasture."

"No, wait. How far is Long Beach to Catalina Island?" I stunk at Geography.

"Just a ferry ride."

"Ferry ride?" *Rosalyn Kohler out at sea.* The missing person article Joyce found mentioned Catalina Island. My pulse danced a two-step.

"Do you know how long she taught there?" I scribbled notes madly in my unique shorthand and captured every word Mrs. Grant said.

"At least one full quarter. The second quarter, a teacher's aid subbed for her."

"Why?"

"I don't really know, to be honest. After spring break, she never returned. She was a rather frail-looking woman, dark hair, dark eyes, rail thin. I wouldn't be surprised if she was ill at the time."

I made notes to contact the University and see if I could uncover any information regarding her departure.

The bell rang, indicating next period. A couple girls came in chattering about last night's *American Idol* winner. "Good Morning," Mrs. Grant greeted them.

"Thank you!" I said, and slipped my notes back in my bag and headed out.

From across the hall, Emma headed straight for me. "What did I do wrong?" she asked.

"Not a thing, sweetie." I held up her essay and poem for her to see.

"Oh, that." She scrunched up her nose and lips.

"I'm proud of you," I said. She shrugged and jogged off toward the gym.

CHAPTER 21

Back in my Jeep, I dialed Joyce, eager to share my new-found information. Hearing the Catalina Island connection from another source, Joyce would pump the air with her fists until her bangles bruised her wrists. She squealed over the phone, "yahoo—awesome" when I told her what Mrs. Grant said. She made me promise to send her a text if I uncovered anything else. She was on her way out to Dodd's again.

I stopped and grabbed a caramel latte at Hot Joe's and a chocolate chip scone. Not exactly brain food, but the carbohydrate blast and caffeine shot guaranteed consciousness while I researched Mrs. Grant's tips. I parked across the street at Gunthers and ran across Main Street, dodging cars like the poor little *Frogger* arcade character.

I bee-lined for my desk, or tried to, but Ondrea extended her desk to the floor with file folders. Four leaning stacks spanned across her desk and spread across her chair with one heap on the floor.

"Can I help?" I asked her. Not that I had the time or desire, but I'd score points for Matt.

"No. I'll find it." She finished flipping through the folder and added it to the stack on the floor.

Simon was out on assignment, so I dropped my tote in his chair, pressed the space bar, and my monitor lit up, happy to see me.

I clicked the web explorer icon, sat down, and pulled my scone from the white bakery bag. In the search bar, I typed, Long Beach State College. The links displayed listed the college athletic sites. Huh. I opened a few, and learned that in 1964 Long Beach State College changed its name to Cal State Long Beach. In 1965, a little over 10,000 students attended the university. Gosh, I didn't need all that, just a professor. If I could find old Joe Deeter in Yardman's population,

I could surely find Rosalyn Kohler.

I searched faculty and staff, and then went to the English Department link where a general information number shimmered in blue highlight and I dialed. Voicemail. I left a message, and bit into my scone. Reaching voicemail must be Karma coming back to bite my backside for the calls I left unanswered. I scrolled the web page and found a list of advisors with links to email. *Choose, choose.* I clicked Office Administrator for the English Department and composed an email.

Until I looked up to review my email, I hadn't noticed the letters E and R failed to show up in my email. Great, my brief introduction and request for information on Rosalyn Kohler read like text lingo. *My nam is Kat Lambos. I'm a pot at City Scop Nws and saching a fom faculty mmb on staff by the nam of osalynn Kohl.*

Hardly readable and the English Department would split their guts laughing. I wanted a Pulitzer, not a Razzie for Journalism. I stuffed the last bit of scone in my mouth and washed it down with my latte, flipped my keyboard upside down, and tapped it on the desk.

"What ya doing, Kate?" Mack said from behind me. His hands braced the back of my chair.

I slapped my hand to my chest, shrieking like a monkey at his sudden appearance. What brand of shoe did he wear that made his left limp oddly stealth? Careful not to knock him off balance, I craned my neck to look up at him. "I think I found a lead to Rosalyn Kohler."

"She in that keyboard ya pounding?"

"No." I laughed. "I got crumbs in my keyboard. I think she was a professor at Long Beach State College in 1965. I'm sending an email requesting info on past faculty."

"Who told ya that?" Mack swiveled me sideways and leaned closer to my monitor to read my email.

"Emma's teacher. It really is a small world, isn't it?"

"What ya say."

Mack's whatever phrase confused me. Like a barking dog yelped different meanings, his idiom meant different things depending on the circumstances. I shrugged it off. Eventually, I'd learn his nuances.

"Can't read much of what ya got written," Mack said.

"Hazards of eating over a keyboard." I tapped it on the desk again.

"Let me help ya with that." Mack pulled the keyboard out of my hands and planted his backside against my desk. I reached for my latte just in time before it spilled across my blotter.

"Sorry." He grinned and pulled a four-inch switchblade from his pants pocket. My brows mimicked Joyce. "Tools for the trade," he said.

"Oh." Made sense. He'd have to slice packages and cartons.

"Good for gutting fish, too." His lopsided grin inched higher, pushing his right cheek upwards and narrowing his eye to a wink. He flicked the blade open and wedged it between my keys, turned the keyboard over, and tapped. Cookie crumbs, lint balls, and pencil lead dust drifted to the floor.

"Huh. Must have been more than one crumb."

He held down the E key and then the R key until two rows of EEERRR stretched across the screen. "Good to go." He put the keyboard down and his thumb grazed the escape key. "Sorry," he said when the cancel box popped with a chime.

"It's okay, and thanks." I tried to scoot back under my desk, but he crowded me.

"These computers squawk like pinball machines. What's it say here? Cancel?" He rolled the mouse.

"I'll do it." I nudged my way closer, but I couldn't reach my mouse in time.

"Got it." He canceled the save to draft and left my email intact. "Ain't so hard." He grinned at me. "I might get me one of 'em yet." He rolled the mouse around, playing with it. The cursor landed on send and he clicked. My email faded off into a rotating envelope zooming across the screen. I slapped my hand on my monitor, reaching out to the virtual world, willing *return to sender*. Hopefully, my chance for a Pulitzer didn't hinge on the email sent to the English Department complete with missing Es and Rs and underscored by a long row of EEEEEEEEEERRRRRRRRRRREEEEEEEEEERRRRRR.

"Oh crap." I whipped around on Mack. "Go away!"

"What happened?"

I pointed toward the door directing him out. "Leave. You just sent that unfinished, unsigned, messed up email off to the college."

"Oops." He hung his head and limped away.

I quickly composed another emailing apologizing for the mishap and continued with my request for information. Live and learn to add the email address last.

"Hey, Kate."

"Joyce? I didn't know you were back." We both stood.

"I snuck in while you were screaming at Mack."

"Who was screaming at Mack?" Ondrea had crashed through the doors with another box in her arms.

"Do you think Mack meant to do that?" Joyce asked.

"Meant to do what?" Ondrea asked.

"He clicked send on Kate's half-finished email."

Of course, Ondrea laughed. My hands rose involuntarily; I almost shot her the bird, but camouflaged the move with a flip of my hair off the tips of my middle fingers.

"Seriously?" We stared at one another. I shook my head. He didn't, did he? Unless he had ESP and arrived at the exact moment my keyboard collected crumbs.

The light on my phone blinked, indicating an incoming call. I hadn't turned my ringer back on yet.

"Kate Lambrose," I answered, and waited. No one responded, but I could hear that same traffic whoosh I had heard in my phone threat. I shivered.

"Hello?" I said.

"Ms. Lambrose. I understand you are looking for Rosalyn Kohler."

"Yes, I am." The woman answered with a sweet British or Scottish accent. I could never tell the difference and it was hard to distinguish through the traffic noise.

"Who is this?" I asked.

"This is Rosalyn."

"Oh my God, you're alive?" I whirled my arm around like a pinwheel at Joyce and Ondrea. "The Rosalyn Kohler, Abby's friend?" I asked.

Joyce bounced up and down. Ondrea flew around her desk and down the row. She stabbed the speaker button on the phone, grabbed a notepad, and slid into my chair.

"Yes. I am very much alive and I'd like to keep it that way," Rosalyn said. "I'd appreciate you just leaving this alone."

Then Joyce scrambled beside me. She clutched my arm and my shock mirrored her expression.

"Why are you hiding from Abby?" Ondrea asked.

"Where are you?" I spoke into the handset I still gripped.

"It makes no matter, dear," Rosalyn said.

"The hell it does," Joyce chimed in.

"Spell your name for me please," Ondrea said. I smacked her on the shoulder and pointed at the whiteboard where I had written Rosalyn's name.

Ondrea hit the mute button. "Smack me again, and I'll amputate your hand."

"Both of you, save the boxing match for later," Joyce scolded.

"We know how to spell her name." I glared at Ondrea.

"Yeah, but maybe she doesn't. You don't know if this is the real Rosalyn Kohler."

Huh. Good point.

"Hello?" the woman said. Paper rustled in the background and the line went deadly silent.

"Oh my God, she's going to hang up. Someone un-mute her." Joyce flapped her arms.

I leaned over Ondrea and released the mute button. "Look, if you're in trouble, maybe I can help."

"Is this a ship to shore connection?" Joyce asked.

"Yes," the woman said. "Please just print in your paper that I am well and leave it at that, sorry for the put out," she said, and hung up.

"Oh shit! I told you she'd hang up."

"Dammit."

"You should have pressed her to spell her name," Ondrea said. "Instead of offering to help. Jeez, Kate, you rescue stray cats in the alleys, too?"

"How was I supposed to know she was going to hang up?" I shot back. "The whole thing about wanting to stay lost to stay alive seemed a bigger priority."

"Wait a minute. Stop arguing." Joyce held up her hands between Ondrea and me. Her bangles chimed, ending our boxing round. "Her accent. It seemed off," she said.

"What do you mean?"

"She was trying too hard."

Joyce snatched my notepad from Ondrea's hand and re-cited Rosalyn's words in a British accent.

"Shit," Ondrea said, "you sound like the Queen herself." Joyce smiled.

"I think you're on to something," I agreed.

"What are you going to do now?" Ondrea asked. "You have Abby wanting to find Rosalyn and Rosalyn wanting to be left alone?"

"I still want Abby's side of the story."

"I do too!" Joyce said.

"I'll find Abby, you'll see," I said.

"The two of you hop on any train headed south. I'd talk it over with Beck for sure if I were you. I see a moral dilemma, someone could get hurt."

I hated that she was right.

CHAPTER 22

Jonathan planned to arrive at seven tonight to take me to dinner. I hadn't talked to him since he left for Connecticut and was eager to hear how his visit fared.

I raced from the office, beeped the horn outside Nora's Nest, and drove Emma to meet George. They planned to attend the concert on the Common and rather than one of us driving a full round trip, we arranged to meet halfway.

I stayed long enough to see Emma off and ask George if he'd agree to a family night dinner, the four us, Emma, me, George, and Ethan. His mouth hung open from my suggestion.

He wanted to know why, and I said it was time. He kissed my cheek, thanked me, and gave me a quick hug goodbye.

When I returned home, I had less than thirty minutes to pick out an outfit and freshen up. I sat on my bed staring into my closet. Did Rosalyn Kohler do the same? So many things about her blew out my tire, leaving me flat and stranded. Questions cluttered my day. Was the call from Rosalyn a prank? Was some joker impersonating her and had that same person threatened me? Why was she hiding? Why the accent? Joyce might be right. Or worse, Ondrea might be right, I should report it to Beck. Southbound train, huh. Well, as long as I didn't see the light in the tunnel, the train wasn't going to hit me.

The best I could do at this point was pray I'd hear from Abby and get dressed. I pulled black dress pants from the hanger and my white silk blouse that shimmered with tiny black polka dots. Adjusted my ladies front and center. One final touch, I draped a silver chain with a black onyx stone around my neck. Nothing too showy.

At seven sharp, the doorbell rang. I spot checked the living room for leftover food and clothes. Jonathan didn't need to know how I really lived. My house looked lived-in and it matched my personality perfectly. Neat and tidy on the outside, a cluttered mess on the inside. I pitched Emma's balled up gym socks upstairs with the accuracy of Cy Young, dropped the trashy romance I had been reading on the floor, and kicked it under the couch. Some secrets were mine to keep.

"Hi," I said as I swung the door open.

"Hi yourself." Jonathan smiled. "Ready?"

Shadows smudged his eyes and I'd swear he had lost weight.

"Starving." I grabbed my purse and black knit sweater off the doorknob. I inhaled his spice-scented cologne and my mouth watered. "Definitely starving." Despite his weariness, he was very handsome. He wore black chinos, a white-black pinstriped button down shirt, and a silver buckled belt. We looked like an old married couple dressed alike. It all made me want to stay home, upstairs, snuggled in bed. Was that boring too? Maybe it wasn't Jonathan after all.

"You sure you want to go out?" I asked. "You look exhausted."

"Yes, I'm sure. It's good to get out."

I monopolized our ten-minute ride with facts from my conversation with Attorney Jackson. I was dying to share my progress on Rosalyn that he'd missed over his two-day absence.

"Wonder what's in the safe deposit box?" he asked.

"It will forever be a mystery," I said. We circled the parking lot at the Red Dragon Restaurant before I saw where we were.

"I thought our reservations were for the Woodfire Inn," I said, although I had wanted to splurge and take Emma and myself to the Red Dragon since they opened last September.

"Would you prefer the Woodfire Inn?"

"No. This is wonderful," I agreed.

I'd rather not waltz through a hotel lobby when my appetite craved him more than food. Huh, had he taken the time to mull that over these last two days? In one respect, it was nice he considered our at-arms-length friendship, but at the same time, I found myself regretting my own rules.

He swung his Lincoln Expedition into a vacant spot under a lamppost.

My stomach growled as soon as we entered. Plush oriental designs carpeted the floors. I wanted to kick off my two-inch black heels and scrunch my toes in it. The lighting moderate, white, and clean shone from paper lanterns above the tables. The hostess seated us at a small circular booth, and a waiter immediately served ice water and brought a decanter of tea.

I picked up the vinyl bound menu and scanned the entrée listings. *Are you kidding me? Who speaks and reads Japanese in Yardman?* My C minus foreign language brain scrambled the symbols and made as much sense as Abby's embossed letters. Great, another puzzle to unscramble. I hunted down characters, trying to match K M B A C O E B L B Y, and frowned. None of the pictures lined up either. Hah, neither did Ethan's art on Abby's card. My stomach roared, protesting my descent back into work mode, until I spotted the word sushi. No thanks, I liked my fish cooked, not handled and rolled in seaweed. Fish that had a pulse should swim free. The dead only needed a breading and a good flash fry.

"I have so much to tell you about Rosalyn and not so much about Abby, but first I want to hear about your trip."

"I'd rather hear your story," he said.

"I know." I waited.

He sighed. He poked at his napkin and slid around in the seat before he blurted it out in one long, breathless sentence. "They have to go into assisted living or more than that. My father doesn't have the patience to deal with my mother's confusion. She needs to be cared for, not bossed around. If he wants to stay in the house alone—that's up to him, but she can't stay there. Therefore, I'm going back to Connecticut on Wednesday for the rest of the week. I've made a couple of appointments at some facilities that cater to dementia patients—that's it." He held up his hands.

I was speechless and wanted to call my mother immediately. Instead, I reached across the table and held his hand.

Our moment broke as the waitress arrived and bowed to take our order. He squeezed my hand before picking up the menu again. I played it safe and ordered Beef Teriyaki.

"So, you found Rosalyn?" Jonathan asked.

"Not exactly, but I did get a mysterious call from a woman claiming to be Rosalyn Kohler."

"Claiming to be?"

"And I talked to the house mouse at the police station about missing person reports."

"House mouse?" Jonathan gawked at me, waiting for answers. I laughed at the question mark on his face.

"A house mouse is the police officer that doesn't leave the building. I'm waiting to hear if he found any missing person reports or not." I pulled out Ondrea's handwritten transcript of Rosalyn's short, rehearsed message. He read it while I explained about the fake accent.

"This is really strange, Kate. Why would someone that is not Rosalyn call and ask you to back off? What would that person have to gain?"

"I don't know, what?"

"Well, if it wasn't the real Rosalyn, then that person obviously has some stake in the outcome of you finding her or Abby."

"Meaning?" I sipped my tea and waited to see if he drew the same conclusion.

"Meaning someone doesn't want the truth known."

"That is obvious, but who, if it isn't Rosalyn? All I can do now is wait to hear from Abby, unless Rosalyn calls again." Our conversation paused when the waitress returned with our sizzling platters, bowed, and left.

"And what's this *sorry for the put out*—a British saying?" He pointed to the note.

"Huh, let me see that." I grabbed the notepad from him. "I didn't realize that's what she said." I tapped my chopsticks on my plate. Where had I heard that saying? Who said that, Sadie Arnold, Joyce, or Mack? "Aha." I tapped the note with my chopsticks. "I know now."

"Know what?"

"Who says this phrase, a lot."

"You're having one of those internal conversations with yourself." He winked at me. "Explain."

"Ha, yes I am. Nora says it, Mack's wife."

"I didn't know he had a wife."

"Neither did I until the other day when I drove her to the train station."

"Whoa, back up, I'm lost in this caper of yours. What does Mack's wife have to do with Rosalyn or Abby?"

"Good question," I said. "But Rosalyn sounded suspiciously like Nora."

I missed what Jonathan asked next as I was grazing the sight of a shorter version of Arnold Schwarzenegger walking towards us. His stonewashed jeans belted tight around his waist and his Dennis the Menace orange and white striped jersey hugged his pecks and ballooned on his biceps. The blonde woman draped on his arm wore more makeup than Bozo the clown. Frightful, and I tried not to stare. They stopped at our table.

"Kate?" the muscle man asked.

As soon as he said my name, my mind panted *Michael Earl*, but he didn't match the picture I snapped into my imagination.

"Yes," I said.

"I thought that was you. I'm Michael Earl," he said with that voice that could light kindling, and he offered his paddle-sized hand to shake.

My lips stretched over my gums, baring my toothy grin, and I wiped my mouth with my napkin, hiding my pleasure.

"Oh, nice to meet you." I shook his hand without any worry that it might be gummy. His ill-fitting jeans and Halloween jersey faded from my mind. He introduced himself to Jonathan. He didn't bother to introduce his cling, and we didn't ask.

"The house mouse," I said to Jonathan, who kept staring at the clown. Michael chuckled.

Officer Earl was *no* house mouse and not a pretty boy either. I fit him into the category of beefcake with brains, the typical bad boy dynamite package I shouldn't open. His smile curved up the right side of his face more than the left side and his deep brown eyes matched his chocolate brown hair.

"I meant to call you, Kate, and let you know that we have no cold paper records dated nineteen-sixty-five or nineteen-sixty-six. You might check with the Historical Society."

"As it turns out, she may not be missing after all."

"Really. Then you found her?"

Miss Clingy tugged at his arm. "C'mon Mike, my babysitta is goin inta ovva time."

"All right." He rolled his eyes. "I'll call you." He pointed to me and sidestepped away. I looked straight back at Jonathan to keep my eyes from trailing Michael Earl out the door.

"Well, that was interesting," Jonathan said. "He must be the circus strong man and she the sidekick clown."

"Oh my God." I laughed. "I think that is the first time I have ever heard a judgmental comment escape your mouth."

He shrugged. "A result of my Connecticut visit." The sadness returned in his eyes.

"I think you need to talk to me." I squeezed his hand.

"You're probably right, but not tonight. So what's been happening with you and your nemesis?" Jonathan asked.

"Who?"

"The name castrator."

I laughed between bites. "You mean Mack. Well, he sort of apologized, saying he was just teasing me. Now he's handing me my mail, calling me Kate, and offered—"

"What did you do? Bribe him?"

"No, I think he just realized how much it annoyed me."

"Seriously, Kate—"

"What?"

"Despite your attempt at a hard shell façade, you tend to trust too easily. People don't change their patterns overnight. It's not like flipping a light switch."

George did. Maybe his was a dimmer switch.

"Well, Mack came around."

"Just be cautious. He's an old man set in his ways. Something prompted his change."

"Change is good." He was being dramatic, looking at people through his microscopic lens, and thinking about his father. "But he was very kind to me the other day after my threatening phone call."

"Whoa, back up." Jonathan raised his chopsticks, food and all. "You didn't mention any threatening calls."

"No worries. People that make threats don't have the guts to act on them," I sputtered, surprised by his sharp tone.

"And it didn't occur to you to call me?"

"No."

"What was said?" he asked, and pulled out his cell.

"Nothing concrete, just some vague voice saying, 'leave it go before you're gone.' I'm sure it was the same woman pretending to be or not to be Rosalyn." I laughed.

"It applies to Abby, I'm sure. No one has ever threatened you before. What did Helen say about it?"

I bit into my beef and chewed while he stared at me. "I haven't mentioned it to Beck yet. Your food is getting cold."

"Did you report it to the police?"

Before I could finish shaking my head no, he flipped open his cell phone. "What are you doing?"

"Calling the police. Kate, do you realize how many oddballs are out there? You need to file a report."

"Nice talk for a shrink."

"You know what I mean."

"No. I don't think I do."

He pushed numbers on his cell phone.

"Stop," I said. "*Stop.*" I spun my chopstick around and pointed at him. The people at the booth across from us stared, eyes wide and utensils paused in mid-bite.

Jonathan flipped his phone closed. "What?"

"Listen, buddy, you don't get to be irritated with me. I can handle myself. I'm not some territory that you can conquer. I make my own decisions."

"Kate—"

I held up my hand and cut him short. "Look, if we're going to have a healthy friendship, you can't take over. A woman doesn't need her man—ah, her friend to fix things. I need to know—trust that I can tell you anything without censoring it or worrying about your armchair analysis."

Oh, damn, a Freudian slip, *her man*. He caught it and winked at me.

"It's a natural male response to want to fix things. I promise I'll make a sincere effort, but you'll have to remind me," he said.

"You bet I will."

I speared a broccoli floret, which reminded me of Jolly Green. Jonathan hadn't heard about my adventure with Rosa Lynn Kohl yet. I filled in the details and summed up the experience with a laugh to lessen his worry. Poked in the eye by protruding nipples was more threatening than an anonymous wheezing voice over the phone. Just the same, when I mentioned my phone call from Bea and my scheduled trip to Arlington on Sunday, he offered to tag along. Good plan.

Over Sake, I purposely left out my planned dinner with George and Ethan. No need to give Jonathan false hope that I was moving past my grief and toward him. Until I made it through dinner with George and Ethan, I couldn't commit to me, never mind Jonathan.

However, I did share my emotional turmoil from meeting with Emma's teacher. My turning point hinged on Emma quietly and eloquently releasing the vent on my pressure-cooked emotions. My eyes watered, and I blamed it on the Sake.

He reached across the table and squeezed my hand. I left my hand in his and savored the comfort.

CHAPTER 23

On Sunday, I dressed in my jeans and my royal blue sleeveless sweater, ready to go by nine. Jonathan picked me up at ten sharp and forty-five minutes later, we pulled into Elderly Assist Gardens in Arlington.

"Nice, pleasant place," Jonathan said when we pulled into the parking lot.

Winding sidewalks circled around attached bungalows in one direction and a three-story building towered behind them.

The sight unfolding on the walkway ahead was either a wheelchair derby gone awry or bumper cars for the elderly. Two male residents faced off in motorized scooters, wheels locked against each other. Their motors engaged at full throttle screeched like a fork scraping across a plate. My teeth hurt and burning rubber filled the air.

"Let me help you." Jonathan reached for the controls.

"Don't touch me, Sonny." The hunchbacked, peach fuzz-balding senior slapped at Jonathan. "I mean to run him off the path. Die, you prune-stealing thief."

"You don't have enough juice!" The other man gummed. "Your chair is as constipated as you are."

I laughed at their banter and sidestepped the rocking scooter battle. Jonathan tried again to intercede, but they both shouted, "Go away."

"Come on." I tugged Jonathan.

"We can't leave them like that, Kate."

I glanced over my shoulder. "Why not?"

"You heard them—"

"They're evenly matched. Besides, their batteries will wear down soon." He still looked concerned, so I added, "You can report it to the staff." We walked through the automatic doors. Air rushed at us, assaulting my nostrils and reminding me of my grandma's house, vitamins and cauliflower.

Twenty feet inside, a four-sectioned circular reception station buzzed with activity.

"So, what are you planning, Kate? Flash your *City Scope* credentials and ask for Bea?"

My credentials consisted of a laminated business card and barely got me into the library. "I'll take a direct approach and ask for Bea. If that doesn't work, I'll go to my backup plan."

"Backup plan? What's your backup plan?"

"Use your doctor credentials." I grinned.

A red-haired woman in purple scrubs stood and scanned Jonathan from head to toe. "May I help you?" Her nametag read Linda and her hair molded like a helmet to her head. Red Hat Society came to mind.

"Yes," Jonathan said. "A couple of gentlemen out front are trying to run each other off the walkway."

"That would be Mr. Carter and Mr. Hershey," she said. "Were they stuck?"

"Definitely engaged," Jonathan said.

Miss Red Hat Society picked up her phone and held it to her mouth like a microphone. Her voice bellowed through the ceiling. "Leroy report to the front entrance. Code Reese."

"Code Reese?" I asked.

She laughed and her cheeks blushed to match her hair. "Carter, like peanuts, and Hershey, like chocolate."

"Oh. Like, you got your peanut butter up in my chocolate." I laughed.

"Exactly." She turned back to Jonathan. "Now, what can I do for you?"

I stepped in front of Jonathan into her view. "I was wondering if Bea is working today." I hoped I hadn't colored Bea's tip with more intrigue than it deserved.

"Bea? Beatrice?" she asked, and I nodded. I shot Jonathan a victory smile. *Who needs credentials?*

"She's working on the Memory Enhancement wing today. Shall I page her for you?" She snatched up the phone before she finished talking.

"No, no, that's okay. If you could just point us in the right direction, we can find her."

"Down the west corridor." She pointed to the left. "You'll have to buzz for entry."

I thanked her, and Jonathan and I headed west.

The tile-waxed floor shimmered under the florescent

lights and my shoes squeaked across it. I would never understand why hospitals and nursing homes insisted on slick as snot floors when the people walking on them could hardly balance standing still.

"How the heck did you pick up what she meant by Code Reese?" Jonathan asked.

"I know my chocolate." At the end of the hall, I peered through the glass door and pressed the buzzer. A woman at the desk waved, the door unlatched, and Jonathan followed me in. Two employees, a man and a woman dressed in stark white scrubs, staffed the nurses' station. The atmosphere was sedate. Six of the eight patient doors were propped open. From one room, a TV announcer from the Golf Channel echoed into the hall. The volume continued to increase and the male nurse hurried off into the room.

The young blonde nurse stood from her chair. "Here to visit?" she asked.

Her nametag said Beatrice. I found my Bea.

"Kate Lambrose." I stuck out my hand. "And this is Dr. Jonathan Dohe. You called me the other day about—"

"No, I didn't call." She ignored my hand. "Dr. Dohe. Are you new on staff?" Her lashes fluttered at him. "I could show you around, if you'd like."

"That's kind, and if I joined the staff, I'd jump at the chance."

Oh boy, he just donned his formal, *I-be-doctor* hat, and his lips twitched, holding back a smile.

"Excuse me?" I held up my index finger. I refused to let her zap me into oblivion.

I should have settled for phoning Bea rather than wasting my time and driving an hour to witness the raging hormones of a twenty-year-old.

"Oh." Bea pouted. "That's too bad."

Jonathan's dimples deepened and his head tilted at her. He was deliberately flirting. Huh, was I jealous? No, but yes.

Since I couldn't douse them in ice water, I did the next best thing. I stepped on Jonathan's foot. "Hello?" I waved at Bea. "Remember me? Kate Lambrose, *City Scope News*. You called me on Wednesday said you may have information on Abby."

"No," she said, singing the O.

"Actually, that was me." The male nurse returned to the

desk. His voice, soft and ultra-feminine, not what I expected from such a burly man. I blinked like a strobe light. His name-tag said Barney. "Mrs. Schwartz can use your help, Beatrice," he said. "She's disrobing in the day room again."

Blonde Beatrice darted off to the dayroom. Jonathan and I followed her progress and got an eyeful of Mrs. Schwartz as she tried to wriggle her elastic-waisted, polyester pants over her Dr. Scholl's.

"I didn't expect you to show up, Ms. Lambrose," Barney said.

"You're Bea?" My mouth hung open until Jonathan elbowed me. "Sorry, sorry, of course you're B. Short for Barney, I bet—says that right there on your nametag." I stifled a giggle caught in my throat and covered with a sick cough. My foot was so deep in my mouth already and my brain backfired. Mike Tyson, my mind chanted, which led to the thought that Barney could box my ears. Big targets. Gosh, I could get lost following my thoughts. I tucked my hair behind my lobes.

Jonathan spared me a *what the heck is wrong with you?* expression and scooted me aside to introduce himself. I jumped on the opportunity to rally my composure and dug deep in my tote for my notepad.

"I apologize for showing up. When you said Bea on the phone, I assumed Bea, like in Beatrice. I didn't mean to blow your cover—"

Barney frowned at me. "What cover? I go by B. Residents find it easier to remember one letter than an entire name."

And in the dark, no one could tell the difference between Beatrice or Barney, but I didn't say that. If I uttered anymore random thoughts, I'd have to have my foot amputated.

"Well, that makes sense," I said. To avoid looking at him, I scanned the room to appear curious rather than dim-witted. "So, how long have you worked here?"

"Seven years," Barney said.

"And you think the Abby who wrote the poem was a resident here during that time?" *Focus on the pigeonhole of charts.*

"Yup. That little poem seemed like something she would write."

"How long ago was that?" I glanced back toward the dayroom. Beatrice struggled to pull up Mrs. Schwartz's pants, while Mrs. Schwartz struggled to pull her head free from a pink turtleneck sweater.

"Three, maybe four years ago."

"What was her last name?" I made notes, not that he gave me anything useful.

"I don't remember."

I flipped through my note pages. "Could it be maybe Molbeck, Elkcomb, Belmock, or Lombeck?" Four names I created from the left over letters—K M B A C O E B L B Y.

"No. None sound familiar," Barney said.

I sighed. A frizzy blue-haired woman shuffled a walker over the threshold from one of the patient rooms. "Any chance you might be able to dig through patient records and come up with a name?" I kept my focus on the frizzy blue-do lady, who smiled wide and waved like a six-month-old at us.

"No. Sorry." Barney shot my hopes down. "Had she been a patient on the Memory Enhancement wing, I could probably dig up medical records—theoretically of course—"

"Gotcha. Patient confidentiality and all..." I nodded.

"Right," Barney said. "But she was a resident on the Active Living wing. Those are basically apartments for seniors..."

I tuned him out and studied my notes.

"Uh-huh," I said when he took a breath. Frizzy blue-do flipped her palm up and arthritic fingers wiggled in the air like crippled worms. Another woman exited behind her.

I squinted, zeroing in on the other woman, and nearly choked on my saliva. Nora? No. Couldn't be, could it? But there she was, dressed in forest green scrubs and a perfectly coiffed dandelion hairdo.

"Do you know her?" I pointed.

Barney turned. "That's Mrs. Gregory, why?"

"No, the white-haired lady." I kept pointing.

"Oh, that's Nora. She volunteers here. She visits with our patients that have no family."

"You're kidding me." Until the day I taxied her to the train station, she'd been invisible to me. Now, I noticed her—everywhere. It annoyed me like a mosquito bite. Once I scratched, it kept on itching.

"Was she here when Abby was here?" I asked.

"Ya know, I think their paths may have crossed." The phone rang. "Excuse me just a moment."

"So that's Nora? Mack's wife? The one you think made the alleged Rosalyn call?" Jonathan asked.

My pencil seesawed between my fingers. "Yup." I grabbed his arm. "Let's go have a chat."

Nora's back was toward us as she shuffled through some large print books on a shelf in the dayroom. In my best British accent, I said, "Hello, Nora. Beautiful day for a visit, don't you think?"

She turned around slowly. A frown pulled her eyebrows close together and pinched the wrinkles in her forehead into deep grooves. "Wha—"

Ah, recognition, I saw it happen the moment it struck her. Her frown disappeared into shock, her stare sharpened, and then the nervous eye shift. It all happened in microseconds before she burst into a shy smile. "Oh my goodness, Kate. You sound funny. Are you catching a cold, dear?"

"No, I—"

"Good. Spring time colds are miserable, must be allergies then."

"I'm not aller—"

"Who is this fine gentleman you're with?" She smiled brightly at Jonathan. "You're not following me, are you? But with arm candy like him, I don't think I'd mind."

"Following? I can barely keep up with you—"

"No need to be rude." Nora sniffed.

Crap. There went the waterworks. How did I become the offender? I let out a sigh, and quickly introduced Jonathan.

"Oh, a doctor?" She winked at me. Then she leaned toward me and without even trying to conceal her words, she said, "A good catch, Kate."

Jonathan chuckled. Heat flooded my cheeks, my ears burned as hot as branding irons, and I flipped my hair from behind my ears.

"Do you have a moment to sit down? I'd like to ask you a few questions," I asked Nora.

She looked at Mrs. Gregory who sat at the card table by the window playing checkers with no one.

"Only for a second, dear, but I don't dare sit. My giddy up will give up." She pushed a chair in and shuffled a few tabloid magazines across a table in a neat row.

"Barney says that Abby may have been a resident here."

"Oh this is about the Abby piece in your column?"

"Yes. Do you remember a woman named Abby?"

"No, dear." Her gaze fixed on an air spot above her head,

then back at me. "People come and go here. I hardly re-member what I ate for breakfast."

"You're sure?"

"Oh, dear. Why? Do you think I know something I can't remember that could help you?" She blinked rapidly and tears filled her eyes.

"How about Rosalyn?"

"Oh my goodness. Do you think she was here too?" Nora clutched at my arm. "Heavens, to think I might have informa-tion for you and can't help. This old brain of mine..." Her lips trembled.

"Nothing to worry about," Jonathan interrupted and pat-ted her shoulder. I shot him a warning squint. "Kate, I'm sure, was just hoping to jog your memory," he said.

The hell I was. I was about to ask why she called me pre-tending to be Rosalyn, but damned if I could figure out how to get her to confess.

Jonathan circled his arm through mine and turned a fierce glare back at me. "We should be going, Kate."

"We have plenty of time." I bared my teeth, smiling. "I just have a few more questions." I faced Nora again. Her wary eyes darted between Jonathan and me.

"You two aren't about to have a spat, are you?"

"No." Huh, she could read my body language as well as I could read hers. But why couldn't Jonathan see it? "Nora, I'm going to tell you a secret." I leaned in close. "Rosalyn called me."

"That's wonderful." Her gnarled hands clutched her chest.

"Not really. She said she didn't want to be found. Why do you suppose she'd say that?"

She blinked rapidly. "I have no idea. Why?"

"Kate, really. We should go," Jonathan said.

Nora fidgeted. "I really should get back to work," Nora said. "Mrs. Gregory is waiting for me to play crazy eights."

I flipped my hair behind my ears and readjusted my tote on my shoulder. "All right. If you think of anything, or re-member anything about Abby, call me."

"Oh, for sure. You're number one on my speed dial now." Wonderful.

"It was nice meeting you, Nora." Jonathan dipped his head to her and looped his arm around mine, propelling me to the door. We stopped long enough at the desk to notify

Barney we were leaving so he could buzz us out. Just before the door closed, Nora's singsong voice apologized to Mrs. Gregory. "Sorry to keep you waiting, dear. I hope you're not put out."

I came to a screaming halt. "Oh my God, Jonathan. It was her." I pulled my arm free from his. "Can't you see that act?"

"I saw you badgering an old lady."

"Oh please."

"Seriously, Kate. You brought her to tears."

"She's playing us." I stormed down the hall.

"Hold up," he called after me. I stopped and huffed. "Let's go over this again," he said.

"I don't want to go over it again. I know it's her. The question is why?"

"All right. If we say your assumption is right—"

"It is."

"Could it be she made a fictitious call innocently to keep you from failing?"

"Failing at what?" George—Mr. Eeyore himself—popped to mind and I cocked my head at Jonathan.

"All right, maybe failing is the wrong word." He back-pedaled.

"What would be the right word then, Jonathan?"

He shifted from foot to foot and ran his hand through his hair. "I think I just experienced an attack of the Kate Lambrose Syndrome," he said. "Mouth engaged before brain."

I slapped my hand over my mouth and screeched through my fingers, laughing. He smiled and pulled me into an embrace, kissing my forehead.

CHAPTER 24

I was starving and needed something to eat, but since Jonathan had insisted on driving to Arlington, calling the shots was out of my hands. I sat quietly during our ride back to Yardman. He said he had someplace to be so I didn't want to ask him to stop at a drive-thru. I still fumed over Nora and tossed it back and forth in my mind when Jonathan turned off the highway onto 126.

"Where're we going? I thought you had someplace to be?" I asked.

"I do. I'm taking you with me."

Now I was peeved that I hadn't insisted he stop at one of the fifteen drive-thru chains we passed. My belly button rubbed against my backbone.

"But I don't like surprises." My voice whined.

"You'll be okay, Kate." He laughed.

God, how I hated he knew I needed control, and with surprises, I lost the upper hand.

"Don't make me suffer." I twisted around in my seat, peering out all the windows like a caged-in dog. A dog, how-ever, would wag its tail, excited by the dense forest whizzing by. I just wagged my tongue. "Does this surprise have food?" I asked.

"As a matter of fact, it does."

"Good. What's the name of this place?" I spat the ques-tion at him, hoping he'd throw me a bone.

"You'll see."

"All I see is trees and more trees. Oh, what's that?" I pointed out the windshield across his vision. "Is that the Alcott house?"

"No, that's the visitor center for Walden Pond. Haven't you ever been here?"

He made it sound like a crime if I admitted I hadn't been

here. "Emma has. School trip. Does that count?"

He smiled, but shook his head, more in disbelief than a no. He slowed and turned left into a gravel parking lot. Across the street, through the trees, sky blue water danced with orange ripples.

Jonathan pulled the hatchback level and exited the car. "Come on, Kate."

I slung my tote over my shoulder and slid out, none too excited about traipsing around on an empty stomach. I shuffled from the car, taking disgruntled Emma-footsteps. I'd die of starvation.

"Are you coming?" Jonathan asked, rounding the car with a red and white cooler in his hands.

My stomach somersaulted and rumbled in joy and I'm sure I licked my lips.

"Lunch," he said. "Grab the rest of the stuff back there." He tossed his head toward the open hatch.

"Is this a picnic?" I giggled and grabbed the blanket, radio, and camera.

"Uh huh."

My inner giddy teenager twirled, screamed, and hoped for peanut butter and jelly sandwiches. The sun baked my shoulders, but the breeze off the lake cooled the heat. Tomorrow, I'd show off lobster red arms.

"This is so nice and it beats sitting in a cold booth with a table between us." Oh boy, that was not what I meant, but my mouth had control. "Awe, you know what I mean, right?" I stammered.

He laughed. "It's getting easier to decipher the true meaning in your words."

"Oh shut up," I teased him.

We strolled down a wood-chipped path that weaved around huge oak trees and zigzagged to the pond. Our footsteps flushed out a mama mallard and her six ducklings sending them waddling to the water's edge. We balanced along the retaining wall following the worn path to a quieter spot past several kids who braved the spring-chilled water. The path narrowed a bit but opened again and we staked out a grassy patch beneath a birch tree. Before we spread the blanket down, I searched for anthills and kicked some sticks away while Jonathan gathered two rocks to keep the blanket from ruffling up in the breeze. I chose my spot next to the cooler while Jonathan emptied the contents.

What goodies to devour first? I grabbed the items as quickly as he set them down. Two deli subs. One turkey and provolone, and one ham and Swiss according to the label stuck to the cellophane. Turkey for me. I handed him the other sandwich and dug into the cooler. The menu was endless. Potato salad and coleslaw, four ice-cold sodas, stuffed olives, cheese cubes, and bless his heart, brownies. And he even remembered cutlery, napkins, and paper plates. And Matthew said he was boring, more like prepared.

"You remember me telling you that I'm going to Connecticut again on Wednesday, right?" he asked.

"Yeah, of course. Has something else happened?"

"No, nothing has changed. I was curious if I ended up having to stay through the weekend, if you'd consider driving down to visit me."

No, I'm not driving to Connecticut, but I didn't say that. "I don't know. George has Emma this weekend instead of his usual, which would be next weekend. I can check with him—see if he minds."

"Oh no, I meant you and Emma both. You don't have to drop kick her out the door for me. I don't mind." He gnawed off both ends of his ham and Swiss. "Uh, unless she minds. Does she mind?"

"I honestly don't know if she minds." I pondered why he ate the bread first and left the filling to savor for later. Maybe he was nibbling away at me, but my mouth was full, thank God, I could not ask.

"You never asked her?"

"I never had to. Well, I take that back. I did ask her last week when you were planning to come by the house for Rubys takeout."

"What did she say?"

"*Okay, whatever*," I mimicked and added the one shoulder shrug Emma often used when she didn't care.

"That doesn't sound good."

"She was fine with it. Besides, she had other things on her mind. She met Nora that day and was excited about working at the pet store. Which reminds me—" I shook my plastic fork in the air, conducting an imaginary orchestra. "I don't think I'll let her continue with that."

"Why not?"

"It doesn't feel good. There is something here in my gut that is unsettled about it and especially after seeing Nora at the nursing home. It all feels put on."

"Or put out." He laughed.

"Ya know, that's it. I do feel put out. I don't even know how it all happened. I just wanted Mack to be polite to me and then I end up with Nora in my life too. I didn't ask for another set of parents to...uhm, juggle. I just meant—"

"To mold Mack into a father figure?" Jonathan asked.

"Maybe, but I didn't expect them to move in on me and dictate how I should or shouldn't do this or that."

"Careful what you wish for." He winked.

I speared a couple olives with my fork. "Do you wish your father would welcome you with open arms?"

"I don't think so. It would change my life. I've lived so long with his silence that I've adjusted to suit the relationship. And I don't see any benefit for it to be different."

"That's sad."

"Why? So I can complain about him dictating how I should or shouldn't do this or that?" He smiled.

"Ha ha, touché."

"You know how I feel about Mack, so I'm not disappointed to hear you complain about him."

"I know. I just don't look at people psychologically like you do."

"And I don't get all crazy about befriending old men," he countered.

"Thank God!" I said.

We laughed and toasted to each other, tapping our soda cans together. We didn't stay long after that, just long enough to finish our sandwiches and watch a few canoes paddle across the water. The sun disappeared behind some dark clouds and rather than wait to see if the rain held off, we packed up and left.

CHAPTER 25

The next morning as I turned down the alley to park, I caught a glimpse of the mail truck pulling away from the *City Scope* building. That alone excited me. A week had passed since I posted Abby's poem with my response in my column. No way I'd wait for Mack to deliver the mail today. After I parked my Jeep and grabbed my umbrella, I ran to the building, jumping over ankle deep puddles. I cursed the rain and humidity for turning my do into a Chia pet.

Simon was the only one at his desk. "Where is everyone?" I asked him.

He shrugged and pointed off in all directions. I dumped my tote at my desk and handed Eugene an update for my Abby copy before Beck put the paper to bed. My update simply stated the search continued for Rosalyn Kohler, but she may have been a professor at Long Beach State College and Abby may have been a resident at Elderly Assist Gardens. I returned to my desk, swiped my lock code list from inside my drawer, and headed for the stairs. I didn't ride the clunky elevator.

A floor-to-ceiling wrought iron gate locked out wanderers from access to the morgue, or as I preferred to call it, the basement. I punched in the four-digit code from the post-it-note and pulled the gate apart, stepped down two steps, and closed it behind me. If Mack wasn't ready to sort the mail, I'd do it myself.

I rounded the landing down the next flight and stopped. A small circle of light brightened the basement floor at the bottom of the stairs. I completely understood the phrase "silence was deafening," and I could have heard a mouse sneeze. Even the pounding rain hushed. On my left, the door to the pressroom remained shut until 5 o'clock and no lights loomed through the window. I turned right down the dim-lit hall past the elevator before the hall opened into a room no bigger than a motel single. A double sink hung from the far left wall and a wooden desk sat beside it. A dozen roll-ends propped against the wall beside racks stacked with old editions. Off to the right, a stairway stretched up to a metallic door. A tree branch whacked against the one-foot square window at the top of the door.

Straight ahead in an adjacent room, Mack's mail cart nestled under a table.

"Mack?" I yelled. "You here?" My voice bounced around the empty room. A spider skittered along the floor a gnat's eyelash away from my foot. I shuffled aside and shivered. I'd let it live for now, at least it was company. I hated bugs, especially ones with eight legs and gumdrop bodies.

I craned my neck to peer into the adjacent room. It seemed inconceivable that Mack would light up his cigar down here, but the stale smoke lingered.

"Mack?" I knocked on the open door. The heavy metallic door thudded against my knuckles. Gosh, a prison door, with octagon wire sealed in the one-foot square window. Newspaper stuffed the doorknob hole.

A paddle lock loop screwed to the door below a broken dead bolt knob. It all put a morbid spin on the man cave theory.

I prowled through the doorway. A four-tiered shelf with at least a hundred mail slots balanced on the six-foot long table. Masking tape labeled slots with our names, as well as the company names on the third floor of the building. I now understood why Mack spent so much time delivering mail. He delivered to the entire building.

Oblong windows lined the wall above the table. Grates covered the windows from the outside and I could see feet to knees splash by on the sidewalk.

Two wire racks stacked with old newspapers lined one wall. Boxes of envelopes and *City Scope* stationery as well as postage paid postcards filled another rack. Two racks along the back wall towered with paper towels, toilet paper, paper cups, and boxes of vending machine goodies. Uhm, grazing food.

Where the mail truck dropped off the mail puzzled me, as the only mail I found was stuffed in the slot labeled *OTHER*. I fingered five or six card stock ads addressed to resident before plucking them from the slot. Another spider dangled from a card and wiggled up its silk. Freaked, I flung the ads into the air. They sailed in every direction across the floor, into the trash bucket, and under the *City Scope* stationery rack.

"Damn it." I hunted around for a broom or anything I could sweep under the shelf to retrieve the mail. Nothing, which meant I had to reach into the dark shadows. I knelt down with my butt up in the air and my cheek pressed to the floor and palmed under the rack.

"Okay, spiders, get out, get out. The next one of you won't be so lucky."

Using just my fingertips and wishing I had stuck-on nails like Joyce, I pulled the runaway mail, cobwebs and all, from under the shelf. That's when I noticed a black square hole recessed into the wall. I half expected some creature to pounce out and attack me.

I slid two cases of paper aside that covered the hidden passage from my view. An opening about the size of a dishwasher dead-ended to nowhere but up. Ropes and a pulley dangled down inside.

I had never seen a dumbwaiter before, but after I moved a couple more cartons, it made sense and explained the sink in the outer room. This must have been the galley or kitchen when the building was a hotel back in 1901. I couldn't wait to tell Dan about my find. He would be down here moving the shelf and snapping photos before I could finish telling him about it.

A door slammed from some far-off place and I jumped to my feet with the mail in hand, but I couldn't decide where to turn. I could run back down the hall, nonchalantly sit in the chair, or hide. My eyes rolled to the ceiling. What was I worried about? I had a right to be here.

I quickly shoved everything back in place and gathered the other pieces of mail. Until then, I hadn't noticed the envelope addressed to me, the same size as the first card I received from Abby. I crushed it to my chest, clutching it with both hands.

"Thank you, thank you." I spoke to the ceiling.

A loud clap thudded on the floor behind me and I twirled around, gasping. "Oh shit!" I screamed.

"What ya doing in here, Kate?" Mack asked.

"Jeez, you scared me."

"Ya, me too. Nobody ever comes down here." He frowned at me. "What ya doing, praying?" He picked up the two mail crates and carried them to the sorting table. "Maybe you got mail from Abby today," he said.

"I think I found what I've been waiting for." I waved the envelope at him.

"How'd that happen?"

I confessed my prowling around and explained how I dropped the mail when the spider spun out at me. "This must have been stuck between the other pieces."

"What ya say." His grin twitched and he fished his cigar butt from his shirt pocket and stuffed it between his teeth.

"Not a problem, at least we have it now." I turned to leave.

"Hold up," Mack said, and shoved a letter opener at me so fast and close, I jumped back. "Let's see what it says."

"Careful." I reached around, took the letter opener by the handle, and ripped open the envelope.

Excitement robbed my breath, however, disappointment stung as soon as I pulled the card from the envelope. A thank you note from the nursing home and not even a recent thank you, but related to the Jack Benny records I found a month ago.

"Son of a gun," Mack said after he finished peering over my shoulder.

"Damnit." I slapped the card in my hand.

"I don't know, Kate," Mack said. "I hear you were at that assist place in Arlington yesterday. How many dead end leads have you followed so far?"

"A couple," I said. "By the way, I appreciate you and Nora wanting to... as you said, keep an eye on me, but it's not necessary." I avoided saying what I wanted to say. It was hard to tell him and Nora to leave me alone.

"Yeah, what ya say."

I just shook my head, mostly at my futile attempt at honesty, and turned to leave, but Mack caught my arm.

"Did ya ever think this Abby person is just some quack?"

"Maybe." I shook free from his grip, which seemed a bit too aggressive.

"Like I said, maybe you got mail from Abby today."

"Maybe." I stared at the mail crates, ready to dive in to help sort.

Mack held up his hand, stopping my thought. "Don't you worry, Kate. If it's in there, I'll bring it right up to you."

"Thanks." I trudged back down the hall and up the stairs with my lousy thank you note.

CHAPTER 26

Back at my desk, I tossed the thank you note in my top drawer and flopped down. The chair whooshed. I grabbed the lever underneath and let it sink as low as it would go. It was only a three-inch plummet, but after the adrenaline rush and disappointment, I crashed like a hang glider without updraft. I was so sure Abby had finally responded. Yet, it was nice to hear appreciation for finding the Jack Benny records, especially after battling with Beck about it. It just didn't set my world on fire, not compared to finding Abby and solving Rosalyn Kohler's mysterious disappearance. Perhaps death had severed all ties for Abby already. That worried me.

I folded my arms, pillowed my head against the desk, and fish-eyed the traced over letters in Abby's poem. Huh, new perspective, and I remained clueless. Keyboards clicked in the background. Simon trilled his bargain ad campaign and from his side of the conversation, *City Scope's* next week edition would offer twenty percent coupons for cremation services. It gave me the willies.

Dan bumped my chair. "What's wrong, Kate? Sick?"

I sat up and eyed the cardboard box he carried. "No. What's with the box?"

"Oh, uh...just clearing out some personal stuff." He opened a file drawer, dug out a football, and plopped it in the box. "From when I coached the pee wee league," he offered in response to my left eyebrow arch. "You got dirt on your nose."

"Huh?" My vision cross-eyed and I swiped my hand across my nose. I couldn't see any smudge, but I did see Dan add some file folders to his box. "What are those?"

"What?"

"Those files you just put in the box."

"Oh. Take home work," he said. "Your phone is ringing."

"No, it—" I turned back to my desk. The red light flashed.

"You're not bugging out on me, Dan. Are you?" I asked.

"You better answer your phone."

"Well, are you?" I lifted the handset, said my name, and asked the caller to hold a moment.

"No. Just cleaning the clutter," Dan said.

I sighed. "Don't go away." I pointed at him. The option for Dan to tell me in his own time why he was being secretive just ran out. "Kate Lambrose," I said to my caller.

"Ms. Lambrose. My name is Alisha Monroe," she said. "I'm a nurse at Mass General Hospital. A patient I'm attending asked me to call you."

Ambulances, paramedics, and car accidents popped in my mind. I mentally ran through my shortlist of people—family— that would list me as an emergency contact. Mass General would be the hospital George would choose if he needed one.

Emma was still with her father. I wouldn't pick her up until tonight. *Emma.* If George were hurt, he'd call Ethan. He'd taken me off his in-case-of-emergency list two years ago. But if something happened to Emma and him, a hospital representative would have to contact me.

"I'll kill him," I said aloud. Nurse Monroe sucked in a gasp. "I'm sorry. Sorry," I said. "What happened? Is my daughter all right?"

"Daughter? Oh no, no. I'm calling for Abby Duncan."

"Abby?" I jumped up, spun around to grab Dan by his shoulder, and nearly hung myself with the phone cord. Abby had a last name. "Abby Duncan?" Where the heck did Dan go? Simon stared at me. I mouthed to him, *I found Abby.* He joined me standing, phone cradled to his ear, and mimicked my movements like an insane aerobics instructor. He mouthed, *Maynard Cremation* and pointed at his phone.

"This isn't show and tell." I swiped at his arm and missed.

"No. It's not. Ms. Lambrose." Nurse Monroe lost her sympathetic tone. "Perhaps I have the wrong Kate Lambrose. I apologize for the confusion."

"Wait. Don't—" Dial tone buzzed in my ear. "Shit, shit."

I stabbed at my phone for a fresh dial tone, but it rang back to me. "Hello?"

"Hello?" the caller mimicked.

"Who is this?"

"Kate?"

"Nora?" *Oh my God, shoot me now.*

"Yes dear. I need a ride."

"Sorry, Nora, I'm busy."

"You sound rushed. Is everything okay?"

"Everything is fine, Nora, got to go."

"But Katie, Helen isn't answering her phone. Is she there? Could you go find her for me or find Bo—Mack, please. I really need a ride."

"You're on your own. I have business to deal with. Good-bye, Nora."

"Oh! What business could be more important than me?"

Oh my God. I stamped my feet. "I got a call from Abby and I have to call her back and you are holding me up."

"Hurry, Kate, what are you waiting for?" she said, and hung up.

I strangled the handset and shook it with both hands. Simon glared at me and backed away from his desk.

With a fresh dial tone and no one on the other end, I dialed 411. It was about time I heard from Abby and I darn near lost my lead with my engaged mouth.

At the very least, I was sure Nurse Monroe thought I was a lunatic.

I scribbled the number to Mass General on my blotter, but chose the "connect me" option. With the phone ringing in my ear, I rolled my chair back and looked around for Beck. No doubt, she still roamed the building. The automatic public address for Mass General played in my ear. I pushed zero on my phone and held it down. Here I was on the line with a hospital in the throes of a figurative heart attack and stuck in automated hell. Where was Beck? I stood up and surveyed the entire newsroom hoping to connect with anyone to share my news. No other heads popped up to meet mine. After my swipe at Simon, he hadn't even tried to copy me. Instead, he eyed me with suspicion and his shoulders hunched.

Zero. Zero. Zero. I pushed and cut off the second replay. I didn't care about what to do in an immediate emergency. I needed assistance now.

"Joyce, are you over there?"

"She is at Dodd's," Simon said.

"I found Abby." I grinned at him.

"Oh-Kay."

I am a lunatic. Simon's expression confirmed it.

Finally, a real person who thanked me for calling Mass

General Hospital came on the line. "How may I direct your call?" the voice asked.

"I need to speak to Nurse—" What the heck was her first name? "One moment please." I searched my blotter for the circle I drew around her scribbled name. "Alisha Monroe." I hollered. Now my heart pounded in double time.

"What floor, please?" the voice asked.

"The one she works on." *Mouth—brain again.* I'll forever be backwards.

"You'll have to be more specific."

"I don't know. The floor where Abby Duncan is located." Beck passed by my cubicle and into her office. I waved my arm at her but too late. Despite the fact we all thought God gifted her with eyes in the back of her head, she didn't see me. I sent a mental "stay" command her way.

"And your name, please."

"Kate Lambrose." If this took any longer, I'd need CPR.

"One moment, please." A computer beeped and her fingers clicking a keyboard snapped in my ear. The line silenced and then elevator music resuscitated me.

"Second Floor, Alisha speaking."

"It's Kate Lambrose. I'm sorry, sorry for the earlier confusion. You said you were calling on behalf of a patient?"

"Yes." Her tone cooled.

Okay, lesson learned. Never say to a nurse I'm going to kill...as a conversation starter. "You said Abby Duncan?"

"Ms. Duncan wanted me to encourage you to visit soon."

"What room is she in?" I asked, and gathered my notes. I peered around my cubicle to make sure Beck hadn't slipped away again.

"Two-oh-three."

"Thank you. Tell Ms. Duncan I'll be there in an hour." I hung up, grabbed my tote, and beat feet into Beck's office. "Knock, knock." I slid her glass door open. No time to stand on formality or shrink from the disapproving frown she threw over the rim of her eyeglasses. "I'm off to interview Abby."

"Wonderful." Beck tilted her head back and focused on me through her lenses.

"Mass General. Room two-oh-three." I grinned. "See you in the morning."

"Good job, Kate," she said. "It's just too bad. It's too late for this week's edition."

I dismissed her backhanded criticism, turned about face, and waved goodbye over my shoulder.

CHAPTER 27

I talked aloud during my ride to Mass General, and not quietly either. The rain pelted the windshield and the wipers droned a steady heartbeat that could have put me right to sleep, so I kept talking. First, I rattled off everything I understood about Rosalyn Kohler. She went missing in 1965 according to Emma's teacher, which corresponded with the Lydia Kohler estate notice and the Catalina Island article. That hop scotched me to what Emma wrote about her father and I cried over her sadness. Then I cried more over how well she wrote. I was so proud of her. I missed her all weekend, but hoped she enjoyed her time with her dad and Ethan. She had no school today because of a teacher's workshop and after the four of us dined together tonight, she'd come home with me. How ironic the ocean scene Ethan drew ended up on the card Abby chose, which brought me full circle back to the excitement of finally meeting Abby. And what about Mack, and him shoving the letter opener at me in a stabbing motion? Or had I imagined it? I reached up and rubbed my arm. Old or not, his strong grip lingered. I could still feel phantom pressure from his fingers. What was that all about anyway?

The biggest question I had, which I would ask Abby, was why she felt it necessary to play games. Why the poem? Why not just call me to begin with? She obviously had that option available to her.

I dug my cell from my tote and dialed Jonathan. He would want to hear that my search had ended. I was about to meet Abby. No answer, which meant he was with a patient. Then I tried Joyce. She should be back from Dodd's by now. As soon as she answered, her painted-on surprised expression popped in my mind like a snapshot. She'd be sitting at her desk holding the handset with her fingertips and brushing her monitor screen with troll hair.

"Guess what? I'm on my way to interview Abby," I screamed into her ear.

"Wahoo," she hollered, and giggled. "Where?"

"Mass General and I won't be back today."

"What is that squeaking noise, Kate?"

My wipers shuddering across a now dry windshield squeaked unnoticed until now. "Oh, sorry," I said, and clicked them off. "It was raining."

"Not here, where are you?"

Ondrea prattled in the background, something about me being the guest of honor in Satan's den.

"Oh my God," I said. "Tell her to shove it. I am so sick and tired of her..." I went off on poor Joyce, and even threatened Ondrea with my brother.

"Kate, Kate stop. It's me, Joyce, not her." She must have cupped her hand over the mouthpiece because she sounded like she was whispering into a tin can.

"I'm sorry, sorry. You'd think she'd be nice to me if she wanted to get in my brother's pants." Like I controlled what he did with his pants.

"What? Your brother's pants?"

"Oh, yeah. You didn't hear?" I asked, but didn't wait for an answer. "She and my brother are doing dinner dates."

"You mean she could become your sister-in-law?"

We laughed after realizing how ridiculous that sounded. But I knew Matthew, and when he got an idea stuck in his head, he'd move mountains to tick it off his to-do list.

"When you get back," Joyce whispered. "I'll hold her down and you can slap her."

We roared and promised to watch each other's backs when it came to Ondrea.

It was after two o'clock when I arrived in Boston and circled my way to the top of the parking garage. I rode the elevator down to the main entrance and signed in. The glum receptionist gave me a sticky visitor pass and instructed me to slap it on my shirt in plain sight. Not that it mattered because the nurse at the locked glass doors on the second floor asked if I had signed in. I tapped my visitor pass that I had stuck on my shirt just below my chin. It disturbed me how robotic the world had become with trained phrases to say rather than using our own insight.

Abby was in a private room and sitting up on her hospital bed when I found her. A privacy curtain partially pulled closed blocked a puddle of sun from heating her bed. Two floral arrays filled with white gardenias and baby's breath crowded the small bedside table to her right. A pump bottle of gardenia hand lotion rested between her legs.

A bandage wrapped her left arm from her hand to elbow and an IV poked through a massive black and blue on her right hand. My stomach flip-flopped at the sight.

An oxygen mask covered her tiny-wrinkled face. A dozen or so wires and tubes protruded from her hospital gown and stretched around behind her like octopus tendrils. Her eyes stayed shut, but she wasn't asleep. Soft jazz moaned from some obscure ceiling speaker and she tapped her feet to the beat. If it weren't for that movement under her blanket, I would have thought she was just a bust in bed.

I sat in the chair at the foot of the bed. I didn't want to speak and startle her, so I waited at least until my tote slipped off my shoulder and thumped to the floor. I grimaced, Abby opened one eye like a doll's eye would flip up, and a wad of silver hair draped across her forehead. She eased her bandaged hand up to push it aside.

"Sorry," I said.

Her hair drooped again, but by then she'd slid her oxygen mask down to her chin. It seemed like too much effort for her to plow her hair back.

"I suspect you find yourself saying that often." Her voice quivered.

I almost said sorry again for saying sorry. If I counted how many times I said it over the last twenty-four hours, she was right. I shrugged and moved the conversation along. "I'm Kate La—"

"Yes. I know who you are. I expected you three days ago."

Again, I bit my lip to keep that word from slipping out. She was frail, but the bite in her words wound my siren.

"I drove as fast as possible after your nurse called me." I smiled at her.

"Oh, Katie," she said. "Didn't you get my poem?"

Huh, only my mother called me Katie and only when she wanted to point out how ridiculous I was acting.

"Yes, I got your poem. Did you read my response?"

"I did. And I thought it marvelous of you to write back to me with a poem so I replied with another poem."

"You did?" Huh, we were talking oranges and apples instead of apples and apples. "I didn't receive another poem from you."

She cleared her throat to speak again, but it erupted into a full-blown coughing spasm.

"You want me to call the nurse?" I asked.

She shook her head and dug an inhaler out of the tissue box sitting in her lap. After a long held inhale, which turned her cheeks amber, she coughed something into a tissue and I bowed my head and closed my eyes. I was no help when it came to spittle.

"Is there a U.S. postal strike again?" she asked. "That would be the only reason you didn't receive my card. What a shame that is. Do you remember the strike in nineteen-seventy? Nixon was President then and didn't he call out the armed forces to distribute the mail?"

"I was seven and doubt I cared or even knew about it then. Now it's just history." I feared she would continue to digress throughout our conversation.

"As most things in my life are now."

"So, Abigail," I said. "If you were able to have the nurse call me today, why didn't you just have the nurse call me to begin with?"

"It's Abby," she corrected, and I jumped on that.

"It's Kate," I said.

She laughed and a gurgle rose from her chest. She eased the mask back up over her mouth and nose and shook her index finger at me. Her eyes crinkled into a smile.

"Sorry." Damn it, I did it again. "Maybe I should come back when you're feeling better."

Abby shook her head and I waited for her to catch her breath. "I may not be here tomorrow. I've already lived longer than expected."

My mind said sorry, but I kept my lips clamped, rolled over my teeth.

"Tell me what you found out about Rosalyn, or are you going to make me wait to read it in tomorrow's paper?" She tilted her head and it reminded me of someone asking me a question who already knew the answer but tested my knowledge.

"She's either dead, missing since nineteen-sixty-five, or

doesn't want her whereabouts known," I said. "Now, why the cryptic poem Abby?"

"Are you always so impatient, Kate? Things aren't always as simple as a phone call."

"Fine, but I don't think I'm telling you anything about Rosalyn that you don't already know."

She listened stone still while I told her what I had found out about Professor Rosalyn Kohler and when I finished telling her about the phone call from Rosalyn, she laughed.

"I doubt she called you, Kate. She drowned."

"Huh?" I heard her, but who drowned? Rosalyn? When? Where? How and why? And what did she need me for if she already knew Rosalyn's burial site?

"I'm sorry," I said. I had arrived too late.

The corners of Abby's lips twitched and her eyes twinkled. "No need. She wasn't a friend. She was my lover's wife."

My mouth hung open and the questions spinning in my head shuffled together, but mostly I wanted her to explain why she had to hide from me. "If you already knew that, then why send me your poem and make me research all this?"

"If you're standing at the top of a hill with a ball at your feet, don't you have to give it a little nudge to start it rolling down the hill?" she asked.

I frowned at her and waited for her to flip the light on her profound analogy. She was interestingly frustrating for sure.

"Well?"

"Yes, Abby." I sighed. I was the ball at the top of the hill, or maybe the hill, but I was about ready to nudge her.

"Let me tell you my story, Kate. Then if I'm still breathing after, you can ask your questions." She paused and inhaled the air from the mask. "At least we will be assured you know the story."

Before death severs all ties. I nodded, listened, and wrote notes for close to an hour while she talked and sucked air after every sentence.

She began her story by telling me that her daughter Luanne was some place in the hospital.

"Probably in the cafeteria consuming a gallon of coffee," she said. "Poor Luanne, she is your age, Kate. You'll enjoy her, but she doesn't know this story."

"I didn't need to know that, Abby."

"Shh," she said.

No way, not for one minute would I be responsible for keeping her story a secret from her daughter—well, we'd see.

"Forty years ago, I was heavenly in love with a magnetic man. Oh, I knew it was wrong, however I was star struck and didn't heed my own intuition," she said.

Bobby, the man she adored, was married to Rosalyn Kohler while she and Bobby carried on their affair. Bobby had invited Abby to California while Rosalyn spent two weeks at Long Beach State College teaching essay techniques.

That explained the geography between *City Scope* and California.

"Is Boston your home?" I asked.

"More or less," she said.

Bobby left Rosalyn at a college function to rendezvous with Abby. They boarded the ferry late in the day for an evening cocktail ride to Catalina Island. That confirmed Mrs. Grant's story and the article Joyce found.

Set my conscience free summed up Abby's guilt for having an affair with a married man.

"Oh how handsome and charming he was." Abby sighed. "He made my heart flutter just to hold his hand."

I smiled at the dreamy memory in her eyes, which disappeared as fast as it came on.

"What we didn't know was that Rosalyn was also on board," she continued.

Find Rosalyn Kohler out at sea.

The weather turned treacherous and the ferry heaved side to side. They were thirty minutes into their one-hour ride when the stars and moon surrendered to rain and wind. Abby admitted she was frightened and ill. However, never as ill as when Rosalyn approached them.

"Even Bobby was stunned into silence," she said.

After Rosalyn began to cuss at him, Bobby suggested they venture outside on deck and speak privately.

"In the rain?" I asked.

Abby nodded. "When he returned without her, I didn't ask any questions, but I think in my heart I knew something awful happened out there."

"Abby, what are you saying?"

She placed the mask over her mouth and nose and shrugged. *Surface the buried lies.*

"Did Bobby push her over into the water?"

She didn't answer my direct question, but continued with her tale.

Bobby told Abby Rosalyn agreed to a divorce, and welcomed the chance to get on with her life because she married beneath her.

"But there was one condition to the divorce," Abby said.

"What was that?" I sat forward in my chair.

"I asked him about it one day years later." Abby closed her eyes.

Again, she dodged my question. I shoved my hair behind my ears and blew a sigh through my lips. I feared my questions would go unanswered. I scribbled the word *conditions* followed by a question mark on my notepad. I had at least a dozen questions, some checked off as already answered.

"Oh, I think Luanne was just five at the time and I finally willed enough courage to handle the consequences of knowing the truth."

I waited for her to continue and after too many heartbeats on the monitor, I said, "Abby?"

Her eyes fluttered open and peered right into mine. "You know how that is, dear Kate. When you know in your heart something is true, but your mind just doesn't want to give in to it?"

It was such a poignant question for her to ask me, as if she understood something about my life. Our eyes locked in a silent understanding. Neither she nor I blinked away. I did know how the mind rejected the truth. For the past two years, I had rejected the truth about George, but for some reason, my heart and mind synced today.

"He admitted the truth," she said.

"He admitted what truth?" Another question—did he push her off the boat?

"And I took Luanne and moved home with my mother. That was the last I saw of him, but I want to go to heaven with a clean conscience, not that I'll know."

She placed her mask over her face and closed her eyes. Her chest rose and fell in rhythm with some machine behind her.

"Abby, it's not up to me to keep your secrets and I certainly don't want to end up like you, wanting to free my conscience." Or like Rosalyn Kohler—dead, but I didn't say that and she didn't respond.

I studied my questions. I needed them all answered and there wasn't one more important than another was. But a new one, more important than any others, popped up.

"Abby, would Bobby have read my column?" The question iced the blood racing through my veins and I shivered.

With her eyes still closed, she nodded.

"What did Bobby admit to you? Did he push Rosalyn Kohler into the ocean?"

She spoke through her mask, her words muffled. "He said he didn't stop her from being heaved over the rail."

My eyes popped so wide my vision hazed to gray. I pictured the boat tossing in the wind and the deck slick with rain. Rosalyn lost her balance, teetered against the rail, arms flailing, screaming for help, while Bobby watched as she splashed into the cold, black water.

"Why didn't you question him then, that night?"

"I had no reason to question him until the notice regarding Lydia's estate appeared in the newspaper and then the personal a month later."

"Did he place that personal?"

She nodded.

"What is Bobby's last name?"

"Maleck."

I wrote it down along with the first name, Robert, which again matched up with the missing letters in the article that Joyce and I read as Robert Mulch. Then it hit me, hard. The bolded letters in Abby's poem K M B A C O E B L B Y spelled Bobby Maleck.

"I don't understand why you didn't have..." I scoured at my notes for her daughter's name. "Luanne look into this for you. Isn't Bobby her father?"

"Yes, but he hasn't seen her since she was five. How would you tell your child the man you married—her father— is a murderer?"

Very gently, the same way I told Emma her father was gay.

"Abby, I can tell your story, but if I do, I can't hide it from Luanne."

She said nothing, apparently leaving the decision in my lap.

"Why the poem and all the mystery, Abby?" I asked, annoyed with the runaround. "It would have saved time to just ask me to visit you."

"I'm old and dying, but not stupid. What would you have said to me?"

"Call the police, no doubt."

"Exactly. I spoke to a detective a year ago. He said if there was a crime, it was forty years old and it was unlikely he'd be able to prove anything. He wrote down the information I gave him and said if he had any questions, he'd come back. He didn't." She opened her eyes then and pulled the mask down. "You were the ball I nudged down the hill, the crime. Without the poem, would there have been any motivation for you to do any research? And now he knows the truth is told." She smiled.

Her conspiracy to feed the reporter, me, a tidbit to get the rest of the story told was brilliant, but it worried me. How vindictive was Bobby? On the premise he was still alive, and he had read the article, perhaps he was my threatening phone call.

"Abby, have you jeopardized my life?"

"Nothing is worth anything without the struggle to obtain it, Kate." Her voice fluttered. "Besides, what do I have to gain or lose? Certainly not life."

Wrong answer. I clenched my teeth to keep from saying something nasty, and thought about smothering her with her pillow. It was all a game for Abby. Free her conscience, I didn't think so. She wanted retribution. She used me and my column, knowing perfectly well a mysterious poem would kick the ball rolling down hill. But why now? Something was missing.

"Why didn't you tell this story forty years ago, Abby? Or at least after you and Luanne moved in with your mother."

"I was granted an opportunity to be a mother, Kate. Nothing was going to take that away from me."

Her breath rasped, reminding me of Darth Vader, and sent chills around my neck. Things came together in my mind and slowly locked into place. Abby feared the label, cold-hearted opportunist, like Bobby. She didn't want her child taken away while she and Bobby spent time in jail. I couldn't blame her for protecting her child.

"One last question, Abby, and I'll leave you alone."

"Oh, I don't want you to leave."

I ignored her plea, mostly to remain impartial rather than

pissed off.

"Bobby told you that Rosalyn gave him one condition to agree to the divorce, right? What was that condition?" It really didn't matter what the condition was because Rosalyn Kohler wasn't around to testify to the truth. It was all hearsay.

"Bobby told me she wanted him to take custody of Luanne. She was just two years old at the time."

I stood straight up and leaned over the foot of the bed. "Luanne is Rosalyn Kohler's daughter?"

She nodded. "She doesn't know that, Kate." Quiet tears streamed down her face.

My mouth hung open and I asked, "You adopted Luanne?"

CHAPTER 28

Silence hung in the air as thick as the antiseptic stench. Abby shook her head.

"Did I hear my name used in vain?" A tall brunette swayed into Abby's room and nodded at me.

Her expression failed to match the sweet tone in her voice. Nor did she smile. She flipped her thin brown hair back over her shoulder. Jovan Musk floated through the air. Her long hair reached to her waist and her black skirt dusted her ankles. She stood at least a head taller than I did.

I extended my hand. "Kate Lambrose with *City Scope News.*"

She shook my hand, but kept her dark eyes glued to Abby. "Luanne," she said.

"Not in vain, dear." Abby smiled. "I asked Kate to wait for your return so she could meet you."

"Nice to meet you," I said, "and nice to have met you, Abby." I picked up my tote, shoved my notebook inside, and excused myself as fast as possible.

"Kate," Luanne said. "I'll walk out with you, if you don't mind."

How could I object? But I tried. "Oh, you're not staying to visit?" I asked.

"I've been here since last night." She leaned over Abby and gave her a kiss. "I need real food and a hot shower. I'll see you later or in the morning, Ma,"

"I might be gone by then," Abby said.

I walked to the doorway, giving them privacy, and waited.

"If you're gone, know that I love you, Ma."

"I love you too my baby girl."

I rolled my eyes wide to air-dry the moisture that gathered and ran my finger along my bottom lids. Abby's tiny voice didn't seem so aggressive now. Although I was still an-

gry she handpicked me to clear her conscience and manipu-
lated me like a chess piece, I wasn't made of stone. Their
emotional exchange smothered my anger, but I still wanted
to smother her with her pillow.

In silence, Luanne and I walked side by side down the
hall and out the glass doors to the elevator.

She was model skinny. Was she ill? Mrs. Grant had said
that about Rosalyn Kohler. Now that I knew Abby's secret, I
imagined Luanne probably resembled Rosalyn.

Inside the elevator, we pushed the number six together
and smiled politely at each other. After two stops to pick up
one doctor and four visitors, we still hadn't said a word. We
exited into the parking garage and turned right. Either she
was following me, or we just happened to have parked on
the same level, in the same row.

"I read her poem to you," she said. "I mean, I read it in
the paper, not to you."

I nodded and struggled for intelligent words to say, but
remained as blank as a blue sky. The facts kept rolling
around in my head like a pair of eight-sided dice. Abby left
me with a sacred secret that now tortured my conscience. I
faced two choices. Tell Luanne now, or never write another
word about Abby in my column. An old cliché skidded into
my head; don't shoot the messenger. My only relief that
postponed an immediate decision was that it was too late for
this week's edition to write Abby's story.

I sighed and stretched my neck, looking up into the sky
for inspiration.

"Long day?" Luanne asked.

"What?" She startled me, breaking into my moralizing.
"Oh yes, for sure."

"Wouldn't it be wonderful to win the lottery?" she said.

"I'm not that lucky." The most bizarre idea zigzagged in
my brain, and I stopped walking. Maybe Luanne was that
lucky. An inheritance waited for her providing she could prove
her identity. Before I finished mulling it through, Luanne
spoke.

"This is me." She pointed to her car.

A Jeep. A black Jeep. Mine was white. Did that make me
the good guy? "Huh," I laughed, and pointed across the lane.
"That's me."

She smiled for the first time.

"You bike?" I asked, and pointed to the bike rack mounted to her Jeep.

"Yes, mountain terrain. You?"

"I've thought about it, but I hike and climb."

"Really?" She smiled again. "I've wanted to try climbing."

The tension between us dissolved and from that point on, we compared our lives. Two months apart in age, we were single and grieved it. However, she lost her husband in a car accident three years back. I shared a snippet of my grief for George and commented that I felt I was over it, which surprised me. She envied me for having siblings, nephews, and a father at least until I was sixteen. We learned my mother was the same age as Abby, which opened the door for me to ask about her father.

"And your dad?" I asked.

"I have no idea if he is even alive." She rolled her eyes. "Why do you ask?"

"What do you know about your father?" I asked, which seemed like a fair question without incriminating me.

"If she is looking for him, Kate, I'd rather you not find him."

"Abby told me he left and the two of you moved in with your grandmother."

"I was five and don't remember anything about him. Did you find Rosalyn Kohler for her?" she asked.

"No, I'm afraid she is deceased." I wasn't going to lie or elaborate.

"Oh," was all she said for a moment, and her hand rested on her chest as she sucked in a long breath. I'd swear her eyes glassed over, but I couldn't be sure. She dropped her head and searched in her purse for her keys.

"Did you know her?" I asked. "I mean, did you ever meet her?"

She shook her head. "I guess they went to school together and had some sort of a misunderstanding," she said. "Can you imagine trying to hunt someone down you knew forty years ago just to say you're sorry?" She rolled her eyes.

I could imagine it and it would be Luanne I'd potentially have to apologize to if I kept Abby's secret.

We traded business cards and promised to call to arrange a time for either biking or climbing. It thrilled me to have a female friend in my life to shop with, bike, or rock climb.

Perhaps Abby was as intuitive as she played.

Before Luanne drove off, she warned me Abby wasn't as coherent as she seemed. If I didn't already have information about RK and the Lydia estate along with the personal ad, I'd worry she fabricated the whole story. That brought me full circle back to the sacred secret I now kept from a new friend.

CHAPTER 29

I drummed my fingers on the steering wheel and mentally sorted my options. If Luanne and I were to develop a friendship, she deserved to know the truth. I had no stake in Abby or her wishes. After all, she had sent me on a wild run when she could have been straightforward with her request. She could have said she was as guilty as Bobby Maleck.

I put my Jeep in reverse and swung out of the parking space. A man four rows beyond my windshield, limped toward the elevator. Nothing unusual, but the man's limp faulted in perfect rhythm to the song "Father Figure" playing on my radio. The old man swung his cane and his fisherman's hat flopped in the breeze. I squinted out my windshield, believing it was Mack's doppelganger limping across the road. From a distance, it did look like him and I worried if he had a health problem that brought him here. Not that I had ever seen Mack use a cane or wear a hat, but he walked with a lean to the left just like the cane man. When he stepped into the elevator and turned to push the button, he flicked a cigarette or cigar from his mouth. I turned right toward the direction he came from instead of left to the exit. If it were Mack, his beater car should be easy to spot.

One right turn and two left turns later, I found what I was looking for—Mack's dust-covered Buick, and I stopped behind it. The license plate meant nothing to me. I never bothered to notice license plate numbers, never mind Mack's plate number, but I recognized the yellow rope wrapped around the bumper. The driver's side door was open enough to leave the interior light lit. Dead battery, and I got out to close his door.

The inside of his car was in worse shape than the outside. The only floorboard visible and not cluttered with trash was the driver's side. In the backseat, each floorboard served as storage for *City Scope* newspapers and the seat collected an assortment of fishing poles and jackets. How apropos I had secretly named Mack the mackerel. The passenger's side floor, the obvious trash bucket, was piled with paper coffee cups, scrunched up fast-food wrappers, cigar boxes, candy wrappers, and unopened mail. I swung the door open enough to slam it shut. The breeze fluffed up some papers on the console and unburied a card with another Ethan original print. "What the hell?" Instead of a lighthouse, the print pictured a white sandy beach and sailboats. I scanned the parking garage, suddenly anxious I was being watched. I pulled the car door open again. It made a high-pitched screeching noise that echoed around the garage. I cringed and quickly snatched the card and its envelope addressed to me, slammed the door, and ran back to my Jeep.

Now I was a thief, or was I? It was addressed to me from Abby. It simply read, *I'm a patient at Mass General, unable to flee. I beg you, Kate, to come see me. Room 203. Abigail Duncan.*

After I drove back around to park closer to the elevator, I scrambled out of my Jeep, jogged toward the elevator, and pushed the call button.

I didn't understand why Mack was here, and in possession of my mail. He must have brought it up from the mailroom, but I wasn't there to get his delivery. Beck might have told him where I went, but it pissed me off that he opened my mail.

The circled lights above the door paused on level three, and then flashed up to five. One more floor. I stamped my feet and stepped on the damn stogie he tossed from the elevator. "Come on. Come on." I stabbed the call button again.

Once inside the elevator, I poked the button for level two and prayed for a direct descent. I huffed and sighed all the way.

The nurse at the glass door buzzed, but not to let me in. I held the door while she exited.

"Did you forget something?" she asked, and closed the door behind her.

"No, but—"

"If so, you'll have to wait ten minutes. Shift change right now and I'm leaving." The door clicked.

I peered around her down the hall. "Did you happen to see a little old man with a cane wearing a fisherman's hat come in?"

"No. I think I'd remember that." She walked off toward the elevator.

"Okay, thanks." I couldn't decide to wait or leave, until I checked the clock on my cell, 5:15. "Damn." If I waited around any longer, I'd run late for dinner with Emma, George, and Ethan.

I would track down Mack in the morning to find out why he was here and why he had opened my mail. Wasn't that a crime or something, to open someone else's mail? Michael Earl would know.

As I was panting *Michael Earl,* my cell vibrated in my hand and I jumped. I spun around, guilty for even having my cell phone turned on in the hospital, and I didn't recognize the number.

"Hello?" I whispered.

"Kate, it's Nora. Where is Emma? She never showed up at the store. I'm worried."

I stamped my foot. Nora was like a buzzing fly that wouldn't go away.

"I told you, she is off school today and with her father."

"Where are you?"

"Mass General." I wanted to say *MYOB* but that would prolong the call for sure. "And I have to leave now, Nora."

"Oh that's okay, dear, Mack just arrived, and I have to go too."

"Uhm, I don't think..." She hung up before I could tell her that she was mistaken. Mack was here, not there.

CHAPTER 30

I circled the block once before I found a parking space in front of the Waterside Beacon Street brownstone where George and Ethan lived. What luck, I didn't have to walk a mile, but I felt guilty for taking some resident's parking spot. It was drizzling again. I dug my brush from the depths of my tote and took a couple halfhearted stabs at smoothing my hair. Ex-husband or not, I wasn't going to arrive looking like a Chia pet. I flipped my rear view mirror sideways and checked my reflection. My lipstick wearing days ended after college, but I never left the house without one quick coat of mascara. But by the end of the day, especially a wet day, I impersonated a raccoon. I dug deep for a tissue, came up with a used stuck together one, and swiped under my eyes.

I took a healthy cleansing breath in hopes to blow out the acrobats somersaulting in my gut. The excitement of meeting and bonding with Luanne in less than an hour made me forget my anxiety about dinner with George and Ethan, until now.

I had met Ethan only once at the end of my driveway in George's car, because I wouldn't allow George to pull into the driveway with Ethan in the car. That was at least a year ago now. What a bitch I was.

I climbed the four steps and rang Lambrose/Standish #400. Emma answered the intercom. "Knock-Knock," I said.

"Mom!" She buzzed me in. "Mom's here," she screamed, and I pulled the door open. I rode the elevator to the fourth floor. Emma was waiting for me when the doors parted.

"I missed you," I said, and hugged her.

"Me too." She pulled free and tugged me through the open apartment door. George paused the video game he and Emma were playing and launched off the plush green couch to greet me.

"Hi, Kate." He crossed the room and gave me a cheek peck. "How was the drive?"

"Not long. I came from Mass General." He took my raincoat and hung it up in the hallway closet—a surprisingly organized closet. When had he become such a neat freak? Or was that something else I never noticed among my own clutter?

"Oh? Visiting and nothing serious, I hope?" he asked.

"I was visiting Abby," I said with my head held high. "The woman who wrote the poem."

I joined Emma in the living room. She un-paused the game and guided a flying dragon over the video field catching coins.

"Dad sucks at this game!" Emma said.

"Hey! Who beat level three, huh?" George said, and punched her in the arm.

It was nice to see where George lived. The living room had a wide-open lofty feel to it with the hardwood floors. Lots of framed artwork hung on the cream walls that I assumed Ethan painted. A slider exited out to a small balcony perched over Beacon Street. Despite the outside drizzle, the slider was open and a small breeze stirred the sheer curtains.

"So, what's Abby's big secret?" George asked.

"It's a mystery for sure and I'm not totally convinced it's the truth." I was more than happy to divulge all the information I surfaced. For one, talking it out might get me to an aha moment, and second, I was pretty damn proud of myself. "In a nut shell, Abby had an affair with Bobby Maleck forty years ago. He was Rosalyn Kohler's husband."

"Awe, so Abby wants forgiveness from this Kohler lady?" George asked.

"Not exactly. Rosalyn is deceased. Abby wants retribution, but I can't figure out why after forty years."

"Retribution against who?"

"Whom," I corrected.

"Who he, whom him, it's all the same."

"Against Bobby Maleck. She claims he caused Rosalyn's death."

"What? He murdered his wife?" George swung around and looked up at me from the couch. "You mean to tell me that you've uncovered a cold murder?"

I nodded toward Emma who focused on the T.V. and I

held my index finger to my lips. George nodded understanding, as always, that meant not for her ears to hear. But it was too late; she heard it all and said, "Oh cool, Mom."

"No Emma, it's not cool. It's not a video game."

"Whatever." She huffed. "It's your turn, Dad."

"Oh, okay. Then I'm done after this round," he said. "Jeez, Kate, what about this Bobby guy? Where is he? And does he read your *In Sight* column?"

"How would I know that, George?" But my gut told me I did know.

"I'm just saying, this could get messy. Have you reported it to the police?"

"I just left Abby, George. You're the first person I've shared this with. Now stop jumping forward, Jeez. I'm not even sure I'll write the rest of the story. Where's Ethan?" I asked, needing an excuse to change the subject as anything.

They both pointed toward the kitchen, I assumed.

"Something smells delicious," I said.

"He's been cooking for hours, Mom," Emma said. "Some top secret sauce."

"Hey, don't go giving him all the credit." George winked and Emma burst out laughing.

"Going to the grocery store doesn't count as helping, Dad."

I left them sitting on the couch bantering and headed to the kitchen. I hoped Ethan wasn't making himself scarce on my behalf. I was the one imposing on his home life. I made myself the outsider. Yet, I invited myself, and George hadn't discussed dinner plans with his partner when he agreed. I'd be a bit perturbed if I were Ethan.

Ethan bent down behind the open double doors on the stainless steel fridge and rummaged for something. His shoulder-length black hair knotted into a ponytail at the nape of his neck. He pulled a large green bowl from the fridge and turned toward me.

"Hi." I grinned.

"Whoa." He juggled the bowl. "You startled me."

"Something smells delicious."

"I didn't hear you come in." The corners of his lips twitched when he smiled.

"Sorry," I said. "I've only been here a few minutes."

"Really, I'm not a bad host. George should have told me

you were here. I could have started the pasta." He wiped his hands on a chef apron tied around his waist, grabbed a handful of spaghetti, and dropped it in steaming water.

I clamped my lips together, held my smirk and the snide remark about George's manners. As satisfying as it was to hear his manners hadn't improved, it was odd to share that with Ethan.

He picked up a ladle from the spoon rest and lifted a lid off another pot to stir. The zesty aroma deepened and my stomach growled. I should ask him if he needed any help, but I couldn't get the words out. It was too awkward to share cooking dinner for the man we both loved.

His simple dark blue tee stretched across his broad back and neatly tucked in his belted blue jeans. He scuffed from stove to refrigerator wearing a pair of dollar store flip-flops. Dramatically, he slapped his hands together before he rested them on his narrow hips. If I had an Adam's apple, it would have bobbed.

"You look like you could use a drink. Wine?" He offered.

"Yes. Please." His long, thin fingers pulled a cork from an open bottle. The diamond stud in his earlobe glinted in the light. "So, you're an artistic cook too."

He stopped midway filling the glass and smiled.

"Oh jeez, that probably didn't sound as complimentary as I meant it." *Keep your feet out of your mouth, Kate.* "By the way, did you hear about the poem I received that was written on one of your cards?" That didn't sound right either, but I left it at that.

"I did." He handed me the glass of wine. "George said if anyone could solve the mystery, it would be Kate." He held his glass up to toast with me.

"He said that?"

Ethan nodded. "Did you find the missing person?"

"She's dead."

"Oh, I'm sorry."

"No, no. She's been dead for forty years, apparently." I waved my hand in the air. "Oh, it's a really long story."

"I got time," he said.

I highlighted the important parts for him, including meeting Luanne and the secret.

"Will you tell Luanne?" he asked.

"I don't know how." I shrugged. "I'd rather just bury the

whole story."

"It will haunt you. You need to just blurt it out."

"Huh, like George did with me when he told me about you?" *Yikes, I didn't just say that.*

"Sorry, Kate." He turned back to the stove.

"Hmm. Must be the wine." I took my first quick sip when he turned back to me. "I meant it to be funny. At least it was funny to me."

He cocked his head to the side, but didn't call attention to my fib. I watched as he chopped walnuts and added them to the bowl filled with lettuce, tomato, red onion, and cucumbers. An awkward silence fell between us.

"About that—"

"Walnuts? You're not allergic, are you?" He was about to whisk them off the cutting board into the trash.

"No. Not the walnuts." I rested my glass on the center island and twirled the stem between my fingers. I wanted to tell him that none of this was easy for me, but I intended to try like hell to take a stab at forgiving and moving on. I wanted to tell him I didn't blame him anymore for George leaving me. He studied me with a calm intensity and I prayed my eyes told him what my mouth couldn't put to words.

He set the chopping knife down, rested his hands on the cutting board, and picked up his wineglass.

"Can I be honest with you, Kate?" He downed his wine in two gulps.

"Please," I said.

"You make me nervous."

"I make you nervous?"

"Yes."

I laughed. "The feeling is mutual."

"So, do you think we can put our hurt aside and be a family?"

For too long I had focused on my hurt and neglected how I was hurting him, George, and Emma. "I'm going to try like hell, Ethan."

He nodded and went back to chopping. He was more intuitive than I expected and nicer to me than I deserved. I hadn't sung his praise, but he still welcomed me. I snatched a handful of walnuts off the cutting board, and he waved the knife at me in jest, our awkward moment now history.

George poked his head around the corner at that moment. "Everything okay?"

Ethan rolled his eyes. "She hasn't beaten me to a pulp."

"Yet," I added. "But the minute he puts down that knife, all bets are off."

George paled and Ethan and I howled. The weight lifted from my shoulders and I could have fluttered around as light as a butterfly.

Ten minutes later, we gathered around the table and passed helpings of salad, hunks of fresh bread, and heaping bowls of pasta with the most fantastic-tasting sauce and homemade meatballs I ever ate. Emma brought me up to speed on The Click Five concert she, George, and Ethan attended. Screaming teenage girls weren't his scene, but he pretended well enough to tout the group, which meant the world to Emma. On Sunday, they had visited the Museum of Fine Art, got caught in the rain, and ate hotdogs from the street vendor. Emma did a show and tell of all the posters, postcards, key chains, and other memorabilia she claimed she would put in a scrapbook. But it would all end up in the shoe box under her bed. While I listened, I admired how George stayed focused on Emma, but still managed to include Ethan's interests. They bonded without me. It made me happy and sad at the same time because I had expelled myself from this side of her life, but no more.

"All right, missy," George said to Emma. "You've monopolized the conversation long enough. Give your mom a chance."

"I'm done anyway." She grinned. "So what did you do this weekend, Mom?"

I hadn't really done anything spectacular and I wasn't about to mention I did some work. That was a sore subject between George and me. Mentioning a picnic with Jonathan didn't see appropriate. Witnessing the elderly bumper car match would have lost humor in my translation, so I focused on how I came to meet Abby.

"Cool," Emma said.

"I helped," George said.

Emma rolled her eyes and mumbled something about his help being the same type he gave Ethan cooking dinner. My daughter was no one's fool.

"Huh. Tell me, exactly how you think you did that, George." I set my fork down and leaned back in my chair.

From the corner of my eye, I saw Ethan splash a little more wine into his glass.

George laughed. "Well, if you remember, I supplied you with the clue Ethan drew that print and don't forget the embossed letters, and since you just came from Mass General—"

"Oh God," Ethan moaned. "One doesn't have anything to do with the other."

"No, please. Let's hear it, Mr. An-a-lyt-i-cal." My head seesawed to each syllable.

"Emma, why don't you help me clear the table?" Ethan suggested. They loaded their arms with dishes while George and I faced off.

"I gave you your starting point," George said.

"What a load of crock. Mass General Hospital was printed on the backside of the card for anyone to read. And that's not how it happened."

"You have to face facts, Kate. I'm valuable to you." His eyes twinkled.

I snorted and folded my arms across my chest. "You're a pain in my ass." I just wanted to slap the fool, but I laughed at him instead.

By the time we teamed up and finished clearing the table and loading the dishwasher, it was eight o'clock. Emma and I faced an hour drive ahead and tomorrow was a regular school day.

The day exhausted me, and the background of my mind reeled with ideas of Abby, Bobby, Rosalyn, and Luanne. Every family tolerated their dysfunctions. For the first time, I was satisfied with my own little clan. George helped me cart Emma's belongings downstairs while Emma hurried to finish one last round on the video game. When it was just us at the car, I gave him the envelope I stuffed with Emma's essay.

"What's this?"

"A gift," I said. "A reminder of the treasure we share." I reached in my pants pocket and curled the pearls into my palm. Before I left the house this morning, I had untangled the string of pearls from my jewelry box and slid them in my pocket. I held on to them all day, not sure until now if I'd give them back. Our bond was stronger than the thread on a borrowed necklace.

He pulled the papers free and began reading them under the streetlamp. I spent a lifetime with George. He was no longer mine, but I knew every emotional nuance that crossed his face. I may not have been a hundred percent sure footed in our evolving relationship, but I trusted the strength of what we shared. Together we sat on the curb, oblivious to the wet pavement. George drew a ragged breath as he read our daughter's truths, the same breathless truths I had read.

I took his hand and closed the pearls in his fingers. "I love you, George."

CHAPTER 31

The drive home from Boston hadn't taken the edge off my adrenaline. Emma played her new Click Five CD the entire way, and I found lyrics that synchronized with my life. Huh, maybe all songs had that potential. Nevertheless, they were catchy tunes. I even hummed a few bars as I packed Emma's sack lunch for school tomorrow. I just finished putting it in the fridge when Emma walked in the kitchen.

"Aha! You like my music," she accused as she filled a glass with tap water.

"All right. Some of it," I agreed. She smothered her grin behind her glass.

"I knew it." She laughed. "Maybe you'll take me to the next concert."

"Maybe we will all go." I held out my arms to her for a goodnight hug.

After Emma shot up to bed, I grabbed the cordless phone and headed to the living room. I wanted to share my day with someone.

Four rings, I almost hung up, but then Jonathan said, "Hello?"

"Hey. What are you doing?"

"Kate? Oh—uh," I liked that confused, caught off guard tone to his voice. "Reviewing patient notes. What are you doing?"

Brimming with excitement, reeling with ideas, wanting your company popped in my mind, but instead, I said, "Unwinding. Want to join me?" I held my breath as he paused. I imagined I could hear actual clicks as he switched from a friend to a therapist then back to a friend in that second.

"Sure. Where?"

"My house."

"Oh, okay. Give me fifteen, twenty minutes."

"Good. See you then."

"Uh—Kate?" He stopped me from hanging up. "Should I bring anything?"

"Just yourself." I smiled and hung up. That was sweet.

I straightened magazines, then folded and put away the lime green crocheted afghan Mom gave me last Christmas claiming I needed more color in my life. A definite eyesore, but Emma and I used it anyway while watching T.V. I couldn't blame Emma this time for having left it sprawled across the couch looking like a leprechaun had melted into a wooly puddle. I snuck upstairs, checked on Emma, and pulled her door shut. Jonathan knocked just as my foot hit the bottom stair.

His plain black sweatshirt and faded blue jeans fit him nicely. I imagined the texture would be as soft as cashmere from multiple washings. I had seen him in his dressed for success gear, and his preppy casual, but never quite so relaxed and comfortable. Damn, he smelled delicious. Despite that I told him to bring just himself, he brought a bottle of wine stuffed under his arm. I teased him for being afraid to come empty-handed. He swore it was from his own stockpile in his fridge. I didn't point out that the yellow receipt from Ziggy's Liquor peeked from his pants pocket.

We crashed on the couch after I hunted down two matching wineglasses and a corkscrew. "Oh my gosh, I have so much to tell you. I've wanted to call you all day, but then one thing led to another and you know how events can just keep spiraling and you don't have time to breathe in between just keep going. But I did try to call you sometime around noon. I think it was—"

"Whoa," he said. The word stretched so long it filled the space as effectively as my rambling. "Take a breath,"

"Sorry," I said. "Sorry." Why did I always do that? Apologize and in plural. "I found Abby! Had dinner with George and Ethan, and,"—I paused for dramatic effect—"I have a new friend." I clinked my glass against his.

"Wow." He smiled wide. "Full day?"

I nodded.

"Tell me." He settled back against the couch.

I told him about meeting Luanne, her relationship to Abby, and our plans to get together. Then I backtracked to my trip to the mailroom, careful not to leave out the spiders.

"Spiders?" Jonathan asked. "You're afraid of spiders? This

from a woman who sticks her fingers in rock crevices for fun."

"I didn't say I was afraid. I just don't like them." I'd for sure remember his words on my next climb. *Damn*.

"Okay." He grinned. "You're fearless, but have strong preferences."

I poked him in the ribs and plowed on with my story, Abby's story, and meeting Luanne.

"So she's terminal? What does she have?" Jonathan asked.

Huh, why hadn't I asked? I frowned. "Some sort of cancer, I assume. Maybe lung. She had this horrible gurgle and in between sentences, she puffed on her oxygen."

"Before death severs all ties—from her poem," he said.

"That's what I thought too. In fact, every line of her poem, now that I know the truth, makes sense. Those bold letters spelled Bobby Maleck. The third prong in their sordid triangle, right in sight."

Jonathan took a sip and nodded agreement. "Just like the crime he committed, which is why Abby covered it up in a word game. The answer is there if you know how to look."

"Exactly. And Abby's intention wasn't so much for me to find Rosalyn Kohler, but for me to tell what happened to Rosalyn."

"And reveal who was responsible." Jonathan finished my thought.

"Well, they are both responsible," I said. "But with Abby on her death bed, she has nothing left to lose. So coming clean now, this freeing her conscience is just another selfish act."

"Don't be so harsh to judge, Kate. When we're faced with our final death, even non-religious people seek redemption, just in case there is more than this life."

I couldn't help but roll my eyes. "You're analyzing a forest; I'm talking about one single tree."

"So will you bring Bobby Maleck to justice?"

I shrugged.

Jonathan stretched out his legs and perched his feet on the coffee table. *Wow, his feet were big*. I took a swig from my wine to cover my grin.

He smiled at me, as if he read my mind.

"You're getting good at this armchair analysis stuff."

"Thanks," I said. "Abby said Bobby told her Rosalyn agreed to a divorce with the condition that he take custody of Luanne."

"Well there's no way you'll ever know that truth."

"I suppose you're right." Her words haunted me again. *Nothing is worth anything without the struggle to obtain it.* She struggled with her conscience for forty years, kept the secret because she wanted a child she couldn't have.

I was given an opportunity to be a mother, Kate. Nothing was going to take that away from me.

"What are you thinking?" Jonathan asked.

"I'm not sure, and I guess it doesn't really matter," I said. "At least to Abby. She's told her story. But what do I tell Luanne?"

"The truth."

"I don't know." I scrubbed my hands across my face. My eyes stung. The emotion filled day all ran together. I didn't owe Abby anything. My sorrow erupted for Luanne.

She doesn't know this story. I recalled Abby's words concerning Luanne. Maybe Abby was manipulating me to do what she couldn't. She knew I'd tell, and she hadn't protested when I debated aloud about keeping her secret.

Jonathan pulled me back to lean against him and wrapped his arm around my shoulder. It was nice, comfortable, and easy. I rested my head against his shoulder and my palm across his thigh. Those jeans were as soft as cashmere, and thin enough I could feel the heat rising from his skin. Our breaths fell in tandem and my pulse knocked out an extra beat per second.

The quiet filled with that bashful tenseness, that moment before the inevitable kiss. I struggled between thoughts of sitting up out of reach and sprawling across his lap. I swear the man could read my mind, because he wasted no time deciding for me.

"Hey." He nudged my head with his and I involuntarily looked up at him. Without another word, he did it. His lips were as soft as velvet when he brushed them over mine. My top lip snuggled between his and he swept his tongue across my lip before locking his mouth to mine. His hand slid under my hair along the back of my neck. I shivered. I was sure he'd feel the goose bumps my scalp donned as his fingers weaved through my hair. My fingers gripped his thigh. His breath caught, stealing mine, and we broke apart.

Twenty years ago, the comfortable pleasure I now enjoyed with Jonathan would have ended in the bedroom. Like the song on Emma's CD, I'm still broken, but I'm free. I finally ended a chapter of my life and ended on the same page as Jonathan. Free, and I told him about dinner with George and Ethan.

I yawned and leaned back against the couch against Jonathan's outstretched arm. "Sorry," I said. "My day just caught up to me."

He looked at his watch. "It's after eleven-thirty." He twirled his fingers in my hair. "You could go in late tomorrow."

"Ya right. You forget. I work for Beck. You, on the other hand, can cancel a few appointments, phone in a few scripts, and call it a day."

He chuckled. "True. But, on the positive side, no more waiting for mail from Abby."

Mail. Mack. "Oh my God. I didn't even tell you." I sat up and faced him. "Mack pocketed Abby's second letter and I found it in his car."

"What do mean you found it in his car and when were you in his car?"

"Earlier. Before dinner with George." I explained I saw a man that walked like Mack and I went in search of his car and found his car door open. "I thought Beck might have told him where I was."

"Kate, you can't just bust into someone's car and take what you want, but what was he doing with Abby's response?"

"It belonged to me to begin with and I assumed he meant to catch up with me."

"Why?" Jonathan asked. "What was the point?"

"I don't know." I frowned. "I thought maybe he was just being helpful."

"You don't believe that," Jonathan said.

"He's harmless," I said, and pushed up off the couch.

"I don't like it, Kate. It would take me all night to detail a psychological composite of Mack to get you to understand."

"Stereotypical." I snorted. "You don't even know him."

"Neither do you." He rose to stand next to me. "There's a reason why psychology and psychiatry work, Kate. There are characteristic traits that are true across the board. What differs is the degree of extremity. All of us to some extent have a psychopath within us."

"You're making my head hurt."

He pulled me into his arms and hugged me. "I told you it would take me all night to explain. Do you want me to..."

Yes, I did. I wanted him to stay the night, but not to explain, and not tonight. I entwined my hand in his and pulled him to the door.

"I can guarantee it wouldn't be pointless." He pulled me back into an embrace and brushed a kiss across my lips. My knees slacked.

I sucked in an unsteady breath. "Oh I can definitely see the advantage." I opened the door, thankful for the cool breeze.

Jonathan blew out a heavy breath. "Lunch tomorrow?"

I nodded.

"Lock up, Kate, and keep the phone close."

CHAPTER 32

I spent the morning nodding off at my desk because an hour after Jonathan left last night, my cell rang. I had fumbled in the dark trying to flip it open before the caller gave up. It was Luanne.

"Sorry to call so late Kate," she said.

"What's wrong?"

She explained through breathless sobs that Abby died. "I never made it home for that hot shower and food," she said.

"What happened?" I asked. A ridiculous question since Abby was terminal, but I was still half-asleep.

She explained that the hospital called her about six o'clock when they discovered Abby. She turned around and went right back. By the time she arrived, the police were there.

"What? Why?" I asked.

"They're not sure it was a natural death."

What? My mind screamed. I understood the phrase "not a natural death" meant murder or suicide, but to say the police suspected that concerned me. My gut overpowered my brain and silenced my lips from asking more. We ended our conversation by promising to talk this morning.

The words unnatural death had kept me awake until three and twisted in my own sheets. My down comforter rooted me to my bed, and my pillows caved hollow with heat. Now at eleven, an hour before lunch with Jonathan, I hadn't yet heard from Luanne. Mack hadn't shown up yet either, and Beck was MIA.

The newest edition of *City Scope News* didn't brighten my mood either. Over the past week since Abby's saga ran, I received twenty to thirty requests, each pleading for help in hunting down a missing person. Although none compared to Abby's request, most wanted me to help them contact loved ones or friends that drifted out of their lives. I had become

Yardman's reunion organizer. Beck, concerned about the direction my column was headed, nixed my plan to search for
these people. It was just as well, the requests were far too
serious to take lightly. However, she did let me write up a
general response in my column and provide several resources they could research on their own.

I opened the paper, scanned for my piece, and found it
on top of page four this week.

Dan burst out laughing and slapped me on the shoulder.
"Kate, I love this." He pointed at my column. "This is great
that you've given each of your requests a title. This one is
really funny." He pointed at the one I titled *Foul by Product
of Fowl.*

"Thanks, Dan."

I had spotlighted two letters that were bizarre enough to
lessen the sting from my boring Abby and RK update. The
first was from Boy Scout Troop 464. Their team leader sent
in a description and picture of a skeleton key they found
while camping. Turned out the key belonged to a seven-
teenth century chastity belt. How ironic, adolescent boys held
a key that could unlock virtue, and I titled that piece, *All
Keyed Up.* The second letter came anonymously and warranted a reply. The sender wanted to know if the foul smell
coming from the church grounds came from dead corpses.
First I advised, as gently as possible, all corpses are dead
and dead things did tend to smell, but last week, the church
caretaker came across unclaimed eggs left over from the
Easter egg hunt several weeks back —the foul smell a by-
product of fowl.

The newsroom door squeaked and Dan and I cranked our
necks to see who came in. It was Ondrea coming from the
cafeteria.

"Nope, not Mack," Dan said.

Earlier, I had asked him to come down to the mailroom
with me to see Mack. I didn't want to approach him alone.
Mack wasn't there, but we kept watching for him.

Just then, Beck showed up. "Good morning, good morning." Her usual greeting.

"Keep an eye out for Mack while I talk to her okay?" I
asked Dan.

"Yup, yup."

When I finished updating Beck on the Abby story, minus

the full names of the players to protect the innocent from the guilty, I returned to my desk. Dan asked if I spoke to Mack.

"No. I didn't see him. Where?" I stood up and looked around.

"Oh, I thought he walked into Beck's office. He was standing in the doorway."

"Damn it. Come on." I grabbed Dan's shirtsleeve and yanked him out the door and down the stairs to the mailroom.

No Mack, but a note taped to his door that read, *gone fishing*. I ripped it off and took it with me to hand off to Beck.

By the time I finished ranting to Beck about Mack's lackadaisical work ethic, Jonathan arrived. I was more than glad to escape to Rubys for lunch. He was disappointed to hear that Abby died and as anxious as I was to hear from Luanne. I kept checking my cell phone for Luanne's call, as if I missed hearing it ring. I picked apart my club sandwich, grazing on the contents, shrugging and groaning at his questions, until he was glad to escape back to his office. I made rotten company, but I thanked Jonathan for lunch and left him at the elevator outside the newsroom.

I had one more edition to my Abby story according to Beck. I decided that I would write her story without mentioning Bobby Maleck and just leave it unsolved as to how Rosalyn Kohler went overboard. The two-week whirlwind that captured my readers' attention needed resolution. Since Abby loved writing poetry, I'd ask Luanne for an appropriate poem, written by Abby. My readers would like that and Joyce would do justice on Abby's obit.

CHAPTER 33

As soon as I swung the door open and stepped into the newsroom, five pairs of eyes stared back at me like mug shots. I froze.

Ondrea, Joyce, and Beck huddled next to my cubicle. Dan sat in his chair, facing my desk, and Yardman's Chief of Police, Carlton Haywood, also known as Bonzie, wedged himself into my chair.

"We need to talk, Kate." Bonzie pushed to his feet.

"I'm paid up on my parking tickets." I laughed.

No one smiled. My pulse picked up pace, heating my skin, and my palms drenched. I hated serious, serious meant death, sirens, and unexpected phone calls, but I hadn't heard either all morning or during lunch. I fingered my pocket for my cell phone, still there. Someone would have called if something tragic happened.

Beck's pop stick skated back and forth across her lips.

Only three of the five W's rushed through my mind, what happened, when, and where? I thought of George and Jonathan, but I just left Jonathan. He was okay. Where was Ethan? If something were wrong with George, Ethan would be here. Emma? Sometimes, Bonzie substituted for the school crossing guard at Emma's school. Had he come from the school? Had something happened? I checked the time. School was still in session and damn, I forgot to tell Emma not to go to the pet store after school.

White noise filled my ears and I said something, or I thought I did. My knees numbed and the air in my lungs wilted. Panic blurred my sight and Ondrea walked toward me through a haze.

"Are you okay?" Her mouth moved, but her voice sounded stuffed in a bottle. "Kate, you're pasty."

"Em-ma?" I managed to murmur through my clenched

teeth.

Like a sprinkler head, I scanned the other four mugs staring at me and then back to Ondrea.

Her hand reached out to me in a 3-D slow motion. Dan sprung up behind me. I hadn't even seen him move, but he stuck a chair against the back of my knees. In unison and from far away, I heard, *not Emma, no, not about Emma.*

My lungs expanded and my head spun. I buried my face in my hands and wiped my relief from my eyes. Ondrea wrapped her arms around me and whispered, "Remind me not to have kids. I thought you were going to drop dead."

"Oh God, me too," I said.

I was a mess. I had dropped my doggy bag, my to-go cup topped with whipped cream, and my tote in one neat pile on my shoes.

"Oh jeez, I'm sorry, Kate," Bonzie said.

Emma and I first met Bonzie at the school. Emma had asked him if he dressed up as Santa at Christmas time. I remember thinking then, that only out of the mouths of babes is the truth spoken.

"Are you okay?" Dan squeezed my shoulder.

"Yeah," I said, but shook my head. "Numb. What's going on?"

Joyce and Ondrea cleaned up my sticky mess and Dan rolled me down the aisle to my desk.

"Didn't mean to scare the hell out of you, Kate," Bonzie said. "I didn't think about your daughter."

"Yeah. Well next time..." I left it at that.

He flipped open his two-inch spiral notepad and licked his stubby thumb to turn the pages.

Joyce and Ondrea stayed at their desks and Beck remained standing behind me, mutilating her pop stick. Dan asked again if I was all right and kept his attention on me.

"I'm here about Abigail Duncan," Bonzie said.

"She died last night." I looked from him to Dan to Beck and back.

"How do you know?" Bonzie asked.

"Luanne, her—daughter called me."

"When did she call you?"

"Wait." I held up my hands. "What, why are you even here about this?"

Mass General was thirty miles east of Yardman in Boston.

It didn't make sense why the Yardman Chief of Police was involved until he explained that the Boston PD had asked him to question me. I was the last person to visit Abby before she died.

"Oh my God." I was breathless again after he told me someone smothered Abby with her own pillow. Shivers spiraled up my spine. A thousand tiny eight-legged spiders scurried around my neck into my hair and I shuddered hard. Oh crap, I wanted to do that—smother her with a pillow—and I searched my memory for anyone I said it to out loud.

"Can you explain your visit with Abigail Duncan?" he asked.

"Sure." I pulled a file folder from my desk drawer. "I can't believe this. Poor Luanne." I handed him the folder that held Abby's original poem, a copy of my column response, and Abby's second note. My interview notes with Abby were private, the reporter's creed.

Bonzie made himself comfortable at the desk next to Dan and catawampus to me. He quietly read each piece at least three times while we waited.

The silence must have been unbearable for Joyce and Ondrea as they popped up to assess the quiet. I slapped my hand over my mouth and squeezed my cheeks to keep from laughing. Ondrea's lips pursed as she shrugged at Joyce. Joyce shrugged back with her ever-ready surprise brows.

"Did you find this Rosalyn Kohler?" Bonzie asked, and shook the note card at me as if he were scolding a child.

"No." I wanted to snatch the card from his waving hand.

"Is that why you went to see her, to tell her you didn't find Rosalyn Kohler?"

"Yes."

"So that's the end of it?"

"Well, it is now," I said.

"Did she explain about this poem, why she wrote it?" He waved the poem at me again.

"Yes, but I'm not sure she was in her right mind. Even Luanne, her daughter, wondered about Abby's stories."

"What was the story?" He turned another page in his notepad.

Dan shifted in his chair and tee-peed his notebook so that it stood up facing me. He had written the word LAWYER in black marker at the top. I frowned and shook my head.

"Abby said she was sure that her ex-husband Bobby had something to do with Rosalyn Kohler's death," I said.

"When?" Bonzie looked up from his notepad.

"When what?"

"When did her ex-husband kill Rosalyn Kohler?"

As usual as all police do, he changed my words around. "I didn't say he killed her."

"When?" he asked again.

"I don't know, forty years ago maybe."

"My almighty," Ondrea said. "You've been searching for a woman that died forty years ago?"

Joyce popped up and added her find. "Not even," she said. "There is no record of a Rosalyn Kohler dead or buried. Just a missing person article, no formal report."

Bonzie turned toward Joyce and scribbled more in his pad.

"What time did you leave Abigail?" he asked me.

"About four-thirty the first time when I walked out to the parking garage with Luanne. We stood around chatting."

"How are you so sure it was four-thirty?"

"Whoa," Dan said. "Does Kate need a lawyer?"

Joyce and Ondrea both popped up and looked from Dan to me.

"Dan!" I said.

"Do you need a lawyer, Kate?" Bonzie asked.

"No. I don't think I do. Do I?" I turned and scowled at Beck. She shook her head.

Bonzie didn't wait. "You said you left at four-thirty the first time?"

"Yes, I was meeting my daughter and her father at his place on Beacon at five-thirty for dinner, but I saw, or thought I saw someone, a friend I knew headed for the elevator to the hospital. Said my goodbyes to Luanne and went back to the hospital."

"To look for this friend?"

"Yes."

"Did you find her?"

"Him."

"Did you find him?"

"No, not at all, so I left."

"Did you see Abigail that time?"

"No, just the nurse. But you already know that, I'd guess."

Bonzie eyed me over his notepad and nodded.

"I asked the nurse if a gentleman came by to see Abby," I said.

"Did you feel threatened by her?"

"Who, the nurse?"

"No, Abby, Abigail."

Again, Dan shifted in his chair and tee-peed his notebook toward me. This time, in black marker he wrote, SHH YOU NEED A LAWYER. I shook my head but kept my eyes on Bonzie. Dan shrugged and pointed to his note again.

"How? Why would a terminally ill patient threaten me?" I scanned the faces staring at me. Was I the only one confused? Beck twisted her pop stick and Dan kept tapping his notebook.

"Are you protecting someone?"

"Oh my God, like who?"

"Maybe her daughter or yourself?"

"No, but you're scaring me." I tucked my hair behind my ears and ran my fingers down my jaw across my chin.

"What time was it when you left the hospital the second time?"

I focused on the ball tip of his nose. I didn't want to do an eye shift, but I needed time to think. "It was about five-fifteen, and I know that because I got a call on my cell phone just as I was leaving."

"What time did Abby die?" Dan asked.

Bonzie flipped back through his notepad. "The Boston PD said time of death was..."

His voice trailed off and I glared at Dan, who was still tapping his notebook. Maybe he was right. I should ask for a lawyer and end this, but I would only answer the questions asked and offer nothing else. Matthew would be proud.

"What time did you walk back into the hospital?" Bonzie asked.

"Well, it was about five, because Luanne drove off and I remember thinking I'd have plenty of time to get to Beacon, but then I thought I saw Mack."

"Mack? The friend you went back to the hospital to find?"

"Yes."

Again, Dan asked about the time of death. This time, Bonzie gave it to us.

"Between five-thirty and six p.m."

That time line left me off the hook for sure.

"One last question, Kate. Is Mack the gentleman you asked the nurse about?"

"Yes."

"So he is a friend of Abby's also?"

"I don't think so. No, he was probably looking for me."

"Mack who?" Bonzie asked.

"Mack, the mail guy who works here," Dan said.

I nodded.

"Why did you think Mack was at Mass General?" Beck asked.

"That's a really good question, which I haven't been able to ask him about yet. I thought you told him where to find me."

Beck shifted behind me and my chair rocked. "No, I haven't talked to him."

"Are you talking about old Mack who works here?" Bonzie asked as if he hadn't heard Dan.

"Jeez, yes." I rolled my eyes.

"Mack," he said again, as if he didn't believe me. "Bobby Maleck?"

CHAPTER 34

My heart beat in my throat so fast that it rocked my head, blurring my vision. My brain flashed back and forth filled with half-finished facts. No one else seemed surprised Mack was Bobby Maleck, but I hadn't shared the sacred secret with anyone yet. I was still undecided about writing Abby's story.

Mack the Mackerel, Bobby Maleck. Just a few too many letters then what I needed to make the connection. I understood now why he turned face to be nice to me. He knew I'd find out about him and Rosalyn Kohler. My God, he went to kill Abby while I hunted for him and I could have stopped him. Killing Abby was useless now that I knew the story. I sucked in a long, hoarse breath. The threat—*leave it go before you are gone*—it was Nora, and Nora was Rosalyn with a bad accent. Abby's second note... He hadn't intended to deliver it to me. He stole it to keep me from finding out the truth. The letter opener thrust at me... "Oh my God." I rubbed my arm. "He killed Abby." I shot up off my chair.

"*Who?*" echoed around the room.

"Mack, Bobby Maleck. And I'm next. I know what he did. Abby told me." I rummaged through my tote for my notebook and dialed into voicemail at the same time. "Listen," I said, and pressed the speaker button. "It's him or Nora."

"Why would Mack—" Beck asked.

I whipped around at her. "Why don't you know?" I was so far up in her face she stepped back. "Isn't he your family?"

"Know what?" she asked.

"This." I shook my notebook at her. "Rosalyn Kohler is dead. She drowned because of him. Luanne grew up believing Abby was her mother."

Dan grabbed my notebook and thumbed through the pages. "Is this Abby's story?" he asked.

"Yes." I swiped my marker off my desk and circled the bolded letters on the white board. K M B A C O E B L B Y.

Joyce and Ondrea trotted around from their desks to see what I scribbled on the board and I rearranged the letters to spell out Bobby Maleck.

"Oh wow," Joyce said.

Ondrea slapped her hand over her mouth and Dan read my notes aloud. The room plunged into silence when he finished. We all jumped when Bonzie bellowed to Beck.

"Where is Bobby now?" He pointed his pencil at Beck.

"He's not here," she said, and ran back to her office. Time stopped or we were too dumbfounded to react, but we watched as she picked up her trashcan, turned it upside down, and dumped the contents on her desk. Bonzie flipped his radio off his belt, yelled a sequence of numbers into it along with his location, and announced he was locking down the building.

Ondrea, Joyce, and I scurried around bumping into each other, attempting to go nowhere, when Beck returned. "Here, he left this taped on the mailroom door this morning. Isn't that right, Kate?" Her lollypop stick fell from behind her ear.

We all tried to grab the note from her, but Dan won and passed it over to Bonzie.

"Gone fishing?" He read. The backup he called for was on its way. The sirens closed in around the building. "Where would he go fishing, Helen?" Bonzie asked.

We stared at her, with our hands on our hips, waiting for her answer. The situation wasn't funny, but I imagined tomorrow when we rehashed the events, we'd laugh at how irrational we reacted. I was the stick figure without knees or elbows dangling on the hangman's gallows.

"I don't know."

"Isn't he your brother-in-law?"

"Yes, to some extent."

"To some extent?" I questioned.

"My husband and he have the same father only. We didn't even know about Bobby until twenty years ago."

"Think, Helen, where would he go?"

She shook her head and shrugged.

The doors slammed open against the walls and four cops burst in with their guns drawn.

"Whoa," Bonzie yelled. Ondrea screamed and sank into the nearest chair shaking and crying. Joyce raised her hands straight up over her head. Her bangles fell to her elbows. I crumpled to my knees. Bonzie ordered the four musketeers to secure the building. In other words, make sure Mack wasn't hiding in some corner waiting to get me. He then radioed for another team to stake out Mack's house.

My cell phone rang and vibrated in my pocket, adding to my already hyper-pulse. I spun around, slapping my hand on my pocket.

"Hello?" I didn't recognize the number.

"Mom, Nora isn't here. The door is locked."

"What? Emma?" I was so confused. I didn't understand why Emma was calling never mind from where. "Where are you?" That familiar traffic whoosh rang in my ears.

"I didn't plug my cell phone in last night so I'm outside Nora's Nest at the pay phone."

I turned to Bonzie, pointing to my cell. "Emma, listen. I want you to go back to the school right now. Right now, you hear me?"

"Where is she?" Bonzie asked.

"Outside Nora's Nest at the pay phone."

"Mom, what's going on?"

Bonzie clicked his radio again and instructed any officer in the area of Nora's Nest to escort the young girl at the pay phone back to the school. He turned to me with a thumbs up. "Good call, Kate, the school is a safe place for her to wait." The radio chirped back. It was Officer Earl saying he saw her, but he was in street clothes and should he approach?

I described Michael Earl to Emma. "Do you see him?"

"Yes, I'm scared, Mom, what do I do?"

"Stay at the school till I come to get you." Just then, I heard Michael introduce himself and he took the phone from her. "Kate, it's Michael, I'll walk Emma back to the school and wait with her."

I then called George to come now to meet Emma. He wanted all the details right then and there. I explained about the C.O.P., Chief of Police, waiting beside me for my statement.

"Just go stay at the house with her." I hung up.

Once the building was secure, Beck told Ondrea and Joyce they could leave. Ondrea bolted out the door without even a *see ya*.

Joyce asked, "What about Kate?"

"She can go when she's finished with the chief."

"I'll wait for her," Dan said. He changed his mind after Jonathan stuck his head in the door.

"Kate, you all right?" Jonathan asked.

Bonzie waved him away. I gave Jonathan a thumbs up answer to his question. He pointed at me then him and pointed up. I nodded. I'd meet him in his office up stairs.

Beck retreated to her glass office, closing the door behind her, and talked to someone on the phone. I couldn't hear her, but her arms and hands punctuated every word her mouth formed. Bonzie sat at my desk with me while I outlined Abby's story from beginning to end. His radio chirped again with information from a neighbor at Mack's house. The neighbor said Mack went to some lake named Lost something, he couldn't remember, but thought it was in Westford.

"Lost Lake, for Pete's sake." Bonzie shook his head. "Radio the chief in Groton, tell him what's going on and I'm on my way. Don't worry, Kate." He rested his hand on my shoulder then left.

I wasn't worried until he said that.

Beck waved me into her office. I just wanted to leave. I didn't even want to go see Jonathan. And now, Beck wanted to discuss the situation.

She didn't want Bobby—Mack's—name in print. It didn't look good for her husband's family. I didn't want Luanne's name in print hanging her personal life out for scrutiny.

"I want to leave," I said. "I'm exhausted."

"I understand," she said. "Let's decide on this tomorrow when we can put our emotions..." She stopped mid-sentence and looked around me.

I followed her gaze, almost afraid to see who caught her attention, but it was Luanne.

"That's Luanne," I said, and waved.

She waited at the door.

"I guess this is my cue to tell her the whole story." I sighed.

"Good luck with that," Beck said.

Not an ounce of empathy softened her voice, which was the major thing I disliked about her. I thought about saying it and I did. "You're not a very supportive person."

Her mouth opened in an O and her brows shaded her eyes. I could have said more, but left it at that and walked out. Either I'd have a job tomorrow or I wouldn't.

CHAPTER 35

Luanne didn't budge from the doorway as I approached her. Her arms folded tight in front of her. Her lips were nearly blue from pressing them in a thin line and I fiddled with the lint in my pockets. She looked like a taper candle; the stare she gave me had me thinking unlit TNT, but I wrapped my arms around her anyway. "I'm so sorry for your loss," I said.

Her hands pushed against my arms. I was surprised to see her and surprised by her chilly greeting. By now, no doubt, she heard an earful from the Boston PD and wanted answers, which no doubt, I had.

"Let's go for coffee." I suggested Rubys across the street.

"Is this where Bobby Maleck worked?" she asked, and strolled around the perimeter of the cubicles.

"Yes. In this building, in the mail room." I pointed out the door.

"You knew he was my father when you visited my mother."

It was hard to tell from her deadpan voice if she was asking me or making a statement.

"I didn't," I said. "I knew him only as Mack."

"But you led him right to my mother."

"I didn't." At least I didn't believe I did. Abby had done that when she wrote the poem, knowing it would end up in the *City Scope News*. When Luanne thought it through, she'd realize that. However, what concerned me most was she'd referred to Abby twice as her mother.

Again, I suggested we go across the street.

"No, thank you," she said. "Is this your desk?" She studied the white board.

"Yes."

"And this is how you found out that Mack was Bobby Maleck?"

"No. When I left the hospital, I only knew that the bolded

letters spelled out Bobby Maleck. I didn't know Mack was him until the Chief of Police told me."

"But you knew he killed Rosalyn Kohler and my mother was next on his list."

"Luanne, I didn't know who Bobby Maleck was or where he was. And it was Abby that told me about Rosalyn." She wanted to blame someone and I was the closest person at the moment.

"The police will find him and then you will have a chance to question him, I'm sure," I said.

She picked up the eraser from my desk and wiped the board clean. It made me think about Emma ripping her pizza to shreds and tearing Ethan from her life.

"The only question I'd ask him is if he wanted life or death."

"I'm sorry," I said. "I have something else to tell you."

She laughed, but not happily. "Haven't you destroyed my life enough, Kate?"

"I know you need to be angry at someone right now, but I'm not responsible for what Mack, Bobby Maleck, did."

"But you couldn't leave it alone." Her voice hit an octave only a dog could hear.

"Leave what alone? Christ, Luanne, I didn't know anything to leave it alone."

She frowned at me. Why was that hard to understand? After all, I had no advanced knowledge who the players were, what they had done, or why. I'm a reporter not a psychic.

She stretched her cardigan tight around her waist and hugged herself. "What do you have to tell me? What's left to say?"

I took a big breath and puffed it out my lips. How could I soften the truth? The only way I could think of was to blurt it out as Ethan suggested. "I don't know if this is true or not, but Abby said Rosalyn was your mother."

She laughed again and stared at me. Her mouth formed many different words. *I, who, her, you,* before she chose, "Why didn't you tell me that you knew that the other night?"

I lied. A tiny lie, almost the truth. "I told Abby you had a right to know, she agreed, and it wasn't my secret to tell," I said without a breath.

"I've known."

"You knew?"

"Yes."

Now it was my turn to form words without sound. I thought back to what she said about Abby wanting to find Rosalyn to make amends for a disagreement during their school years. I decided to leave it alone and let her keep her hidden truth.

"I needed a passport back in high school," she said. "And you need a birth certificate to get a passport."

Huh, that would never have occurred to me and I bet Abby never imagined the difficulties of sustaining a lie.

"You never told her?" Obviously not, I rounded my eyes.

"I suppose if I had, she would have left well enough alone."

I followed her well-said cliché and left well enough alone. At least she wasn't blaming me for that.

"And..." I paused. "You may have an inheritance waiting for you." I might as well confess to everything and get it over with.

"Abby had nothing," she said.

"No. From the Kohler side of your family. See, Lydia Kohler was your grandmother, Rosalyn's mother, and back in nineteen-sixty-five, a lawyer placed a personal ad looking for the last remaining relative—Rosalyn. I'm guessing Lydia didn't know about you."

"I don't know. I was only two then and if I'd met my grandmother, I wouldn't have remembered."

"Here." I pawed through my notes for Attorney Able Jackson's phone number. "This is the attorney in Arizona you'll want to contact. He said there are valuables in a safe deposit box he is paying for."

"What kind of valuables?" She studied his name before folding the paper and stuffing it in her pants pocket.

"I asked him, but he wouldn't tell me, but I'm guessing it's something pretty valuable if the rental of the box hasn't exceeded the contents value after forty years."

She stared at me or through me, not what I expected, but in fairness, she had just learned that her father allegedly killed both her mothers. I could understand her reluctance to jump overjoyed at the prospect of a financial boon. For Luanne's sake, I held on to the hope that Lydia Kohler had stashed away personal insight along with valuable monetary items.

"You'll call him, right?" I asked.

"I'll consider it."

Good enough for the moment. "Coffee?" I asked.

"Would it be too creepy to ask to see the mailroom?"

"Yeah, it's creepy, but if it helps you, I'm okay with it." I understood about having to face the creepy things.

She nodded and I led her down the stairs through the hall into the empty room that wasn't so empty anymore.

"Huh, that's weird." The shelves stacked with boxes of newspapers were moved.

"What's weird?"

"These were all in there the other day." I pointed.

Luanne peeked into Mack's mailroom. "A dungeon. Perfect place for him."

"Watch out for spiders," I said while she rummaged through papers and mail stacked on the table.

The last time I had been down here, I believed Mack was my friend. He could have stabbed me with the letter opener and no one would have known.

"Luanne, let's get out of here."

"Wait, look at this, Kate." She held up a copy of my first article with Abby's poem, cut neatly from the paper.

"Okay, that's creepy, let's go," I said again.

"And this." She opened a bi-fold cardboard photo frame and turned the black and white photo toward me. "I think this is Rosalyn." She pointed to the younger woman on the right.

I studied the photo then Luanne then the photo. My eyes darted back and forth, cataloging differences and similarities. "Could be." I took the photo from her and inspected the other woman more closely. "And her?" I tapped the image with my fingertips. Neither of us had the answers, but took turns guessing and pointing. The strangest game of show and tell I had ever played.

"That has to be Lydia."

I squinted, trying to morph Luanne into the version of her grandmother. "There definitely is a resemblance." Especially if she grew a mustache, but I didn't say that.

Luanne unburied two more faded news articles. One, the original article from Lydia, and the second, original article I thought read Richard or Robert Mulch.

We stood side by side reading them. "Take them and let's

go," I said. "I'm starting to get a bad feeling."

"Yeah, me too."

I turned toward the doorway just as a loud bang, metal on metal, vibrated my eardrums. We screamed. The door closed us in the dungeon.

"Come on." I grabbed her arm and stuck my fingers in the doorknob hole.

We stared at each other stupefied when the door jammed. I pulled again, this time with both thumbs.

"Let me try." She laid the picture and news article back on the table. I pulled again, then Luanne tried to no avail.

"Shit. Shit," I said.

"Yeah, not good."

"You have your cell?" I asked.

"No, you?"

"No."

"Shit. Shit," she said.

We laughed before we screamed and pounded on the door. No one would hear us through this damn door, but we pounded again.

"Wait, wait. What time is it?" I asked.

"Four-thirty or five maybe, why?"

"The press room gets cleaned every Tuesday night. Someone will be coming down those stairs soon." I pointed out the window in the door back down the hall. "But we'll have to keep watch because they don't come this way."

"So what you're saying is, don't panic yet?" Luanne asked.

"Right." I wasn't worried until I replayed the scene in my head. How had the damn door closed from the inside out when neither of us bumped it or swung it shut? I was about to discuss it with Luanne when a shadow blotted the light streaming in the door window and I jumped. Mack's face peered in at us, framed in the small window. "Brosy, Brosy." His cigar wiggled and his sneer grinned at us.

My breath caught in my throat. "Damn it, Mack," squeaked from my mouth. I heard a click and remembered the padlock. "Oh no."

"What?" Luanne asked.

"I think he just locked us in. Open the door." I yelled. "Don't be stupid."

"Make him open the door, Kate." Luanne hit that octave again.

"Me? He's your father." I pounded on the door. "Mack, this is your daughter."

"Open the damn door you stupid ugly asshole!" she screamed.

I swung around and gawked at her. "That is not what I expected to hear out of your mouth."

She shrugged and we laughed. I guess it was true—laugh in the face of adversity.

Mack shook his head then disappeared from our view. "Okay, he's gone," I said.

"So, we just wait for the cleaning crew?" she asked.

I wanted to tell her yes, but I wasn't so sure anymore myself, but Jonathan would miss me. He was probably already wondering why I hadn't shown up at his office. And if he went into the newsroom, he'd see my tote on my desk and know I hadn't left. I hoped.

Two or three loud clangs echoed outside the door and I stood on tiptoe to peer out the window thinking the cleaning crew kicked a bucket, but it was Mack. He tipped over two racks filled with newspapers and kicked them around the floor.

"What's he doing?" Luanne asked.

"I'm not sure, but I'm sure it isn't good."

Luanne turned and shoved the table up against the wall, climbed up on it, and banged on the windows. "Christ, these windows are like ten inches thick."

Mack stuck his face up at the door window again. That smirk that I hadn't seen since he stopped calling me Brosy curled his lips. Jonathan was right—Mack was helping himself, not me. He lit his cigar and puffed it until smoke curled up, hiding his face.

Luanne screamed a few more colorful metaphors at him and he stepped back from the door. I spun around, scanning the room for the hidden axe that always showed up in the movies, but there was nothing.

"You can't do this Mack." I had no idea what he could or couldn't do or what he planned to do, but my intuition screamed that I was about to find out how vindictive Bobby Maleck was.

"Yeah, what ya say, Brosy." He pulled his cigar from his mouth and looked down at his hands, doing something I couldn't see. A flash of light burst in front of him and he heaved something at the door. Glass shattered to the floor outside the door; smoke snaked in around my feet. I jumped back and flames fingered the window, blanketing my view.

"Oh shit, oh shit." I staggered back against the table. Another puff of smoke seeped under the door like gloved fingers waving at us.

We weren't laughing now, in fact, we were too calm about our predicament, and that worried me. Luanne was still on the table and stared down at me. I felt the same blank expression on my face that I saw on hers. I was trying to think, but I could only think about trying to think. My pulse wasn't even racing and it should be scared into third gear by now. Thank God, time slowed when the mind blanked out.

I stared at the smoke curling in through the doorknob hole this time. "Can you see out the window from up there?"

She turned and gawked outside.

"No, the door window," I said.

She spun around, her eyes bugged wide. "Yes, all flames."

"The newspapers," I said.

"The walls are concrete."

"The ceilings aren't." I searched around for anything I could use, but for what?

"What are you looking for?"

"I don't know, anything. Why are you so calm?"

"I don't know. Shock?"

"Give me your sweater," I said.

She whipped it off and tossed it down to me. My mind finally clicked into gear. The adrenaline rushed through my stomach. Nausea hit my throat and my pulse boxed my ears. My vision blurred and I shook my head.

"Why are you up there?" I yelled at Luanne.

"I don't know."

"Get down." I waved her off the table. "Look around for water, something, anything not flammable. Look back there." I pointed to the shelves where the vending machine supplies were stacked.

I could stuff the sweater under the door if I could wet it down. I was scared enough to pee on it, but feared with all the wine I drank last night that would make it flammable.

CHAPTER 36

The flames fingered under the door and I screamed. "Shit!" I wanted to break a window to yell for help, but that would fuel the fire and pull it into the room faster.

Luanne ran back to me, lugging a case of lemon lime soda cans. Why I was giving the orders, I didn't know, but I continued.

"Shake them. Aim and spray under the door."

I ran back around where she found the soda, grabbed the last six-pack and an old shirt hooked on the wall.

"This isn't working, Kate." Her soprano voice returned.

I soaked the shirt and her sweater with soda and stuffed them under the door. We still had the doorknob hole to seal. It wouldn't stop the fire, but it might buy us some time until the fire alarm sounded.

I pointed to the doorknob hole. We nodded and scurried around searching for anything other than more paper. I shook another soda can and let it loose in the hole.

"Here." Luanne ran back toward me with a grungy pair of boxer shorts pinched between her thumb and index.

"Oh God." I grabbed them, soaked them in lemon lime, and stuffed the hole. I didn't understand why the alarm hadn't blared yet, unless Mack was the one to fix it. That would make sense. He'd fixed it for sure or was Beck in on it too?

"I feel like a Cornish hen in a Dutch oven," Luanne said.

I spun around and grabbed her arms. "Oh my God, Luanne, we are in the kitchen." I jumped up and down. "We are climbing out of here girlfriend."

I pulled her over to the *City Scope* stationery rack. "Help me move this."

I pulled and Luanne pushed, but it wouldn't move, so we jerked it top down and toppled it to the floor.

"What is that?"

"A dumb waiter, I hope." I climbed inside, grabbed the dangling ropes, and stood up. I didn't have time to worry about the cobwebs that snapped across my face. I pressed my back against the wall, stretched my leg up and out against the opposite wall. The space cramped in me, small enough to prevent me from straightening my legs, which was a good thing. A sliver of light gleamed above to the right.

"How tall are you?" I yelled down to my feet. From Luanne's viewpoint, she could only see me from my knees down.

"Five-nine maybe, why?"

I calculated Luanne's height plus the three-foot table she scaled to peer out the window and added another two feet from the top of her head to the ceiling. I figured we had to climb about twelve or thirteen feet to reach the floor above us. It looked further, depending on the thickness of the floor above us.

"Let's go," she said. "The smoke is getting thick and I think my sweater is on fire."

I pulled on the ropes and two of the three crumbled down on my head. The pulley clanged to the floor and rolled out.

"Damn it."

"That's not good."

"The ropes are rotten." I twisted the third rope around my arm and pulled. It held. I then lifted my feet off the floor. It still held.

"Hurry, Kate."

"We're going to have to crawl up the wall in a sitting position. Ya know, with your back pressed against one side and your feet—"

"Okay, okay, I get it."

"And wrap the rope as we go," I said. "Take your shoes off. Down to bare feet, then get in here."

I did the same. I could probably shimmy up enough to stand on Luanne's shoulders. That would make us about eleven feet tall and another two feet from my shoulders to my outstretched arm. I hoped I could reach the slice of light and it wouldn't be fire.

Every nerve in my body pulsed on its own and none beat in rhythm with the other. I patted the walls, feeling for texture. Smooth like tin until above my head it lipped over to wood. Great, splinters.

I hadn't felt how narrow the space was until Luanne

climbed in and stood.

"Dark," she said.

"Yeah." We stood breast to breast.

The smoke followed us and we coughed. I wrapped the rope under her arms across her back and knotted it at her chest.

"I hope you know what you're doing." She coughed. "And if you get us out of here, I'll give you half of whatever is in that safe deposit box."

"Less words, less breath, less coughing." I took both her wrists, placed her hands on either side of me against the wall, and pushed to let her know to brace herself. Next, I reached above her head, wrapped the rope around my forearm once, and pulled on it. It held.

"I'm going to stand on your shoulders."

"Okay."

I grabbed the rope with my other hand, pressed my back against the wall between her arms, and lifted my legs, straddling her with my feet pressed against the wall above her shoulders. Another coughing fit and spasms rippled my abdomen. Luanne teetered from the pull on the rope and her head slammed into my pelvis.

"Sorry," she said, and regained her stance.

"Shh." I could barely hear my own breath over the drum roll in my ears and the flames snapping too close for comfort.

George taught me to climb slow and methodical. *Breathe in before each exertion. Exhale evenly, slowly when you push or pull up,* he would say. However, fire wasn't chasing us then.

I pulled myself up onto Luanne's shoulders. From my squat, I stood and slammed my head into something hard and sharp.

I screamed, grabbed my head, and slammed forward into the wall.

"Kate, I'm losing you." Luanne gripped my ankles and followed my lean into the wall. "What happened?"

I couldn't breathe, never mind talk. My jaw tightened, absorbing the pain, and my fingers were warm and sticky. "Stabbed ...my head...don't move." I grunted.

I probed my scalp, hoping for just a surface scrape and not an extra hole in my head. The tiniest head cut always bled like a gusher. No hole, but one crevice-size gash and I pinched it to disperse the pain. Blood trickled down my scalp around my ears and I shivered.

"Okay." I exhaled and reached around in the darkness for what I ran into. "There's a pipe." I talked through my clenched teeth. "Some kind of metal rod hanging down about five feet above your head."

"Okay, careful."

"Yeah." My head stung worse than a hornet sting and throbbed in rhythm to the pins and needles in my arm and hand from the rope wrap. Tears blurred my vision, but I couldn't see anything anyway.

I stayed close to the wall and reached, waving my hand around for any more surprises. My fingertips found the ledge I hoped for, but it was higher than I thought.

I could feel Luanne shaking under my feet. I needed to move fast.

"I'm pulling on this pipe. Be prepared."

"Yeah." She coughed more and that worried me.

I wanted to tell her to fill her mouth with saliva, but it would take too much air to explain how to gleek the salivary gland under her tongue if she didn't know.

Not only did the pipe hold, but also a lopsided cross bar just above my head provided a handy hold.

I pulled and snaked my hand up the rope, hooked my elbow over the cross bar. I was finally off Luanne's shoulders. My legs were shaking and my hand was numb to the point I couldn't feel the rope.

"Kate?"

"Okay, come on," I said. "Watch for the pipe."

Luanne grunted and I held the rope as steady as possible for her. The smoke stung my eyes and I was scared to death that we would become ash in this chimney. Not that it mattered, but I tried to think how much time elapsed from when Mack threw the flames to now. It seemed like hours, but we moved fast, so maybe only fifteen or twenty minutes.

"I got—the pipe," Luanne said.

"Okay. Feel for the cross bar."

"Got it."

"Loop your arm over it if you can."

"Got it."

The slice of light was an arm's length away from me, but right in sight. Luanne and I were face to face, but I had to pull my feet up and straddle her.

"I'm moving, you stay," I said.

I grabbed the pipe above my head and walked up the wall. My feet hit the ledge and I braced my back against the wall. After I looped the rope tight around my arm, taking up the slack, I kicked at the exit to the dumbwaiter repeatedly. It finally split in half, but stuck in the opening.

"Crap."

Although more light streamed in our chimney, more smoke choked us. I looked down at Luanne. Her face was splattered with my blood. Sirens squealed in the distance and the fire truck horn blew.

"Kate, you hear that?"

"Yeah. Can you get up here next to me?"

"I'll try." She wedged her way up between my legs.

"Wait, stay there."

Luanne's back was against the split opening. Where were we exiting? I drew a mental map in my mind. I was facing south into the cafeteria but never saw an opening anywhere in there, which meant it was behind the soda machines or the refrigerator.

"On three, you push your weight back into the opening."

She nodded and coughed.

"One, two, three," I said, and kicked with my legs as she pushed. A high-pitched, rusty whine, much like Mack's mail cart, screeched.

"What the hell is that?" Luanne asked.

"I think we are behind the refrigerator in the cafeteria."

"I tell you, Kate, after all of this, there damn well better be a fortune in the safe deposit box."

We laughed and shoved again, this time with more strength than I imagined either of us could muster. The split boards fell free to the floor. The refrigerator coils were in full view with just enough space for us to wedge one leg through the opening onto solid ground. On three, we shoved our shoulders against the damn refrigerator until we had enough room to fall to the floor.

Luanne and I crawled on our hands and knees through the cafeteria door into thick smoke. The lights in the building flickered then everything went black. I couldn't see two feet in front of me. Luanne took the lead. I could hear her choking in the distance and yelling my name, but I couldn't move.

"Kate, Kate." She grabbed my shirt and slid me along

with her as we dog paddled down the hall.

"Where the hell is the damn door?" I coughed.

"Here, here. Come on."

Something crashed behind us and we screamed as flames roared, glass shattered, and the smoke rolled back over our heads like storm clouds.

"Oh my God, hurry." I screamed. "The floor behind me. It's gone."

"Shit." We somersaulted through the front doors and crawled down the steps face first like twisted Slinkys.

My lungs pounded against my ribs, begging for clear air. The next thing I knew, George and Jonathan were hauling Luanne and me across the sidewalk into the street. Paramedics ran across the street toward us.

The entire Yardman Fire Department battled the fire from all directions. Paramedics and police used Gunthers' parking lot as a staging area.

"Is there anyone else in the building?" A firefighter intercepted us. "I don't know—Helen Beck?" I rasped.

"She's out. She's with the chief over there." He pointed.

My legs stopped working and I fell to my knees doubled over, and coughed until stars burst behind my eyelids. I clung to George's neck with one arm and he hugged me tight around my waist, keeping me from doing a face plant. Jonathan carried Luanne. His white shirt was stained gray. Luanne, paler than usual, had black soot streaked across her cheeks and arms mixed with blood. Someone slapped oxygen over both our faces and we were handed off to paramedics. I was suddenly off my feet, cradled in strong arms. Michael Earl carried me the last several yards to an ambulance.

"Emma?" I croaked through the mask. I braced myself against the ambulance door until the paramedic gave up and pushed me down to sit on the bumper.

"She's with Ethan," George said.

"Where?" I struggled to get up. I whisked my head around, worried she was watching. My head spun and I gagged.

"With Ethan." George pressed his hands on my shoulders. "She's okay. They're at your condo."

I didn't have energy to protest or even thank God at that moment. Paramedics pushed George and Jonathan back behind the police line.

"Breathe in and stop talking," Michael ordered.

Stars burst in my vision, tiny pulses like static electricity. If my head wasn't throbbing and my lungs weren't burning, I might have taken a moment to admire the oddity. Behind me, Luanne was retching and swearing all the best swear phrases and I laughed. I tried to focus on George and Jonathan. Their lips moved, but I couldn't concentrate on their words. Breathe. I was back on automatic pilot. The scene unfolded like a muted movie on television.

Windows on the first floor exploded. Glass showered the sidewalk and flames licked out the windows. I imagined the hewed ceiling logs rolling, an upside down campfire, and I shuddered. We had been so close to becoming toasted marshmallows. Firefighters sprayed water streams through the broken windows. Damn, I would need a new tote bag. A new cell. A new job. The hook and ladder truck deployed and a two-man team exited the cherry picker and searched the building's upper floors.

I hoped everyone escaped. I tried to remember what day of the week the dance school held classes. Did the fire alarm sound?

I felt pressure on my arm—a blood pressure cuff. Someone else probed at the gash in my head. The pain jolted me. A roar filled my ears, my teeth chattered, and my body shook.

"You should go to the hospital," someone said. I shook my head no, which was a really bad idea. The world spun and I closed my eyes and forced down a nauseous wave that burned my throat.

Someone wrapped a blanket around me. It was Michael Earl. I very slowly turned my head to check on Luanne inside the ambulance. She had one arm wriggled free from her shirt while she smiled and laughed with the paramedic who sponged the muck off her face, and he winked at her. She turned her head and whispered thanks, but from my perspective, it looked like she brushed her lips past his ear. He was a tall, thin blond and they looked like a matched set of salt and pepper.

"Are you flirting?" I yelled to her.

"Yes, I am. It's good to be alive." She laughed.

"But you're bleeding," I said.

She glanced at her shoulder. "Pipe," she said. "I found it."

I nodded. Then proving she was a self-taught tyrant, she slid off the gurney despite the paramedic's protest and scooted next to me on the ambulance bumper. We clasped our hands together.

"Did you get his number?" I asked.

"I will."

George and Jonathan were corralled several feet away from us. The threat of jail for interfering kept them both sputtering and arguing.

"My ex-husband and my wanna-be-boyfriend." I explained to Luanne.

"Good timing," she said.

"Not always," I said, and we both laughed. We zoned into that comfortable quiet friendship spot where no words were needed and paid no attention as the paramedics cleaned our cuts, slapped gauze on our wounds, and checked our vitals. Bonzie jogged toward us; his belly jiggled. He was in shape for a crosswalk guard, but not a full-out jog. Was I going to have to give up my ambulance bumper to him?

"Are you okay, Kate?" he asked.

"Did you find him? Or Nora?"

"We're still looking."

"He set the fire. Locked us in the mailroom."

"I hope he burned," Luanne said. She stared across the street. The second floor windows burst and rained glass.

Bonzie and I blinked. Luanne's words came out flat and her expression stone cold. I didn't wish death on Mack, but a long life in a six-by-eight cell, preferably shared with a Freddy Krueger impersonator.

Bonzie sidestepped over to Luanne. "And you are?" he asked her.

"Luanne."

"Abby's daughter," I said.

"Duncan? Maleck?" Bonzie asked.

"Oh, hell no." Luanne stared Bonzie in the eyes. "Formerly Duncan, now Hamilton. Never Maleck."

Bonzie licked his pen and took notes. She supplied dimension and emotion to the back-story I related earlier in the afternoon.

"He meant to kill us," Luanne finished.

I shuddered. Mack roaming the back alleys of Yardman, watching, waiting for me, or traipsing around the bushes in my backyard yelling, Brosy, Brosy, terrified me. My gaze darted through the crowd as I scanned heads and searched for the fisherman hat. Bonzie's radio sounded with a voice announcing the building was clear.

"He got away." Luanne and I both jumped to our feet and grasped each other's hands. I searched the crowd packed on the sidewalk in front of Gunthers. She scanned the street.

"We'll find them," Bonzie said.

"I've heard that before," I said, without thinking. The chief didn't respond but nodded and thumbed to the officers that were squabbling with George and Jonathan to step aside.

Free from their restraint, George and Jonathan joined us along side of the ambulance. They both speared me with an I-told-you-so expression on their faces, but spared me the words. I sucked in a breath without coughing. "George, Jonathan. Meet my new climbing partner, Luanne." We winked at each other.

"Yeah, and our next climb will be at thirty-five thousand feet," Luanne announced.

In perfect vaudeville comedic rhythm, we coughed and sputtered. "We're going to Arizona, right?" I said, and added a high-five.

ABOUT THE AUTHORS

Elaine

Margarete

Collaborating writers on opposite coastlines is no obstacle for Elaine Braman and Margarete Johl. They share the passion for writing a witty mystery, heat waves, hot flashes and Palm trees but beyond that, they couldn't be further apart than Florida and California. They met one time four years ago by chance in California at a business meeting and became fast friends mixing like paper and pen. Although they haven't seen each other since, they have written three novels together and continue to plot their next.

Born in Pennsylvania to parents whose native language was German, Margarete started writing early in life perfecting English grammar; for obvious reasons. Now residing in Palm Springs, CA. (where anything under 80 degrees is sweater weather), Margarete and David, her husband enjoy their grown daughters and two dogs. Margarete writes fiction and poetry every free hour she has and works for a telecommunications company full time. Stage fright is her enemy, but give her a keyboard or a stubby pencil and she'll create a world.

Originally, from Massachusetts, Elaine migrated to Florida for family and job. Her background in technical writing provides skills to organize a logical plot. In addition to winning place in the 10th annual Writers Digest short short story competition she has written instructional articles for career professionals, contributed proofing and editing (dialogue) services, for such publications as The Florida Writer, RPLA, Connections Magazine and the johnyraygun Comic Book by Rich Woodall. For the past four years, Elaine has been a member of the executive board of directors for FWA. Elaine and Darrel, the love of her life, enjoy their Florida home, grown family, and grandchildren while she continues to perfect her craft. Elaine's philosophy is, *teach what you know to learn what you don't know.*